WOLFSONG

Louis Owens

American Indian Literature and Critical Studies Series

Gerald Vizenor and Louis Owens, General Editors

UNIVERSITY OF OKLAHOMA PRESS: NORMAN

Library of Congress Cataloging-in-Publication Data

Owens, Louis, 1948–2002
   Wolfsong / Louis Owens.
      p. cm. — (American Indian literature and critical studies
series; v. 17)
    ISBN 0–8061–2737–6
    1. Indians of North America — Cascade Range — Fiction.
I. Title. II. Series.
PS3565.W567W65   1994
813'.54–dc20   94–36435
                                              CIP

Wolfsong is Volume 17 in the American Indian Literature and Critical Studies Series.

The paper in this book meets the guidelines for permanence and durability of the Committee on Production Guidelines for Book Longevity of the Council on Library Resources, Inc. ∞

Oklahoma Paperbacks edition published 1995 by the University of Oklahoma Press, Norman, Publishing Division of the University, by special arrangement with West End Press, P. O. Box 27334, Albuquerque, New Mexico 87125. Copyright © 1991 by Louis Owens. All rights reserved. Manufactured in the U.S.A. First printing of the University of Oklahoma Press edition, 1995.

3 4 5 6 7 8 9 10 11 12

For Polly, once more.

1

The rain fell onto the downswept branches and collected and fell to the hard undergrowth with a steady hammering. The old man climbed slowly down in the near dark, edging each thick lug sole into the wet humus, leaning back against the push of the slope to balance the weight of the rifle. Water soaked through his frayed mackinaw, through the flannel shirt, and lay next to his skin, familiar and comforting. The years eased away as the drumming on the brush deepened. Then he stopped and frowned as the dancers began moving again in the undergrowth, swaying and stepping, back and forth, watching him. He moved his eyes between the wavering shadows, feeling the drops of water running down his cheeks from the wool watchcap, and he tried to fix the faces again and again he failed.

"I have work to do," he said in a soft, flat voice. "Go back."

His forehead creased and his black eyes tried to focus. Now they seldom left him alone. In the last weeks they had come only on rare, solitary nights when he camped in that drainage, but now they were nearly always there, beckoning, waiting to begin the dance again. Once he had been drawn in, stamping his heavy boots and shrugging his old shoulders, moving with them in the darkness and chanting. They were becoming harder to resist, more demanding and insistent.

He turned away, his short, heavy body shifting with a precise grace. Stiff, silver hair hung straight from the black roll of the cap, and deep in the square face his eyes glinted. Wrinkles cut like old wounds around the eyes and pulled the corners of his mouth up and back and then dropped them. The skin on his cheeks stretched over blunt bones, and when he grimaced yellow teeth gleamed in a face the color of red cedar.

He stabbed the bootheels into the soaked duff and descended a dozen yards with stiff, measured plunges before stopping behind a log nearly as high as his chest and covered with thick moss and ferns and small trees. The undergrowth rustled behind him and the rain filtered through the trees. His elbows sank into the moss and rotten bark and the log seemed to grow up around them. He rested the ancient 30-40 Krag on the log and it, too, sank into the decay.

In the clearing below, their roar muted by the steady rain, a D8 caterpillar gouged at the red earth of the mountain, and behind it another pushed a raw moraine toward the white rapids of the Stehemish River fifty yards further down the slope.

The Krag exploded through the rasp of the dozer engines and the engines stopped and the drivers disappeared.

"The crazy fucker's back!" The shout came from behind one of the machines.

"Got mine this time," a shout answered. "Splintered the shit out of something."

The Krag fired again, and the whang of cutting metal winced through the narrow drainage and across the river.

"Sonofabitch is going to hit somebody pretty soon."

A big man came around the back of the machine that had been cutting at the mountain. He glanced skeptically down the road to where a line of caterpillars and dumptrucks and graders crouched. Then he turned and spat before he looked up at the mountainside. Behind him a new road stretched into the trees alongside the river, the rusty earth torn and uneven where the gravel trucks had not yet reached. The man lifted a dented aluminum hardhat and pushed a large, very dirty hand through tangled red hair where a matted line encircled his head.

"What the hell you doing?" a high, squeaky voice shrilled from behind the other tractor. A black baseball cap rose over the cat's track and the voice squeaked, "'at 'ere Krag put a hole in you big enough to drive this fuckin cat through."

The big man sighed and squinted at the trees above him. "Hell, Jim Joseph ain't going to shoot nobody—he wanted to shoot somebody you and me'd been shit out of luck a long time ago. That old man could give a fella a running start and shoot his pecker off at a hunnerd yards, even a little bitty pecker like yours. He's just pluggin at these machines." He shifted a lump inside his lower lip and shot another stream at the road.

"Ain't that right old man—you're just shootin at these here caterpillars?" His shout vanished into the purr of the rain and river and settled into the forest. Above him, above the gash they'd carved out of the base of the mountain, the forest leaned in a black wall, wet and impenetrable.

He set the hardhat back on his head and cupped his hands over his mouth. "Hey you old fool," he shouted at the mountainside, the words emptying in the damp air. "What the fuck you doing up there? You hurt somebody you know they'll be hell to pay." He watched and waited for the shout to dissipate. "Come on down and we'll give you a lift into town. Buy you a beer." Again the silence filtered in like the rain after his voice.

The tall man wiped the rain off of his forehead, leaving a muddy streak across the heavy red eyebrows. Then he shook his head and shouted again, "We know you, old man. Now come on down before somebody gets hurt. This ain't cowboys and injuns." Somewhere in the timber above him a raven barked and he shifted irritably. Cupping his hands, he continued. "We can get Taylor's hounds, and you know you cain't get away from them hounds, old man, just like you cain't stop this here road. Now come on down outa there."

The baseball cap bobbed over the track of the other machine again and the second man's face, with small, possum eyes, moved back and forth.

"Like hell he can't get away from them hounds," the voice behind the tractor yelled. "Leave that crazy-ass injun alone, Leroy."

Leroy hooked his cracked, mudcaked fingers behind the suspender straps on his big belly and watched the trees reflectively. "Shitfire," he said softly. "That old man ain't going to shoot nobody except hisself. He's just nuts, that's all, crazy as a July rabbit. Crazy fuckin Indian."

He looked at the rain-reddened dirt and scuffed one vibram-soled boot. "That's we get for being dumbfuck stupid enough to work on Saturday."

Behind the green log, the old man stared through the trees. The voice was like the boulders in the river; it caromed off the fir and hemlock and cedar trunks and drifted into the shadows. Sunk deep into the moss, the rifle pointed down at the big man's center, and the dark eyes lined up the sight at the end of the barrel, a stiff finger feeling the curve of the worn trigger. After a moment, he straightened, lifting the rifle and turning back toward the forest. Then he began working his way up the mountain between downed timber with rootwads twice his height, gripping the gun in the downhill hand and clutching at bare roots and small hemlocks for support with the other. A foot slipped and he grasped at a huckleberry branch.

"Hold on tight, uncle," he said aloud. "It ain't cowboys an injuns." He chuckled.

A hundred yards from the log he became a shadow, and then he disappeared.

For two hours he worked his way through the dripping forest, following the game trail along the contour of the ridge, weaving between windfalls and barriers of undergrowth. Once a gray bird flitted into the shadows, a feather falling to the earth behind it. The old man stooped and picked up the feather, smoothing it between thumb and forefinger and placing it in the mackinaw pocket. The hollow whistle of a thrush cut through the rain, and his boots sank into the forest floor.

In a small hanging valley high on the ridge, shut in by gray-black timber, the old man stopped. Around the clearing the straight, old-growth trunks leaned inward, their branches beginning a dozen feet or more from the ground. In the center of the clearing a half-submerged log lay in a sunken triangle of earth and ragged spring snow. At one edge of the clearing, a clear plastic tarp angled from the ground to form a lean-to against a pair of hemlock trunks. In front of the lean-to, a blackened coffee can hung with baling wire from a tripod of green branches over a still-smoldering fire.

The old man stopped beside the log and leaned the rifle against it, glancing toward the tarp and then above, to where the rain had lightened to a drizzle that floated from the clouds at tree top. He folded his arms across his chest and closed his eyes, thinking of the boy again. The nephew would be on his way home soon, he could feel that. He wondered if he had taught the boy enough. There was so much that he, himself, had never learned. He couldn't even speak the language anymore. In the government school they had cut out the tongues of Indians, sewing in different tongues while the children slept. He'd awakened at night in the dormitory and seen them doing it, with their pale skin like ghosts in the dark. When he'd tried to shout no sound had come, and he'd understood. For several years he'd watched the white teachers' dogs grow fat from thrown-away tongues, and he'd felt his mouth swollen and dry with someone else's words. When he returned, he hadn't spoken for a year, taking that time to listen and test sounds like bird wings on the farthest tip of his new tongue. The older relatives nodded and watched, used to the silences of children stolen to school. At the end of a year, alone in a clearing like this, he'd had the courage to say his real name aloud, and after that he could speak again, but it was never easy, and it was always the old signs twisted into another language. Across the circling years, working as a choker-setter and faller and bucker in the woods, he'd grown comfortable with his new tongue and had even grown to enjoy the strange directions it took at times. He'd learned to tell stories with it, and he'd told them to the nephew, along with a few of the old words that hadn't hidden from him.

He whispered a word, hearing his real name for the first time in many years. The people had come to this house. A boy, he had crouched inside against the cedar-slab wall, shy in the shadows, and watched the grandfather, a singer. And the singer reached out, and the fire sent tongues of darkness up the inner walls of the house. Outside, the animals listened and the boy felt their spirits draw closer.

The memory tired and he opened his eyes. Between the trees the shadows began to move. First a flicker like the waving of a branch or a ghost of rain or moth, and then a steadier movement and finally they began to come out into the spaces between the trees and weave and step. The chanting began. He fixed his eyes where the earth heaved up between patches of hard snow and he tried not to hear the voices, tried instead to think again of the nephew who was gone. "I am too old," he thought. "Too damned tired." In the old days, a man might be thrown away by the people. Today, it seemed sometimes that the whole world was being thrown away by the whites.

He began to move in time to the chant. The hands rose an inch or two and fell, and the boots touched the earth one after the other. High in the trees a raven shouted raucously and dove in looping flight. More shadows rushed from the forest to crowd at the edge of the clearing and weave through the rain, and the chant grew deeper and more urgent around him until he moved faster and didn't hear as the clouds rumbled and the rain grew harder until it droned through the trees.

On the ridges the wolves ran again, and he saw black feet

driving into the spring snow and long black necks stretched hungrly. The voices drummed along the ridgetops and out over the drainages. The boy listened and fasted beside the lake, and when it was time he dove seeking the vision. The wolf rose on two legs and beckoned, and for a lifetime he followed, far out into the world of men.

When the old man fell, his head struck the rifle and together man and gun lay across the patch of unmelted snow.

After a while, Leroy turned from the trees and said, "Come on out, Dinker, the old fart's gone."

The quick head jerked into view again, and a small, nervous man appeared. Dinker walked rapidly to where the bigger man stood, Dinker's small blue eyes darting around the clearing. Barely over five feet, Dinker moved like a hunting weasel, wiry and quick. Thick black hair curled below the baseball cap and above the collar of his green, neopreme raincoat, and his small hands clenched and unclenched.

Dinker looked up at the timbered slope. "Maybe he's jest waiting to blast us new assholes," he said.

"Naw. He never takes more'n a couple shots." Leroy rubbed the reddish-gray stubble on his chin with the back of his hand and let out a long breath. "Serves us right for working our asses off out here while everybody else is in town. Fuck the overtime."

"You're crazy trying to talk to that old man." Dinker squinted through the rain from under the brim of the cap. "Maybe he's still settin up there. Nobody knows what crazy people'll do, specially crazy injuns. You remember Split-Lip John?"

"Shitfire, Dinker." Leroy spat at the ridge of a caterpillar track. "That old man could've blowed us both two ways to Christmas a hunnerd times. Course I remember John."

Leroy stuck two fingers behind his lower lip and pulled out a brown ball and threw it to the ground, looking with interest at the way the snoose blended with the red earth. He reached a round tin from his shirt pocket, pried the top off, and squeezed a pinch of the tobacco between thumb and forefinger. He settled the new load behind his lower lip and began to work it with his tongue, sighing as he did so.

"Snoose?" He pushed the tin toward Dinker, who waved it away with a disgusted snort.

"You ought to take up snoose. Might mellow you out some. You put a touch of brandy in it, let it soak in real good."

"I don't need no goddamn mellowing out. We ought to get them hounds like you said. Run that crazy bastard down before he blows us to kingdom come. Thinks he owns the whole goddamn state cause he's a injun." Dinker shoved his hands into the baggy pockets of his Ben Davis jeans and glared at the trees. The rain had increased, and silver beads formed and ran together on the bill of his cap. He pulled the stiff collar of his raincoat tighter around his thin neck.

"Thought you said couldn't even dogs catch old Jim." Leroy closed one eye and looked down at Dinker, imitating the smaller man by shoving his own hands into his jeans pockets. The rain had dyed his shirt a deep blue.

"Know something, Dinker? It occurs to me that old Jim Joseph might just be after you instead of these machines. He's getting on in years and maybe he ain't the crack shot he used to be. Maybe he heard you insulting his ancestry."

Dinker's face jerked toward Leroy and then back in the direction of the timber.

"Yeah," Leroy went on. "I thought he was just plinking at these cats, but . . ." He looked up at the old-growth on the mountainside and back at Dinker. His face slackened. "Ah hell," he said. "Let's get the fuck out of here and find a beer."

"Why'd you say maybe he was after me?" Dinker's eyes narrowed to a glint of blue that turned moon-gray in the rain. "Thinks he owns the whole goddamned woods cause he's a injun."

Leroy studied the forest that rose above them in a black wall. "Didn't mean nothing at all, Dinker. I was just blowing off. He might just as well try to stop that river down there as this here road." He jerked his head toward the sounds of the glacial river through the trees below the road. "Didn't mean a friggin thing."

"J. D. ain't going to like him shooting up two more machines," Dinker said. "He ain't going to let that old man keep shooting up his machines."

"Well, I don't see one whole hell of a lot J. D. or anybody else can do about it, personally." Leroy lifted the hardhat and ran his hand through hair again. "Seeing as how Jim Joseph done run circles around Will Baker and his boys."

"Hounds'd find him," Dinker answered.

"You sure change your tune, Dinker. Come on, let's go tell J. D. he's got a couple more invalid cats out here and hit the Red Dog."

Dinker swatted at a horsefly that came roaring out of the rain. The fly banked away, and Dinker stared after it in amazement. "You see that sonofabitch?" he squeaked. He lifted the baseball cap and resettled it. "Don't you plan to tell Will about that crazy bastard first?"

Leroy picked up his slicker and lunchpail from beside the seat of his cat and looked from the mountainside to Dinker. "You know, Dinker, you ought to wear a hardhat. You might get your head squashed without it someday. You remember the Knudson kid, don't you?" He walked to the pickup and tossed the raincoat and box in the bed of the truck. "Don't see no point in telling Will. J. D.'ll do it fast enough."

Dinker watched Leroy walk toward the battered Dodge and shouted after him, "Them tin hats make my head sweat. Danny Knudson didn't get his head squashed, he got his whole self squashed. You ain't dragging your heels just because of that girl of yours and Tom Joseph, are you?"

Leroy returned to the caterpillar and gathered loose tools from the gravel nearby. He bent and rose with an enormous crescent wrench in one hand and looked at Dinker. Then he pulled himself over the cat track and onto the seat. He ground the ignition once and nodded with satisfaction when the motor failed to catch.

"That what you think?"

Dinker glanced toward the river. "Hell, I don't think a goddamned thing. Besides, everybody knows about her and Buddy."

Leroy climbed off the tractor and tossed the wrench in the back of the pickup. As Leroy slid behind the steering wheel, Dinker hurried to get his own lunchbox and scramble into the other door of the crumpled truck.

The ignition sputtered and caught, and the truck rattled down the new road away from the machines. Gravel caught in the tread and flew from the mudtires.

When they had gone two hundred yards, Leroy cranked the window down and spat into the rain. The truck's one wiper trailed a fragment of cracked rubber and smeared rain across the glass in front of him, making the road a blurred gash through the forest of the narrow drainage.

"D'you know you can't strangle a dog?"

Leroy turned to look incredulously at his friend.

"What?"

"You can't strangle a dog. Jake tried, says he couldn't do it." Dinker turned to watch through the side window, and Leroy frowned at the wiper blade, shaking his head.

A small deer leaped off the road and vanished into the fir and vine-maple. Leroy watched it bound out of sight and said, "Shit."

"Huh?" Dinker had been watching the rows of silver culvert pipes stacked along the side of the road, admiring the way they gleamed in the rain, admiring the road they'd carved out of the upper Stehemish drainage. Hell, he thought, if it wasn't for the wilderness area they'd go on and push the road right over the Cascades and down to Stehekin. Fuckin sahara clubbers. He could see the route it would take, right through Cloudy Pass and down to the lake. That'd be something to tell the grandkids about.

"Jim Joseph could take on a army with all the hounds in the world in these mountains," Leroy was saying, "and have hisself roast hounddog for supper every night."

"What?" Dinker usually didn't bother to listen until the second or third time. If a thing wasn't worth repeating, he figured, it probably wasn't worth hearing.

"Nothing."

"What'd you say?" It had occurred to him that Leroy might be talking about the Indian again.

"It's a damned shame, that's all," Leroy said, "a friggin shame."

"What is?"

"Aw for chrisesake, Dinker."

The scarred black body and rattling red fenders of the pickup bumped down the gravel road, trailing an uneven stream of black smoke, disappearing beneath the rows of old-growth timber that leaned in over the painful gash of new road. Then the truck vanished in the rain-whitened shadow of a turn.

It was dusk when Sam Gravey found him. He lay on his back, the rifle beside him and both eyes staring toward the dim opening where the rain slanted between the trees. The first flush of dark rippled out from the wall of trunks, sending shadows dancing across the old berry-house clearing, and the whistle of a thrush hung in the air.

Sam took down the plastic tarp, folding it carefully and pushing it inside a wood-framed backpack that leaned against a tree nearby. He lifted one of the two ragged Army wool blankets from its moss mattress and folded it before slipping it into the pack. Next, he emptied water out of the coffee can and placed it in the pack on top of the blankets. With the toe of his boot, he stirred the cold fire, spreading the embers so the rain would touch them all evenly. He returned to the log and picked up the Krag, tying the rifle on one of the packboxes on the mule. Then he went back to the lean-to site and picked up the second blanket. Working carefully, he wrapped the body in the wool blanket and then lifted it across the packmule, passing a rope around and between the stiff hands and beneath the mule before tying the rope to the feet and anchoring the body. Last of all, he tied the pack on behind the topload. Then he led the mule down toward the river, feeling the weight of his friend's body lying heavy over the drainage, from the glaciers where the river began to the rapids where the river curved back toward the new road and distant town.

2

The bus slid into sight on the coast highway, trailing a mist
as the tires threw rain off the asphalt. Above the red bank where
the road cut across the cliffs, tall black firs stabbed a layer of
cloud. The rain slanted in on the wind, streaking across the window, and the ocean slashed at the base of the cliffs, throwing
seaweed and polished logs and debris against the land. A hundred yards out, columns of black rock, pocked by wind and
water, guarded the empty coastline and mists of gulls lifted in
uneven lines before settling again. The wind cut the tops off
the waves and wove whitecaps around the broken stone.

A cramp worked its way into his shoulder and he shifted
against the hard vinyl seat, trying to shelter the raw nerve. Staring out the rain-streaked window, he could feel the vastness
of the rain, sensed the water gathering in the high country, sliding down the granite peaks and running into channels that fed
streams that fell to rivers that consumed the rocks, earth and
trees until all was disgorged into the sea and the sea threw it
back at the land. As soon as they had left California the damp
had closed in, working its way through the bus till it found him
and settling into his bone and muscle like a contented, wet cat.
Now it purred shivers up his spine and probed the pinched
nerve of the bad shoulder. He thought of the funeral, but his
uncle wasn't in the thought. It would be in the rain. He couldn't
see his uncle in the vision he evoked of the old cemetery, and
because he couldn't see it there was no loss or sadness. He
imagined the old house, his mother and brother. He thought
of the valley with its timber, the granite and ice, two rivers,
Karen. There was a great sense of going home.

He straightened his back and squared his shoulders and
looked out at the sea distorted by raindrops. Out there now the
salmon were gathered and heading for the river mouths. Hump-

ies, kings, silvers. His eyes picked out the shape of a seal's head rising and falling with the breakers as the bus rose and fell on the winding road.

He watched the seal, and the bus hissed north along the highway, parting the wall of rain. The heavy timber leaned far out over the road toward the Pacific, shining and black beneath the ceiling of clouds.

The bus headed inland up the Willamette Valley, through forests so green after the parched landscapes of southern California that they hurt his eyes. Small farms filled squares hacked from the timber. Cattle grazed in damp fields between giant, hollowed-out stumps, and the violet fireweed grew dense where the black-and-white or red cattle could not reach.

Through the window he saw the wavering outlines of small houses and pickups, the trucks perched on big tires like waterbugs high above gravel driveways. Blackberry skeletons coated the banks along the highway, and a thin stream ran in the ditch on his side of the road. A crow lurched up from a flattened rabbit, and he watched as it rowed itself raggedly into the low branches of a fir to wait for the bus to pass. For a while he played the old game from childhood, sliding the razor-edged blade out from the bus and lopping off everything in its path, seeing the telephone poles fall in neat lines, the timber mowed like grain before the inexorable blade. When a dull farmhouse appeared, its yard full of rusting objects, the blade magically retracted and then shot out again faster than the eye could see, precisely missing the house that reminded him of all the Indian homes he'd seen. When a shining, two-story brick house swam into view, however, the blade sliced it neatly in two, soundlessly and without resistance.

He closed his eyes. The salmon had entered the rivers and were massed for the run upstream. The monstrous bowed backs of sea lions rose and fell in the river mouths as the predators gorged. Upstream, Indians readied their gillnets and loggers got out their poaching gear while the fish and game people prepared to save as many of the spawning fish as they could.

By the next day, after an all-night bus ride and a change in Seattle, he'd be in Arlington, and then a thirty-mile hitch would get him home in time for the funeral. Again he tried to picture his uncle in a box that would be buried beside the river, but he could see only the ferns and vines and great trees of the old Stehemish graveyard and the stone with his name.

The bus reached Island Crossing at midday, grinding down off the freeway to stop in front of an A & W Rootbeer stand and a pair of clean-looking gas stations on each side of the road. Behind the buildings in pastures stretching off toward the range of peaks in the east, cattle raised their heads as the airbrakes belched. The driver announced the stop in a bored voice, and Tom Joseph stood and dragged the guitar case from the overhead rack. Within the case were three pairs of undershorts, one pair of fairly new Levis, four pairs of socks, two shirts and a novel by Jack London. McBride, his Flathead roommate, would be pissed off when he found the case missing, but the thought of carrying his clothes in a paper bag had been too depressing.

A few passengers watched as he carried the guitar case down the aisle and out the sighing doors, but no one showed much interest in a long-haired Indian kid getting off at Island Crossing in the rain. Outside, he hurried to get clear of the Greyhound and then set the case on the wet gravel beside the pavement and stood still, letting the small, sharp rain hit him full in the face.

The two-lane road ran perpendicularly away from the freeway. Shining with water, it raced off toward the Cascade peaks, a jagged grey-and-white line that disappeared into clouds a few miles away. He flipped the corduroy collar of his Lee Stormrider jacket up and buttoned the top brass button; then he watched as his jeans turned blue and finally black with the rain coming in waves across the fields. The bus groaned back onto the freeway toward Canada, and he glanced at the rootbeer stand and thought about the way the weather always came from the southwest. The people always watched Whitehorse; when the mountain put on a cloudcap, rain came quickly. Overhead, flat gray clouds promised plenty of rain for the funeral. He watched the dizzy streaking of the rain and thought again of his uncle who could not be buried in dry ground. A sign over the rootbeer stand said, "Best burgers, prettiest girls."

As the bus faded, he heard a log truck come humping off the freeway and slow for the turn onto the narrower road. He looked up to see what he knew would be there: one trailer stacked on top of the other and a gleaming chrome bulldog balanced on a shiny radiator.

He stuck out his thumb and stepped onto the asphalt to catch the driver's attention before the truck picked up speed again. The companies didn't allow hitchhikers, it said so on the door of every truck. But it was a boring, kidney-crushing job and the drivers picked them up anyway.

The truck stopped and the driver waved him over. He trotted across the road and around the dusty blue Peterbilt cab, pulling himself up the step and dragging the door open. He threw the case on the floorboard on top of a raincoat and orange hardhat and climbed into the seat just as the driver began taking the tractor back up through the gears. The fields and cows started to flow past, and the dice hanging from the mirror swung erratically. The radio muttered a song about an Okie from someplace called Muskogee, and he thought about Rana.

With a quick glance the driver shouted above the throbbing deisel, "Where you headed?" his voice barely audible over the gears, slashing tires, and radio. The driver's short, bulky torso filled one side of the cab, the striped hickory shirt rolled up over big forearms and his belly straining shirt and suspenders against the steeringwheel. His pants were stagged off high on the ankles to keep them from fraying and getting tangled in the brush the driver remembered from his days in a logging unit. Instead of corks, the driver wore thick wool socks and moccasins.

The driver rolled down the window and spat into the rain and then turned to grin, tobacco juice gleaming on his yellow teeth.

"Forks," Tom Joseph replied, knowing that the driver already knew. There was only one town on the road, and that was where the road ended.

The driver reached to turn down the country-western drone of the radio, and Tom watched the wipers make broad, clean sweeps across the big window. He tried to remember the last time he'd been in a truck with wipers that worked.

"Planning to get on in the woods?" The driver's glance covered the battered guitar case and straight black hair that hung from the wet wool watchcap to the turned-up collar.

"Maybe." He waited for the driver to recognize him, rolling the window down a few inches to smell the damp air with its growth and decay, logging mills and mist, air so thick after Santa Barbara that he felt like a man at the bottom of the sea. Diving back home, going down and down toward some kind of dark center. The truck passed a tiny headquarters office for a different tribe, and he tried hard to look through the unlighted windows, seeing only a blurred reflection of the truck.

"Getting tough these days," the driver said, taking the truck up another gear. "Outfits closing down right and left. About the only show in town these days is K & M and, hell, it ain't even really K & M anymore since J. D. Hill bought 'em out. Used to be that a young guy like you could walk onto a landing and start setting chokers right then and there. Nowadays they's men been fallin twenty years can't get work. Fallers fighting for choker-settin jobs. Gettin damned hard for a logger to make a living in these parts what with most of the trees done cut and what's left crawling with sahara clubbers."

Tom's thoughts drifted in the liquid air, settling finally on the approaching peaks. McBride had tried to talk him into joining the Sierra Club in Santa Barbara, but he didn't like to join things. McBride, an eighth Flathead but enrolled, with pale skin, light-brown braided hair, and a beard, joined everything. President of the Native American Students Association on campus, McBride was going back to Montana to get married. He planned to give the bride's father ten horses. It would have been different going home if you were McBride, he thought. "It's not the Flathead tribe," McBride said often, "it's the fucking Confederated Salish-Kutenai tribe." McBride liked to point out the Salish part and say, "We're related, man. You Stehemish folks are Salish too. We're bros, man." But when he looked in the mirror, he had trouble thinking of himself and McBride as bros. The only bro he knew was large and dark and waiting for him upriver.

The road left the flat fields and swung in beside a fast, green river. Bigger timber crowded close to the road, and steep slopes rose toward glimpses of granite mountains. The river narrowed and quickened over boulders and logjams. The truck moved into a straight section, and the driver turned for a long glance.

"You're Sara Joseph's boy." The driver's eyes drew back a little, his voice grew cautious.

"Hello, Amel. I was wondering how long it would take you." He tried to smile. It was strange hearing his mother's name. It wasn't a name he thought of, and he hadn't heard anybody say it in more than a year. And it wasn't his mother's real name anyway.

"I'll be damned." Amel laughed, nodding his round head toward the windshield. "Must've been the hair. You're starting to look like a old-time Indian, a whole lot like a picture I seen once of your uncle when he was a kid."

Tom watched the second-growth speed by beside the road, the thin trunks receding quickly to darkness as the forest rode the sides of the valley up toward the peaks and beyond, into the wild country.

"I'm sorry about your uncle," Amel said after a moment. "I guess you come back for the funeral."

A possum shuffled to the edge of the road and stopped, blinded by daylight, its pink nose shining in the rain. Then it plodded onto the asphalt and Tom felt the thud. The rain bent across the line of trees, and he looked ahead toward the droplets that came driving in toward the windshield. He was surprised at the white man's care in not mentioning his uncle's name. Most white people didn't know things like that.

"Damn," Amel said. "I sure hate to do that."

"You couldn't help it," Tom replied.

"He was a good fella. There ain't never been nobody knew this country like he did."

Tom looked back out the window, trying to see the possum.

Amel frowned at the road. "When I was a kid your uncle showed me how to make showshoes and how to use 'em." Amel glanced at Tom. "Couldn't nobody figure out what happened. Maybe he just stayed out there in the woods too long." He paused and then blurted a final attempt. "I never thought he was nuts. I knew him since I came here with my family back in the thirties. There was more of your people back then."

A silver mailbox glided toward them at the end of a blacktop driveway that wound into the trees. Tom thought about Amel's words, and he remembered a song that said, "Let my people go." Who were his people? It seemed like they'd been let go a long time before. Then he saw J. D. Hill's house. Quarterback on the high school team, J.D.'s son, Buddy, had been the best athlete in the school and could talk like a duck. Huddled in the rain, a thousand points behind and facing third-and-long against Granite Falls, while the fat-assed coach thought they were planning one last great play, they'd listened to Buddy tell the one about Mickey and Minnie Mouse getting a divorce. Rain puddling and dripping through the shoulder pads and making their asses itch, they broke up on the punchline: "I didn't say Minnie was crazy. I said she was fucking Goofy." He grinned to himself. On the team they called him "Chief," but it was okay. He was the best fullback in the conference, and they knew him. It was different at the university; there only McBride could say it the right way.

The telegram had said, "Our uncle is dead. Funeral next Thursday." Jimmy's name was on it. A Kenworth loaded with cedar logs shot past out of the valley and Amel waved. It was traditional to wait four days for the funeral. He wondered where they were finding the old-growth cedar. Cedar was sacred.

"You see them logs went past?" Amel jerked his head in the direction of the other truck. "Ain't nobody seen logs like that around here in a coon's age. Taking 'em off the rightaway for that mining road up the Stehemish."

So that was it. The copper company had finally gotten the go-ahead for the open-pit mine in the wilderness area. He was surprised to realize that for almost a year he hadn't even thought about it.

The truck spun around a corner and faced for an instant a large white sign with black letters proclaiming, "Tractors die and rust forever. Jesus died so you may live forever." Below the sign two iron-wheeled tractors sat in the blackberry vines, rusting. In the middle of the clearing a man hacked at the vines with a machete.

"Old John's still the same." Amel grinned. "Ain't missed a lick since you been gone."

Tom gazed at the tractors and the man with the knife, his mind still on his uncle and the new thought of the mine. The man jerked up and down like a stickfigure in a green slicker and tin hat. One hand rose and fell with the machete and the other pulled the cut vines and tossed them behind.

"Old John don't dick around," Amel said. "He works them vines. That's job security."

Tom focused on the scene. John Hanson had been Mad John since the Korean War, carrying steel fragments in his body and a metal plate in his skull and a sermon about Jesus, all tangled up in a battle between Jesus and the valley's demons. Sometimes confusing Indians and demons. As a child he'd been terrified of the stringy white man with eyes like floodwater. When the old man, as hard-edged and angular as a barn hinge, had come pounding up the steps to his mother's house, spitting steel splinters and shouting about the devil, he and his brother had run to the brush to hide, burrowing into the salmonberry vines and listening while his mother laughed and offered the crazy man a cup of coffee.

"He keeps dropping pieces of that Plymouth all over the valley. Still scaring sin out of folks. Preached a sermon in the Red Dog one day standing on a barstool. All about how they was demons in the wilderness, things he'd seen, two-headed snakes and devilbirds and wolves that walk on two legs like a man. Every so often he'd spin around on that stool and keep preaching as he went around. Got Floyd so dizzy he fell over."

Tom grinned at the picture, wondering how the white man had heard those Indian stories.

"Sam Gravey finally shut him up by threatening to take him out and tie him to a tree and leave him there."

Sam Gravey now. Tom thought of his uncle's old friend. The truck slipped past the clearing, and in the instant of passage the man cutting vines paused and straightened and looked into the cab of the truck. A pair of gray-brown eyes locked onto Tom's, and then the truck sent them hurtling backwards. Tom shivered and wondered if Sam would be at the funeral.

The river eased up beside the road, half-white and flashing between breaks in the trees. On either side of the narrowing valley, peaks appeared wherever the timber had been cut back from the road. Then the dull, woodframe Baptist church came into sight, and the truck slowed at the edge of a shallow pool of wooden, one-story buildings lapping against a wall of granite at the end of the valley.

Around the town a halfcircle of peaks stood with their heads in the clouds and fingers of ice and snow running down their sides. He named the half-hidden peaks to himself as they slipped into view: Whitehorse, Skullcap, Stujack, Three Fingers, Pugh, Sloan—trying to recall Indian names for the mountains and remembering only one. Up the sides of each peak, arrows of forest ran to meet the descending fingers of snow. Clearcuts broke the ribbons of timber into patchworks, the residue of high-lead logging, even helicopter-logging in the steepest places. He strained to see the big mountain, Dakobed, up the Northfork drainage, but the mountain lay behind the same clouds that sat on the tops of the lesser peaks.

At Forks two rivers collided and ran side-by-side for a moment before pushing off toward the sea in different directions. The Stillaguamish fell in a clear, fast stream from the mountains and turned sharply at the town to follow the valley to Puget Sound in the southwest. A heavy, green river, the Sauk came rolling out of the mountains in two branches that came together above the town and made a deep, impatient stream that cut its own valley through the mountains to join the great Skagit to the north. In the triangle formed by the rivers, Forks squatted nervously, one eye on the trees left to cut and one on the rivers and rock.

"Your family must be mighty proud of you going off to college," Amel said as Tom opened the door and started to climb down from the truck.

He nodded. "Thanks."

"Take it easy."

He dropped to the wet gravel and waved toward the cab as Amel started the truck in the direction of the mill. Then he turned to look in the dusty window of the Fir Tree Cafe a dozen feet away, past the mud spattered along the bottom of the glass, beyond the beaten cardboard that insisted half-heartedly that the cafe was OPEN, through the flaked yellow title that arced from one corner of the glass to the other. He recognized the thin silhouette moving behind the counter and looked for a second figure, but all he saw was Ida drifting away from the three shadows hunched over the counter. A big doug fir drooped its branches over the shake roof of the little building, and a couple of four-wheel-drives with gas cans and chainsaws in the back nosed each other on the gravel near the door. He turned away and closed his eyes and listened to the soft rain, feeling the granite face of the peak they called Whitehorse leaning over the town. In the gulley at the peak's base were the icecaves, where you could sit against rock and ice with arms around knees and feel that you'd climbed down to an old, secret heart of the valley, a place without echoes where shadows moved cool and smooth along the walls.

He flipped his collar up once more against the drizzle and crossed the paved road in front of the Fir Tree, entering a gravel road that dove straight into a thick stand of small fir and alder tangled here and there with vine maple. He'd dried out some in the truck, but now the damp came back through the coat and jeans. The jacket's wool lining began to itch through his shirt, and he smelled the rain on salmonberry vines, a damp, familiar smell mixed with the stench of the mill a couple of miles away. Moving into the narrow lane he felt as though he were passing from one world to another. This damp, darker world didn't have anything to do with the one he'd left in California, or much to do with what was closer, as close as Seattle or any of the white cities. As he walked, he felt his body becoming heavier, more solid, as if he'd stepped out of one of those x-ray machines that made everything a shadowy silhouette of bones. A Canada Jay squawked at him from atop the berry vines and then swooped away laughing.

Startled, he kicked a round river pebble into a puddle, listened to his boots on the wet gravel, noted the glimmer of the slick salal leaves close to the ground, felt the weight of the clouds and remembered the droning of the bus all the way from Santa Barbara. The bobbing head of the seal slipped into his memory, and now he thought he could see brown eyes watching him in flight.

When he looked up, the house was there, a block of gray through the dark trees. On one side of the road the abandoned railroad tracks cruised off through salmonberry, blackberry, and wildrose vines toward an obscure destination. On the other side a small clearing in the trees exposed the old house, alone in a wet forest at the edge of the town.

He rounded the wall of trees and saw his mother in the straight chair on the porch. Even with a blanket over her shoulders, he could see that she'd grown heavier. Her plump hands worked back and forth with knitting needles, making what people called authentic Indian socks and caps to sell to the tourists who streamed into the valley to stare at the mountains. He'd hidden in the trees beside the house when the tourists came out of their stationwagons to bargain. They'd see the sign at the end of the road, and they'd come sniffing down the gravel drive in big cars. They always wanted to bargain, as if that was part of what they purchased. "You should've seen the squash blossom necklace I got down in Arizona," he heard one man tell another. "I talked a Navajo squaw down to damn near nothing." "Like Mexico," the other replied. "You have to; they expect it." When they spoke to his mother, they used words of one syllable pronounced slowly and carefully, the kind of speech they'd heard in western movies. They were words, he'd realized even then, designed to cross huge distances and return unmarked, as simple and compact as bullets.

But they always paid the same price, no matter what words they used. He hadn't noticed the sign. It was either overgrown or gone. The vines took care of things quickly.

The porch roof sagged like a broken bird wing. One support post swung free beside the steps, while the other bowed toward the road with drunken dignity. The drizzle made a silver fringe around the porch. In the windows on either side of the screendoor, more panes had given way to plywood. The moss had thickened on the roof, and he saw a hint of gray smoke coming from the tin chimney where a broken guy wire pointed toward the low clouds.

His mother bowed her head over the knitting, and he approached slowly, noting each detail, enjoying the deep red of the blanket against the dark blue of her cotton dress. The mocassins on her feet were the same one's she'd been wearing when he left, the fleece-lined ones he'd bought at REI in Seattle.

A transmission peeked out of the weeds close to the step, and a pile of bald tires leaned awkwardly beside it. Ferns and weeds jungled in the humus and dirt of the tires, and rusty orange water sat in the hollows and cracks of what he could see of the transmission. A fat, brown boletus grew at the end of the transmission, and he wondered why his mother hadn't picked it. They were her favorite, like mushroom pies.

He stepped over a pile of melting cardboard oil cans and noted the two new wrecks sprawled beside the house, tires gone and rusty drums on chunks of alder. The vehicles eyed him through shattered headlights, blackberry vines reaching up the sides of both cars. One vine had wrapped around a windshield wiper, allied with the rain.

His mother's hands moved more slowly than he remembered, and her skin seemed to have darkened while he was gone. She looked exotic, like someone from another country.

The hands paused, and she laid the knitting in her lap and reached to the warped flooring for a can of Rainier Ale. She took a short, quick drink, tilting her head back for an instant, and then set the can back on the boards, never taking the squinting eyes from the wool in her lap. Her hair, more silver than the shining rain, pulled tight against the sides of her head and slipped in thick braids down either shoulder over the blanket.

Seeing the eyes, he thought of his own almond-shaped eyes. "Ching-chong Chinaman," the white kids had sung, "sitting on a fence, trying to make a dollar out of fifteen cents." He'd never even seen a Chinaman back then, and probably few of the other kids had either, since the Chinese had all been chased out of the valley years before. And he couldn't understand then why the white kids called him that, since they knew his family was Indian and not Chinese. Ching-chong Chinaman, sitting on a rail. Along came a white man and chopped off his tail. Hiding in the woods, he'd tried to imagine people with tails, and eyes like his own. What he'd imagined was a devil. "They made a thing called a sundown law," his uncle had explained. "Then they rounded up all them little guys and shipped them right out of town on the railroad the little guys built. No yellow people here now, just red and white." His uncle had pulled the cleaning rod from the gun he was oiling and grinned. "No blue ones yet. And I'm still waiting for them to make a sundown law for old-growth Indians." He'd imagined, back then, an army of white men chanting Ching-chong Chinaman as they converged on the Indian people who had lived in the valley forever, never anywhere else.

His mother didn't pause again until he set a boot on the porch step. Then she heard the creak and looked up, her eyes swimming out from the round face until they saw him. A spark flickered in the nearly black eyes, and the corners of the lips lifted until a smile appeared. He saw that she didn't have her teeth in.

"Tommy," she said, dropping the knitting and staring at him. Her voice was barely audible.

"Hi Mama." He stepped to the chair and knelt to kiss her cheek, smelling the green beer. Inside the house a scratchy record started up and Lefty Frizzell sang, "If you got the money, honey, I got the time." Far away, a heavily loaded truck began to work up speed for the trip from the valley, the gears whining in deepening pitch.

"Who is it, Mama?" His brother materialized behind the screen door, distorted by the torn and rusty wire so that he looked like a dark ghost. Then the door opened and Jimmy stepped out, his bare belly protruding between the dirty white teeshirt and beltless jeans.

He reached out his hand toward his brother. The round, familiar face with its two chins mimicked the color of the rusty screen on the door and spread into a wider grin. When Jimmy reached to shake hands he felt the familiar soft touch of the Indian handshake. In Santa Barbara he'd learned to grip hard when he shook hands. McBride had explained it. "They'll think you're queer if you shake hands like that," he'd said. "This isn't any reservation or bushwoods Indian camp. This here's the Native-American-economic-opportunity-big-time, Chief. Scholarship of broken treaties."

In the background, Lefty Frizzell warned, "When you run outa money, honey, I run outa time." His brother's face had softened and taken on the first plastic sag of the alcoholic. He'd gained at least thirty pounds.

"That record's so old it's probably worth a fortune," he said. "You ought to frame it instead of playing it."

Jimmy shrugged. "That's about the last of Uncle Jim's. Most of the rest are broke or so scratched up you can't understand them. Not one Jimmy Rogers left," he added sadly.

He looked up in surprise at his brother's carelessness about the name, and then he looked back at his mother, who was watching him alertly. She'd grown a lot older in a year. He tried to remember her age. She must be around sixty, he thought, but she looked older. Married late to the obscure man who'd been his father, she'd seemed old as long as he could remember, not like the mothers of the kids in town and not like the tanned women in California whose one goal seemed to be to become as dark as an Indian. His mother's teeth, he knew, would be on the shelf in her room. From the first day she'd complained that they hurt her.

"I'm sorry," he said loudly. "I came as fast as I could." She looked harder at him and nodded once, her eyes becoming more distant. The music ran out, and he heard the rain and the river behind the house. The sliding current softened the sharp edge left from the bus and log truck, and he looked toward the doorway, hoping the fire hadn't gone out in the stove.

"Come on in and dry off," Jimmy said, running his free hand through his burr haircut. "You come on in, too, Mama. It's too damned wet out here. She always wants to sit out here in the rain, and I keep telling her she's going to get pneumonia again." He looked past Tom and frowned. "Got to fix those posts one of these days." Then he noticed how wet Tom's clothes were. "You should've called Ida," he said. "I would've come and got you."

"Still got the Ford?" Tom looked around for the old truck.

"Just put a new clutch in, heavy-duty. It's around back with a load of alder."

Tom took the knitting from his mother as she rose with effort from the chair and followed his brother into the house.

The house smelled of mildew and fungus in spite of the fire in the pot-bellied stove in the center of the room. The windows, half plywood and dirty, skimmed the brightness from the gray day, and the bulb that hung in the middle of the room splashed light around ineffectually upon the bare floor and few pieces of furniture. At one end of the room, a heavy mahogany table covered with faded oilcloth stood near a sink and an enamel counter piled with dirty dishes. A sack leaned against the cabinet door beneath the sink, overflowing with crushed beercans and coffee grounds, the bag stained dark and wet at the base. A crumpled pink bag of sugar sat on the corrugated countertop.

Near the front door, an overstuffed couch sagged against the wall, cotton protruding from the arms and a tattered blue chenile spread draped over the back and cushions. Where the spread pooled on the floor, a muddy vibram boot track stood out on the tufts. The coffee table he'd made in high school woodshop, its lathe-turned legs uneven and wobbly and its varnish peeling, squatted before the couch, two open beer cans on one end and a newspaper with a mess of carburetor parts on the other. He looked around, surprised by the condition of the house.

On the wall above the couch hung a plastic crucifix, blood dripping from the plastic thorns down emaciated plastic ribs. The crucifix had been a gift from Mad John who'd told Sarah that he'd gotten it in a trade over in Concrete for a book about a crazy man and a whale that he'd gotten from a Lummi woman in Lynnwood. An Indian family like theirs, Mad John must have thought, needed a crucifix like that on the wall. Their mother had liked it and their uncle had hated it, taking to the woods for a week in protest. Next to the crucifix hung a beautiful cedar basket.

As his eyes moved along the side of the room, he saw his high school graduation picture on the wall above the television. He was preposterously dark and solemn in the black robe and cap, with a gold tassle for getting the highest grades in the school. There was no picture of Jimmy, because Jimmy had dropped out in his third year to set chokers for a gypo outfit that folded a year later. On the wall near the graduation picture an out-of-date calendar advertised Stihl chainsaws with a picture of a grinning Swede bucking hardwood. On an upturned cable spool, the record player spun the silent Lefty Frizzell record, the needle making ghost sounds against the center.

Jimmy turned off the record player and went to a small white refrigerator at the end of the counter. Taking a screwdriver off the top of the refrigerator, he jammed it into a hole where the door handle had been. The door jumped open and Jimmy took out a can of Rainier Ale.

He motioned with the can toward Tom. "How about some green death?"

When Tom nodded, Jimmy took out a second can and swung the door closed with his foot. The door caught and Jimmy tossed the screwdriver on top of the refrigerator.

"They had a sale at the Serve-U," Jimmy said. "Two-fifty a sixpack." He glanced toward their mother on the couch and sidled closer to the stove, hunching his shoulders with the heat. "It's good to see you, Tommy." He handed a beer to his brother and popped the top on his own, taking a quick drink and saying, "Kinda thought maybe you weren't ever coming back up here." He nodded toward their mother, who had taken up the knitting at one end of the couch but sat staring at them with motionless hands.

"She hasn't said a word about it since Sam brung him in. Hasn't even cried. You know, I half expected her to cut her hair and all, but she ain't done nothing except some smudging."

"What happened?" He kept his voice low to match his brother's.

"Heart attack, the coroner said. Sam found him up the Stehemish where that old berry-house used to be. The place he showed us that time." He took a long swallow and belched silently, his cheeks puffed like a red squirrel's.

"He was acting funny the last couple months. Since they started cutting that road up the Stehemish." He frowned and looked toward their mother.

"He was pretty nuts about that mine." He paused and looked at Tom, but seeing his brother's blank face he went on. "Last three weeks he was staying out in the mountains. Came in once or twice at night for flour and stuff, but nobody but me saw him. He was living out in the woods somewhere, and when I caught him sneaking in here for stuff one night he started raving about wolves and roads and a bunch of that old junk he used to tell us when we were kids. He said they were coming back."

"Who was coming back?"

"I don't know. He wouldn't exactly say. But I think he was seeing things out there, and he carried that old Krag around with him. People were talking about catching him and sending up to Cedro Wooley, especially after he started shooting the tractors." He set his beer on the television and went to the stove, opened the door, and shoved a stick of alder into the fire.

"Stove burns this stuff like paper. I'd get some maple, but hell, that'd be like putting tuck'n roll in a Rambler." He reloaded the stove and closed the door and then swivelled for the beer.

"What tractors?" Tom glanced at his mother, who seemed to be studying him from across the room.

Jimmy followed his glance and spoke more quietly. "He was taking potshots at the guys working on the road out there. He wasn't shooting at them exactly, just knocking out headlights and tires and stuff like that—enough to make those guys pretty nervous and J. D. Hill pretty mad."

"What's J. D. got to do with it?"

Jimmy belched softly and scratched under his belly. "Good price on this," he said, nodding at the beer can. "J. D.'s got the contract to put that road through. J. D. owns everything in the valley now."

"Couldn't you talk him into staying here when he came in at night?"

"You ever try to make him do something?" He looked nervously toward their mother. Lowering his voice further, he said,

"Look at her, way she's staring at you. That's all she does now, sit there and stare at something, or nothing, or sit out there in the rain and knit."

Tom took a swallow of the bitter beer and felt the wet wool of the jacket lining through his denim shirt. He set his beer on the floor and peeled off the jacket, laying it across the kindling box near the stove. When he stood up again with the beer, Jimmy went on.

"Sheriff went after him but never found nothing. He took a couple of shots at Leroy and Dinker two days before Sam found him." He belched and then edged his voice close to a whisper. "You should've seen Dinker down at the Red Top telling about it. Like it took the goddamned calvary all over again to save his ass."

"At Leroy?" He lowered his voice further. "Have you seen Karen?"

Jimmy picked up his brother's jacket and hung it on the back of a kitchen chair. When he turned around he said, "Yeah, I seen her." He straightened the pile of kindling in the box and added, "She'll probably be working with Ida down there tonight."

Tom nodded. "How'd they know it was him?" He backed closer to the stove.

"Who else would it have been?"

"Amel Barstow gave me a ride from the freeway," Tom said. "He told me they were cutting the right-of-way through for the mine." He shivered and turned to face the stove.

Jimmy rubbed his stiff black hair with his fingers. "Before he went out there he started telling folks around town that he wouldn't let them do it, that it was sacred land up there and that kind of stuff. Made people pretty pissed off. With the mill damned near shut down and logging almost dead, people need the jobs that mine'll bring in. Already some guys are cutting the road through and hauling out timber, and a couple of guys are even doing something up at the mine site. And when the snow melts up there they say they'll hire a bunch more guys. I tried to explain all that, to let him know how folks felt, but he couldn't even hear what I was saying."

Tom edged still closer to the stove. "Remember the time we camped up where that berry-house used to be, and he told us about the old days, about the singers?"

"Sure. I guess I remember some of that, but that time's long gone, Tommy, and he just wouldn't admit it. And couldn't nobody tell him."

"That country was sacred to him," Tom said. He felt odd speaking in the past tense about the man who had raised them after their father got hammered into the duff by a widowmaker. Besides, he thought, if it was a sacred place, shouldn't it be sacred to him, too, and Jimmy? He tried to imagine his uncle haunting the Stehemish drainage like a sleep-walker, but he failed.

"They tried to get Bayard to help catch him, but Bayard wouldn't do it. Bayard said couldn't nobody find him if he didn't want to be found. Bayard was the only one in the valley who didn't seem like he was pissed off, except Sam of course, but nobody ever knows what Sam's thinking. Hell, nobody ever sees Sam anymore either. Seems like he's living out in the hills too."

Tom turned to warm his front side and then sniffed and said, "You using cedar in there?"

Jimmy shook his head slightly. "She's been burning cedar branches in here since he died. You know, keeps the ghost away." He shrugged. "It's been a little spooky around here, with her smudging like that every night. And the last few nights there's been some big goddamned dog messing around outside."

"A dog?" Tom looked curiously at his brother. There were always dogs prowling around the valley. Sometimes they packed up and killed livestock, usually a pack of mongrel shepherds and coon hounds.

"The biggest goddamn dog you ever saw. I found his tracks out back the morning before Sam brought the body in, and then last night he made so much noise on the porch I thought he was going to come in the front door. I got the shotgun but he was gone before I got out there. The tracks are probably still in the mud by the porch."

Tom turned and noticed the steam rising from his Levis. He finished the beer and tossed the can into the kindling box. He imagined his uncle shooting at machinery. The 30-40 would make quite a hole. As a kid, he'd listened to his uncle's stories with big eyes. "I ain't supposed to tell you all this stuff," his uncle said. "It's bad medicine, heap bad luck." Talking like an Indian in an old movie, he'd grinned like he always did, but the grin held little humor. Then he'd listened to his uncle's stories in the dark, almost believing he could see the wolf spirit, *staka'yu*. But even then the few old words his uncle used had been confusing, an other-world language connected with strangeness and magic. He'd felt the words cutting him off from something at the same time they brought that something closer. And he'd sensed that the words balanced painfully on his uncle's tongue, twisted and sharp-edged, so that he drew back from those utterances. But he'd learned that the wolf spirit brought deer to the man who possessed it. It wasn't complicated. The man just had to walk up to the deer who came to give itself. The deer liked to be taken by such a man, and afterwards, if all was done properly, if their bones were sunk in a stream or pond, they would come back. "That's the way it used to be," his uncle said. "In the real world, before everything became crazy." When he hunted with his uncle in the now-crazy world, they'd fought their way through slide alder and vine maple and cursed the devil's club like everyone else, but they'd always gotten a deer. His uncle had been the best hunter in the valley, and when he was young people called him "Wolf." Nobody knew when that name got started. Some said it came from the Upper Skagits.

They'd been sitting on a downed cedar near the headwaters of the Stehemish, listening to the milk-white river rolling boulders like thunder when his uncle had told him about the spirit. A story that perhaps shouldn't have been told.

Up that far, miles from the nearest road or world of men, the river roared down from the icy mountain, a shock of waves and silt that cut the drainage like a knife and flashed away in leaping, creamy white angles and creases. Everywhere, fir and hemlock trees lay fallen and tangled by the wild river, branches torn away and tops pointing downstream while roots clung hopelessly to the caving shore. Even ten feet from the water, a cold mist lay over everything, and moss coated tree and stone. Tom had watched his uncle's face grow sharper and more intent. He'd seen the same wildness later in the face of a Choctaw student at the university, Jacob Nashoba, who was named, he said, for the wolf. Tom had wanted to tell Nashoba the story of *staka'yu*, the hunter, but he had no words.

He'd tried to tell his brother about *staka'yu* once when they'd sat on a windfall fishing for dolly varden trout, but Jimmy had laughed and said, "Forget that old crap. That stuff's for old men and crazy longhairs. You forget about wolf spirits and all those other things—Knife Man and Cedar Man and Old Man Raven and all that crap—and learn about chainsaws and carburetors. That ghost stuff is for movies." Jimmy had spit a wad of Redman chewing tobacco into the stream and grimaced. For a week he'd been trying to learn to chew, and he'd felt sick all week.

Tom had watched the floating tobacco with disgust, casting his salmon egg well upstream to let it drift past the trout, thinking it was a good thing he hadn't told Jimmy about the land of the dead reached by paddling across black water on a rotten log.

The heat prickled his back. Jimmy had become silent, nursing his beer and staring at the cracks in the floor. A mosquito whined in Tom's ear, and he thought about the trips with his uncle up the Stehemish to where the trail ended. They'd had to skirt the rocky edge of the glacier-silted river by jumping from rock to shore, rock to log until they reached the broad upper drainage where the whites never went. There they could see the muddy tail of the jumble of ice called the Chocolate Glacier, and they could see the cloud of dust that hung over Dusty Creek where the creek ate away at the pumice of the Great Fill. In this hidden cirque the forest was thick old-growth, well inside the wilderness boundary, with Dakobed, the big white mother mountain, standing above them. They'd shoot a deer, remove the meat from the bones, and let the river take the bones, his uncle praying. Then they'd pack out the deer's flesh without anyone knowing. "These white people are funny," he would say over his shoulder as they walked. "They want us to shoot old, tough bucks instead of young does. They don't want us to catch fish with nets because they want to stand out in the streams in rubber pants and catch them with chicken feathers. We eat the fish, but they stuff them and put them on their walls. I've seen that, Tommy, fish on walls. Even just fish heads sometimes, with their mouths open like grizzly bears. It made me laugh." He'd turned and grinned. "They took everything, you know, and said they would pay us. Now when the government gives us money, they say Indian people are on welfare. The white people could never pay enough, no matter how much they paid or how long. If they all went away tomorrow and gave us back the whole country it wouldn't be enough. But they don't give anything back. It ain't their way."

When he was twelve, his uncle called him "Little Wolf" and laughed, and sometimes then, when he caught a reflection of his lean, pock-marked face in a window in town he thought of the name and his slanted brown eyes became wolflike.

He wondered how it had been for the old man, dying alone in the woods. The stories said that a man couldn't die before his guardian spirit left him. And the spirit would have come to him, Tom Joseph. "I'm willing this spirit to you, Tommy," his uncle had explained. "That's one way we can do it, you see. Sometimes these spirits just do whatever they want, and go anyplace they want, but this is a good one and will do what I ask it to." Tom shivered again and felt the nerve stab his shoulder and realized that his shoulders were tight and hunched in spite of the heat. Night after night he'd swatted mosquitoes and listened to the stories while Jimmy, followed by his tilting shadow, ran off down the gravel road to play with the white kids in town. He'd tried to imagine what it would've been like to have been a real Indian, before the whites came and began to cut the trees—and pay Indians to cut the trees—and everything changed. In the winter, when the valley was stiff and quiet with snow, his uncle and mother told the funny stories about coyote's tricks, about fox shrinking the animals so the Indians could hunt them, about the tall, bearded hemlock that stood near Concrete on the banks of the Skagit and stole the souls of foolish Indians who came too close, and threw the souls across the river to another tree which threw them back until the person died. And once his uncle had pointed the tree out when they'd driven past on the way to Cedro Wooley. It was the tallest hemlock he'd ever seen, its scaley branches drooping and malicious.

"Have another beer." His brother was already holding a can toward him.

He nodded his thanks and pulled the tab and took a drink, stepping aside so Jimmy could shove another stick into the stove.

"We got a venison roast in the oven but it won't be done for an hour," Jimmy said. "I can fry up some spam if you're hungry. We could have some sandwiches." He straightened up and continued. "You got here just in time. The funeral's tomorrow."

"No thanks," he said.

"What?" Jimmy looked at him curiously.

"I can wait for the roast. Thanks anyway." He drank more of the hard beer and said, "Where?"

"The old place up the Stehemish. Going to be hell to pay getting down that road with all this rain."

Tom glanced across the room toward a doorless doorway leading into a colder recess of the house. The rain picked up its tempo again and tapped on the rotten shake roof.

"You stop at the Fir Tree?"

When Tom shook his head, his brother said, "She'll be there later." And after a moment's silence he added, "When you going back to school?" His brows furrowed, and his mouth puckered at one corner where he chewed on the inside of his cheek between sips of beer.

"I'm not."

Jimmy looked at him with surprise. "That's crazy," he said finally. "You stay here, Tommy, you'll rot like me and all the rest of these guys. Go back to the land of opportunity. This valley's dying." He paused again and then said, "And you shouldn't think she's waiting for you."

Tom watched as his mother rose, leaving the blanket on the couch, and walked to the kitchen end of the room. She bent stiffly and pulled a sack of potatoes from beneath the counter. He followed and placed a hand on her shoulder.

She set a potato on the counter and said, "It's good you're back. We'll have a talk later."

When he looked back at his brother, Jimmy was staring in surprise. Outside, the valley lay deep in rain.

His uncle's room was at the end of a short corridor, with their mother's room at the other end and Jimmy's in the middle. After dinner, he left his brother washing dishes and his mother reading her Bible on the couch and, mumbling a few words about how tired he was, he went into the small room and shut the door behind him. His mother watched him go with a worried expression.

In the dark, he felt for the string beside the door and pulled. A bulb winked on in the center of the room, flushing tall shadows from the corners. In the dead quiet, the river splashed softly toward the house. Hearing the water, he stopped. He'd missed it without knowing what it was he missed. He'd gone to the ocean at night and watched the waves hiss with phosphorescent edges into the tar-coated beach, but the ocean wasn't the same. It didn't flow.

In one corner a small, neatly made bed sat in a wood frame that still had the axe marks from its creation. A red blanket stretched across the bed, and beside it an upended apple crate held a small tin lamp with no shade. Two rifles hung in a hand-carved cedar rack on the wall near the foot of the bed, with boxes of cartridges on the bottom shelf of the rack. Stopping at the bed, he took down the smaller of the guns, a worn twenty-two with the stock nicked and polished smooth. A hair-triggered single-action, it was the first gun he'd fired, the one he'd taken grouse, snowshoe hares and squirrels with. He ran his hand along the barrel and it came back stained with rust. He replaced the twenty-two and lifted down the heavier rifle.

The thirty-forty Krag was long and bulky, an old military gun with a cutdown stock. He held the gun and tried to remember how old it was. Older than his uncle, as old as the Spanish-American war. The Krag wasn't rusty, and when he lifted the military sight that could be set up to sixteen hundred yards, his thumb and finger came away smudged with oil.

He set the rifle in the rack and looked around the room. His uncle's snowshoes hung on the wall across from the bed, the frames gray under a tattered coating of lacquer, the rawhide dry and brittle. Beside his uncle's hung his own Black Forest shoes of aluminum tubing and neopreme webbing. Lighter and more maneuverable than the old wood-and-leather bearpaws, they looked dead and evil hanging on the papered wall. By late spring the snow was hard enough to walk on without snowshoes. It was then that the Stehemish had made their long walks across the mountains.

He returned to the bed and sat on the edge, where the wood frame came up an inch above the sagging mattress. In other times relatives would have come and taken these things away, to keep the dead one from coming back for his possessions. In difficult cases, with a stubborn ghost, they would have burned the house. But now the only close relative was Aunt Jenny, and Jimmy wouldn't have let those things happen anyway.

He felt for his uncle's presence, searched for a ghost in the corners. But he was aware only of the dampness in the walls and floor, the river distant through the trees, and the rain lying heavy on the mossy roof.

His uncle's backpack was in the corner beneath the snowshoes, an old green canvas bag on a wooden frame stained with mud. His own Kelty pack was gone, probably traded away by Jimmy during the winter.

He lifted the pack off its nail and leaned it against the wall. From the canvas bag he pulled an Army blanket which he unfolded carefully before dropping it to the floor. He slid a tightly folded square of clear plastic from the pack and beneath the plastic found the burnt coffee can and wooden spoon his uncle always carried in the woods. Inside the can were a plastic bag of salt and a few yards of parachute cord.

He stuffed everything back into the pack and hung it on the nail. He thought of his uncle, alone in the mountains, shooting at machines.

He found the cleaning rod, oil and rags in a box beneath the bed and lifted the guns down one at a time, running an oily rag along the barrels and shoving an oiled patch down the inside of each barrel with the cleaning rod. The acrid smell of the gun oil freed a rush of memories, and he sat for a moment before rubbing each stock with the same rag until the rifles shone, metal and wood. He placed the smaller gun in the rack and picked up the box of thirty-forty shells. He shoved four of the cartridges into the magazine of Krag and closed the bolt with a satisfying jolt. Then he ejected the shells, opening and closing the bolt with hard, quiet jerks of his wrist.

He put the Krag and ammunition away and lay down on the bed, his hands behind his head and his boots dangling over the rough, split-cedar board at the foot. He realized with a shock that he was taller than his uncle. He remembered his uncle as a tall, big man, one of the biggest men he'd ever known, but he knew that he, Tom Joseph, was not tall.

His thoughts eddied. He had a sudden impression that the peaks surrounding the valley had shifted to block the way out. He wouldn't be able to leave. He focused on the brittle-looking lightbulb, then he closed his eyes and watched the spots fade in back of his eyelids. Images finned in the dark pool of the valley, and the old house settled in the rain. The hemlock hurled souls across the wide Skagit and he felt himself arcing over whirlpools in the green river.

With his uncle he canoed the rivers and pushed through masses of blood-red and orange salmon leaving the rivers to spawn far up in the headwaters, in the bright water upstream.

Beyond the room the rain brushed the leaves and branches one last time before giving up, and the sound of the river rose on a thin wind and subsided. Canoes flew from treetops, hurled back and forth over a wide river by tall trees. Bones and bits of flesh and hair spilled from the canoes and became the swarming salmon. His uncle stood in one of the canoes and sighted the Krag and fired at nothing and then began to dance. Tom Joseph climbed an icewall, chipping steps with his knife, dreaming that he lay in his uncle's bed on a rain-stilled night, dreaming the rising howl of the wolf, moon-bright snow, and a running shadow. In his dream, voices spoke in a language he couldn't understand, a fragmented jumble of disordered words aimed directly at him. When he tried to reply, his tongue was swollen and he could taste the blood.

He awoke to the sound and lay on the narrow bed listening to the silence of the room and the valley. Then the scratching came again, along the wall outside the room, and the sigh of a deep breath drawn in difficulty or haste. He rose and lifted the Krag from the rack. In the dark he located the cartridges and slipped three into the rifle's magazine. Noiselessly, he moved out of the room and down the little hall and through the front room to the screendoor. He eased the door open and slid out of the house, crossing the porch and stepping down into the yard. The half-moon lined the posts and weeds of the yard as he walked around the corner of the house toward the back.

Near the woodpile he saw it. A few feet from the wall of his uncle's room, it paused and looked up at him, the scattered moonlight sparking in yellow eyes. He raised the rifle and aimed it in the animal's direction, and it turned slowly and began to walk toward the trees and river. As it passed the pickup, it stopped and looked back at him, its broad head even with the top of the truck fender, the ruff on its shoulders erect and its eyes fixed on him. The legs were long, and the deep chest swept back to narrow hindquarters. For a moment he stared back before the animal turned and moved away into the thick second-growth. He watched it disappear and then he turned and walked toward the front of the house. The moon made black stitched lines of the crevasses on Whitehorse above the town and sent the spiked tops of the fir and hemlock in jagged shadows across the yard. The river grew suddenly loud in the sleeping valley.

"You see it?" Jimmy stood in his shorts and teeshirt in the middle of the room.

He hesitated a moment, shifting the rifle to his left hand and angling it toward the floor. "Yeah. Looks like somebody's dog prowling around."

"Somebody's damned big dog," Jimmy said before shuffling back toward his room.

Seated on his uncle's bed, Tom emptied the shells from the

gun, and then he lay back on the bed with the rifle beside him and thought of his uncle, the cold peaks, where he was and where he had been. He heard the creaking floor of his brother's room and his mother sigh in her sleep.

3

The scarred hearse spun in the mud and gravel at the end of the road as it turned to clamber onto the blacktop. The rain gleamed on its bug-like shell and beaded the curtained windows and dripped from the rain-gutters to the road. As the hearse picked up speed, the rain wisped out behind. In front of the Fir Tree, a short, round old man wearing overalls, a red mackinaw, heavy boots and a thunderous white beard shouted at two boys who jabbed at the asphalt with picks. Rain dripped from the moss-green edges of the man's bowler hat as he gesticulated toward a spot between two big holes six feet apart in the pavement. As the boys stood side-by-side and flung the picks indifferently at the blacktop, the old man raised his round arms like a flightless bird and let them drop. It seemed to Tom that the little man rose a foot or two off the asphalt before settling again. Then he took off the hat and wiped his bald head with his hand before pushing the hat back into place. As the hearse swerved to miss the holes, the old man jerked the hat from his head and held it to his chest. The boys leaned on their picks and stared as the black vehicle passed by, and then one of them pressed a finger to his nose and blew.

In the pickup, Jimmy swerved behind the hearse and shifted into second, clutching the round black shift knob lovingly as he shook his head. "Floyd's digging more holes," he said. "I hope he finds it before the whole damned road's gone and we can't get out of the driveway."

"Calling that a driveway is stretching it," Tom said. The picture of Floyd made him feel like laughing and crying at the same time.

Tom turned to watch Floyd replace the hat and begin waving his arms at the two boys, fluttering like a heavy butterfly over the pavement. When Tom turned back, he could see the mud from the side road spattering off the hearse's tires and up the sides of the vehicle. He felt his mother breathing heavily beside him, the three of them crushed into the cab of the pickup because she wouldn't ride in the hearse or her sister's car. He turned with difficulty, rotating his shoulders as far as he could without dislodging his mother so that he could look back at the shiny Buick that followed the pickup. His aunt Jenny's new husband, the blocky Upper Skagit from Cedro Wooley, drove the car with both hands divided over the steering wheel, his dull face intent and his black hat on his head. Aunt Jenny was half-turned to listen to something the Baptist preacher was saying from the back seat.

"Phony bastard," Tom thought as he caught a pale glimpse of the preacher's face. They'd all be saying a lot of crap about his uncle. Jenny hadn't been in Forks for two years, though she lived only thirty-five minutes away. But it was Jenny who'd insisted on the preacher, and his mother had sided with her. A lot of the Indians on that side of the mountains were Shakers, but the Josephs had been Baptists for three generations. It would have been four but for Tom and Jimmy.

In the Buick, the preacher was saying from the back seat, "It's a shame about Jim; he was a good man." And he was thinking, I wish I'd worn my boots for this one. He just hadn't thought about the mud. Why in thunder did the Indian cemetery have to be so far out in the sticks? A place that wasn't even really a place.

"Jimmy was the nicest one in the fambly," Jenny said, nodding her head as she smoothed the black dress over her broad lap and regretted having to wear a raincoat for the ceremony—even though no one would really be there to see the dress.

"Folks say he went nuts, crazy as a coon," the husband

replied flatly, his eyes fastened like brown barnacles to the road ahead.

"Gordon!" Jenny glanced back at the preacher.

"Hell, that's what I heard. That's what everybody says. Just went craziern a coon and took to running around the woods shooting at people. There's blanket Induns and then there's nuts, and if that's not nuts I don't know what is. Trouble with Jim Joseph was he wanted to be a backwoods Indun all his life. Didn't want nothing to change. That's the trouble with a lot of Induns in these parts. Hell, he could've had a good job with that mining company. I heard they offered him one as a consultant or technical advisor or something. Could've made plenty of dough and fixed up that excuse for a house and got a new rig like this one." He patted the wheel with his left hand and the corners of his mouth smiled.

The preacher turned his hat in slow circles on his knees. The Indian driving the car was unfortunately right and it made him uncomfortable. The deceased had been, in fact, crazy, and the talk only made things worse. "The poor man wasn't well," he said. In a yard beside the road he saw a white dog lunging at the end of its chain, snarling at the car with a mouth as red as blood. The dog's coat shone with rain, and its feet were braced in two inches of mud. On the ridge of the frame house behind the dog, two ravens watched with cocked heads.

The three vehicles left the asphalt and rattled along a Forest Service road, the tires kicking small rocks up to ping against the pickup and Buick. Jenny's husband slowed to get out of range of the pickup tires, cursing softly when the first pebble rang from the car's bumper. The Buick's wide, heavy wipers swept clean swaths across the windshield, and the rain beaded on the waxed hood.

After half an hour along the straight gravel road between narrow lines of tall, dark second-growth, the hearse slowed and turned to the right on a wide path of mud and clay hacked from a wall of vine maple and alder and vines. The hearse stopped twenty feet from the gravel road, and Jimmy stopped the truck with its nose close to the other vehicle. On the road, Gordon braked the Buick and he and Jenny peered through the broad windshield like heavy, curious fish in an aquarium.

The driver got out, shutting the door carefully, and walked back toward the pickup. The clear plastic raincoat over his black suit and the plastic on the black yachtsman's cap glistened in the rain, and as he reached the truck's fender he tried to frown. Tom watched as a fat bead of rain dropped from the back of the cap and landed inside the plastic collar. A flicker of irritation touched the driver's face for an instant like the involuntary shiver of a mule bitten by a fly.

The frown deepened as the driver realized that his shiny black shoes were sunk an inch deep in the sticky mud. He stopped beside the window on the driver's side and Jimmy rolled the glass down and said, "What's wrong?"

The man motioned toward the mass of branches and vines that seemed to almost choke off the road a few yards in front of the hearse. He moved a lump inside his cheek and turned to spit in the direction of the graveyard.

"I ain't driving in there," he said, working the tobacco. "Them vines'll tear hell out of that paint job. Probably get stuck in the goddamn mud, too." He sucked at his teeth as he spoke, and Tom could see the brown juice at the corners of his mouth.

Tom watched his mother watch Jimmy's face darken. "It's only a couple hundred feet," Jimmy said, "and this road's got a good bottom. You won't get stuck."

"Can't do it. Hell, this place don't even look like it's been used in a hunnert years." The man shoved his hands in the pockets of the plastic coat and spit before looking back at Jimmy.

"I don't understand. What do you mean, you can't do it?" Jimmy looked as if he might cry. "You got to do it. This is a funeral and that's the cemetery."

The man stared impassively. "Might as well back this heap onto the road so's I can get that rig out," he said.

"What do you expect us to do?" Jimmy asked, pronouncing each word softly.

"That's your problem. Maybe you can carry him in there, but I sure as hell ain't driving in."

Tom opened the door and walked around the front end of the truck, being careful not to slip in the slick mud. When he stood next to the driver, he said, "What's the problem?" his voice calm, almost friendly.

The man shifted his attention, and Tom noticed that the driver's face was wet and that water clung inside the creases of his neck. Then he realized that his old suit, the one in which he'd graduated from high school, was soaking up the rain.

"I ain't driving any further," the driver said. "The sooner your brother backs this heap out of the way, the better." He hesitated, and his voice rose an octave. "The vines'll scratch hell out of that rig, and I'll get canned."

Tom looked toward the cemetery, still invisible through the trees. Now he could hear the river beyond the trees, muted by the rain. The thimbleberry and salmonberry vines grew close on both sides of the wide path that was supposed to be a road. Somebody—probably his brother—had come recently to hack off the alder and maple branches and thick vines, but it wasn't a good job. The driver was right. It did look as though no one had made a deposit in the old cemetery in a long time. But the hearse could get through with only a few scratches if the driver was careful.

He turned and watched the man's face for a moment and saw the blue eyes begin to fidget.

"I'd like to talk to you for a minute," Tom said, taking the driver's elbow and stepping away from the truck. The driver jerked his arm free, but followed as they both slid in the mud.

A few feet from the truck Tom faced the driver and the wall

of vegetation. He felt the water seeping into his thin soles, and the fact saddened him.

"You know," he said quietly. "I guess it used to be easier. Our people used to put their dead up in trees, in canoes, in special places. I heard they used to do it right here. But that's illegal now. White men came along and made a law against it. Now the law says we have to pay somebody like you to help put us in the ground. Isn't that incredible? You people came to our country and told us that what we'd been doing for a thousand years was not legal. I have trouble understanding that sometimes." He wiped rain from his forehead and looked over the driver's shoulder toward the thicket.

"If I had a couple hundred bucks," he said softly, "I'd just give it to you and tell you to get yourself a new paint job when this is over. But I don't have five bucks, so what I'm going to do instead is suggest that you look around. You're in Indian country right now." Tom almost smiled as he watched the driver begin to realize the tough spot he was in. Except for the preacher, who didn't count, he was surrounded by Indians. A few hundred feet away were more Indians, lots of them, maybe even scarier ones.

The driver sized up the Indian kid without moving his eyes. He was taller than the kid by six inches, but the kid had a massive chest and shoulders and heavy fists. They probably weighed about the same, but twenty pounds of his was beer flab, pork muscle. There was a fifteen or twenty year age difference and the Indian was in his prime. It probably wasn't a bluff because these Indians didn't seem to play that way. He'd once seen a Skagit they called Skookum Joe, a man in his thirties built just like this kid, nearly take a guy's head off. After a few thousand years of pushing dugouts up the rivers these Indians were tough. The Indian in the truck was even bigger than this one, and the one back in the car might, probably would, get involved.

The driver looked at the hearse. It was old, and the company had a couple of new ones in Arlington. The piece of shit was ready for the scrap pile, or they wouldn't have given it to him for this job. Hell, they probably expected it to get fucked up or they wouldn't have assigned it to him.

The driver sighed and spat into the rain, wondering why he'd been stuck with the job. These Indians didn't even put their dead in real cemeteries. If it wasn't for the law they'd probably still be sticking them up in trees and letting them rot, dropping bones all over the place. The woods must have been a great place for picnics back then, he thought, with fucking corpses falling out of trees on you.

"All right, kid," he said, raising his eyebrows beneath the brim of the cap and looking off toward the trees. "Didn't know it would upset everyone like this. Let's get on with it."

Tom felt the rain leaking through to his shoulders as he walked back to the pickup. He wondered why he didn't have a raincoat. It seemed like the people who lived in rain never had rain gear, except the loggers who seldom wore theirs. In Santa Barbara everyone had umbrellas and it never rained.

As he climbed into the pickup, the hearse was already creeping down the road beneath the shadowy canopy of evergreens, the vines trailing along its sides. He glanced at his mother, who stared straight ahead, and he wondered where she'd found the money. It must have cost a couple years' worth of knitting. He knew his uncle would have prefered to be still lying where Sam had found him, spread across the drainage, the mountains.

"What'd you say to that guy?" Jimmy asked, his eyes fixed on the muddy road and hearse ahead of them.

"I just explained how important it was."

Jimmy snorted.

Tom wondered about his mother's long silence. Maybe she was thinking about all the people who wouldn't be there. It wouldn't be like the other burials she'd seen in the old cemetery, including those of her parents and husband. Three generations of Stehemish were planted over, under and between the long, twisting hemlock, cedar and fir roots. He thought of a story his uncle had told of the time when the first whites began drifting into the country. Even before missionaries reached the valley, the local tribes had heard of the religion adopted by some of the Puget Sound tribes, a religion that led them to eat a sacred powder from the ground-up bones of a very old body and drink the blood of this holy person who'd been dead a long time. Revolted but curious, the people had sent runners to talk to the tribes who had already converted. Everyone laughed for a long time when the runners came back with stories of bread and wine. That had been a favorite story among the people. In the beginning they'd had little use for the new religion. How could you separate the spirit from life and call it religion?

The tribes and clans had melted like July snow, with people drifting away to lumber camps and mills and the slums of Seattle, dying on the skid road that became skidrow. Burials in the graveyard had become far between.

The graves hung on the edge of the Stehemish River, moss-eater stones and rotten crosses tilted out of a mad growth of ferns and vines and the broad-leafed devil's club. Here the old-growth had never been taken, and the cedars towered on trunks eight and ten feet through, while enormous, sagging hemlocks dripped needles and moss upon the hidden graves. Mushrooms, orange chantrells and brown and red boletus, sprouted beside carved stones lying flat in the fern and salal and bunchberry, and the forest buried the dead in layers of humus and tangled vegetation. The people vanished while the river, milky with glacial silt, gripped the air so tightly it was difficult to breathe.

Visible in pale sketches through the forest, the river gnawed at its banks, taking a little more each moment. One day, after a big rain or heavy snowmelt, the current would cut through and sweep the Stehemish people away, tumbling the bones

smooth and dropping them on sandbars and gravel bottoms.
Steelhead and salmon would slip through shallows where the
bones of the people trembled in the current.

He thought of the importance of water in the stories. The
most powerful spirits lived in the water, and water separated
the worlds of the living and dead. The world was an island in
a great ocean. "You can see how it makes sense," his uncle had
explained carefully. "The rivers keep leaving but they're always
here. People keep dying but there's always more of them." He'd
grinned. "Especially white ones."

With the driver and Gordon on one rope and Tom and
Jimmy on the other, they fought to keep the box from slipping
and turning over. Jimmy had dug the hole a couple of days
before, and the raw red ends of roots lined the sides of the cut.
As they lowered the coffin the roots brushed the sides lovingly.

As Tom stepped back from the grave he saw the others, who
must have come down the road on foot while they struggled
with the ropes. Sam Gravey stood a little behind Jenny, and
beside Sam stood a large man he recognized as Leroy Brant.
Karen stood beside Leroy, a couple of steps back and almost
hidden by the huge bulk of her father.

The minister's voice had begun to match the monotone of
the slow rain as he read about the sun going down and coming up. His suit was sticky and uncomfortable inside the raincoat. The problem with raincoats was that without them you
got soaked and with them you sweated like a pig. He pondered
the injustice of this fact as he spoke the words and wondered
idly about the three people who had just appeared. The short,
round man with the thick gray beard and shining black eyes
he recognized as Sam Gravey, dressed today in a ragged red
mackinaw over what looked like a black suit. It took a moment
to place the big man as someone whom he'd seen often in town
in the two years he'd been minister of the church. The girl
worked at the Fir Tree.

Tom watched Karen out of the corner of his vision while he listened to the words and thought that his uncle would have liked them. "When I die," his uncle had said once, "maybe I'll be a wolf. What do you think?" When Tom had pointed out that there were no wolves any longer, his uncle had shaken his head. "Never doubt the wolf," he'd said. "Just keep your eyes open."

The lumps of clay and river gravel rattled against the box, and the rain became hard again. After the coffin disappeared under a thin layer, Gordon whispered in Jenny's ear. Jenny shuffled solemnly to her sister's side and whispered. Tom saw his mother stare impassively ahead. The preacher said some quick words, and then with Jenny and Gordon he hurried up toward the Buick while Tom and Jimmy continued to fill the hole.

By the time the grave was filled and mounded, the Buick had gone and the rain was already beating down the piled humus and exposing bits of silver gravel and the redder fragments of root. The driver got into the hearse and worked to get it turned around to squeeze it past Jimmy's truck, and Sam Gravey shook hands wordlessly with Jimmy and then Tom. Sam turned and walked back up toward the Forest Service road, his suit pants spattered with mud and ending at the tops of his boots.

Leroy shook hands with Jimmy and then rested a heavy hand for a moment on Tom's shoulder. "Good to see you," he said, and then, glancing at his daughter, he followed Sam toward the road.

Jimmy nodded at Karen, and then he and their mother also walked up the hill. Tom leaned his shovel in the dirt and looked at her.

She wore her long brown hair in a tight bun and held a collapsed umbrella. The rain glistened on her hair and beaded on the shoulders of her brown raincoat. The cheekbones were the same, strong and high, showing the Cherokee blood common in the valley's North Carolina transplants. The spray of freckles across the bridge of her nose and cheeks seemed less distinct in the gray, watery light of the cemetery, and the lips were more serious than he remembered. The green eyes still seemed to smile independently of the rest of the serious face.

She stood on the opposite side of the grave and waited.

He let the shovel fall behind him and took a step toward her before feeling his foot sink into the raw earth. He jerked back and looked down at his footprint in the grave.

"My father's waiting," she said. "I have to go." She turned and took a step and stopped. Looking back, she added, "You just expected me to wait, didn't you?"

Before he could think of the right words, she had disappeared after the others.

When they were all gone, he walked a few feet from the new grave and stood before a granite marker that leaned awkwardly in the spiny salal growth. As always, seeing his name on the stone made his stomach knot. As a child he'd stared again and again at the one photograph of Tom Joseph, a dark figure in a long, gray overcoat and formless hat, more shadow than man. He knew his father was Indian, Stehemish, but the man in the picture didn't look like anything, or he looked like everything. The face was any stranger's, shadowed beneath the tilted hat, and disturbing. The overcoat seemed designed to hide everything about the man, so that he was formless and a part of nothing around him. Tom had never gotten any closer than the photo or stone. Tom Joseph, he knew, had worked the tugboats and then logged, marrying a thirty-year-old wife whom others had passed over and giving her two children in three years before being killed by one of the big falling limbs they called widow-makers. The grave, sunken and probably nearly empty, was another thing he didn't know about. Sometimes at night, when he lay in bed and tried to figure it out, he felt as if he were descended from some madman's dream. Indians rode spotted horses over golden plains after buffalo. They lived in the light of the sun, where nothing was hidden and earth rose up to sky, in tipis, not in cedar-slab houses crouched in the bowels of a rainforest They sat horseback against the infinite horizon, bare-chested and challenging their disinheritors. Those were the Indians they studied in school. How could the remote, disturbing figure in hat and overcoat be part of that? He was unreal, as were all of them.

On the gravel road, the rain drummed on the metal shell of the pickup, and the wiper smeared water across the windshield in front of Jimmy's stolid face. The other vehicles were gone, and the tired pickup rattled along the narrow strip by itself, a bit of movement lost between walls of green-black timber rising to vast, dark ridges. The river moved away to the south a half-mile to cut close to the ridge, and they no longer caught glimpses of it through the trees. Occasionally a raven flapped slowly up to sit on a fir branch and scold as they passed.

In front of the ranger station a plywood Smokey Bear, brown with blue overalls, pointed a moveable finger at "Low Fire Danger."

"Low Fire Danger," Jimmy said.

"Damned low," Tom answered, noting, however, that the rain was letting up again and that over the top of Whitehorse patches of broken cloud had replaced the solid gray. Between the clouds shreds of vague blue appeared, sucker holes from the southwest. The granite peaks ripped the clouds and left tattered mares' tails behind in the evening sky.

They drove the last mile without speaking, pulling up in front of the house and climbing out of the truck in silence. The front door had blown open, and a spattering of rain had drifted in to puddle on the floor and seep through the cracks. The house was dark and cold, and Tom thought of the burned cedar branches.

Inside, Jimmy began stuffing newspaper and kindling into the stove. Tom helped his mother sit on the couch and draped the red blanket across her shoulders and lap. Then he went to the end of the room that served as the kitchen and began to make coffee, dumping the grounds from the last pot into the sink and hearing the sodden weight of the grounds against the earth below.

By the time Jimmy had the fire going and was mopping up the rain, Tom had thrown two handfuls of coffee into the enamel pot and set it on the flat top of the woodstove, ignoring the gas range at the end of the counter. He watched his mother rise with the blanket over her shoulders and walk across the room to turn on the television. Returning to the couch, she stared blankly at a young, blonde woman weeping on the screen. A man in a plaid sports coat was touching the woman's shoulder and bending close to her ear.

The fire cut yellow and red lines through the joints and grate of the stove, and Tom stood with his back to it watching his mother. Was the television as effective as cedar branches, he wondered? Could the figures on the screen, obviously acting out a story of loss, maybe death, keep ghosts away? Did she really believe that a ghost would come back for those it loved, the way the old ones had thought? Maybe, he thought, the power to believe is diluted with generations, the way McBride's skin had lightened as his Indian grandfathers and grandmothers had slipped further away, despite his desperate attempts to keep them close. Maybe his mother could only believe half as much as her own mother, and he, her son, half as much yet. Maybe being a Christian and watching television left only a certain amount of room for belief.

The coffee exploded onto the stove, and he grabbed the pot and jerked his hand away. With a corner of his black coat he carried the pot to the counter. Pouring milk into a cup of coffee, he noticed the end of his blue tie soaking in the coffee and he took the tie off and shoved it into a coat pocket.

His coat already off and lying on top of the carburetor parts,

Jimmy nodded when Tom handed him the cup. "He's leaving her. For a woman who's a legal secretary," Jimmy said, nodding at the screen. "She makes good money." He sipped the coffee. "His wife wants kids and he don't. They still love each other, but the secretary don't want kids either."

Tom set a cup on the coffee table in front of his mother, and she smiled at him and looked back at the television. Jimmy got up and stood with his cup close to the stove. When Tom stood next to him, Jimmy said, "I feel kind of like burning some branches in here and waving them around myself. This house sure feels like it has a ghost in it. Maybe he's having trouble finding his rotten log." He grinned weakly and raised the cup to his face.

"I didn't know you knew that stuff," Tom said.

"Who do you think he talked to after you left?" He took a drink of the scalding coffee and grimaced. "Folgers sucks. I don't know why I buy it. I keep thinking I'll try French Market. It's on the shelf right next to the Folgers, says it has hickory in it." He blew into the cup and went on. "I'll tell you something else he said, too, something I wasn't going to tell you because it's too weird." Jimmy spoke still more quietly. "He told me that when he died the wolf spirit would go to you, that you would get the power, that kind of totem thing. He said I didn't need it, so he was going to give it to you. He was worried about you, worried that you wouldn't come back and worried that you would."

Jimmy took another sip of coffee, holding it in his puffed cheeks and swallowing slowly. "Man, that's hot coffee," he said.

"He told you that?" Tom watched his brother's eyes as Jimmy nodded.

"I told you he was saying all kinds of crazy stuff," Jimmy said. "Want to drive down to the Red Dog for a beer?"

"I don't think so." Tom shook his head.

"I don't mind if I do," Jimmy said. He disappeared into his

bedroom and came out in workboots, jeans, and flannel shirt and denim jacket like Tom's. He waved a hand as he went out the door.

When the screen door swung back against the house, Tom saw that his mother was watching him. He cupped his coffee in both hands and tried to think of something to say.

"We missed you," his mother said. "He used to talk about when you would come home." On the television the blonde woman was sitting on a love seat and sobbing. "You have to be careful now. He loved you very much, and so this is a dangerous time for you. Later maybe we can pray to our Lord Jesus together. It is a bad time for you." She watched him for a moment, and then her eyes lost their focus and she leaned back and closed them. He felt for the warmth of the coffee and shivered.

4

Floyd poked at the cherry-rhubarb pie and frowned at the counter and tried to remember. Years swirled in his memory as dark as the coffee slowly revolving in the cup in front of him. Paths turned into dirt-and-gravel roads that disappeared under layers of asphalt. And beneath the confusion of asphalt, somewhere, lay a water pipe that had finally burst. The question was, did the pipe run under the road in front of the Fir Tree or was it down at the intersection fifty feet away?

"Good pie, Idy," Floyd said as he became aware of the woman refilling his cup. Crumbs and drops of coffee were woven into Floyd's beard, and he brushed a pudgy hand across the beard to merge crumbs and liquid.

"Thanks, Floyd. Made it myself." Ida tightened her lips in something close to a smile and winked at the old man. A tall, big-boned woman of fifty, with graying brown hair tied back and a frank, tired face, Ida moved to the end of the counter and began wiping it with a cloth.

The pies came in twice a week on a truck from Everett, but that wasn't what Floyd was thinking about. There were three holes in the pavement outside the cafe, and no sign of the pipe. It was there somewhere and it was busted, for nobody down toward the ranger station was getting any water. If he dug another hole the truckers would raise all kinds of hell, and the town would be trying to take over his waterworks again.

"Say, Idy," he called. "You remember that pipe I put crost the road here back in forty-nine?"

"Nope. Me and Oscar was in Alaska back then, remember?" Sure was pretty up there."

Floyd snorted in the full cup of coffee. "Guess I'll get them boys and try down to the intersection." He laid several coins on the counter and spun slowly on his stool. "Makes it hard when they go putting that blacktop all over creation."

"Maybe you ought to fill them holes before you dig any new ones," Ida said from the end of the counter. "Harve ain't too happy already with his customers having to dodge them holes."

"I guess I better do that," Floyd muttered as he took his jacket off the rack by the door. He pulled a red bandana out of the jacket and rubbed it across his face, looking curiously at the bandana when he'd finished. "I better do that."

"Luck, Floyd," Ida called. When the round old man was gone, she turned toward the kitchen and said, "Floyd's gonna dig up this whole town someday." In the kitchen, someone laughed.

5

It was dark when Tom left the house. A quartermoon glimmered between the clouds blowing across the valley, and in the faint light an appaloosa sky stampeded over the range of ice and rock.

As he walked, he looked toward the outlines of peaks, and he sniffed the smells of sawdust and mildew and vegetation and listened to the crunch of gravel under his boots. Except for the distant bark of a hunting dog and the whine of a revved-up car working its way through four gears on the straightaway outside of town, the whole valley lay silent. He fingered the lint in one corner of his pants pocket and hunched his shoulders in the denim jacket.

When he looked up again he saw the yellow light of the cafe's window and the blocky shadow of a truck in front of the door. Before he could have recognized the truck by its outlines and told who it belonged to or if it announced the presence of an outsider. But now he stared at it blankly.

He walked past the rotting cabin and abandoned orchard where he and Jimmy had picked plums a long time before. The trees huddled in clumps of shadow beneath the taller evergreens. He thought about his uncle up in the Stehemish drainage during the last days and wondered if he'd felt his aloneness out there, if he'd closed his eyes at moments and felt the distances surrounding him. A frog croaked in the vines beside the road, and another replied from further on. The valley felt shrouded, heavy.

At the end of their road he stopped and looked across the blacktop and into the yellow light of the cafe. Behind the window, Karen glided like water toward the other end of the counter.

He entered just as she vanished into the kitchen. Hanging his coat on the rack, he crossed the small room and sat at the

opposite end of the counter from the other customer. He'd for-
gotten how small the cafe was: the kitchen, the counter with
eight stools, four small tables with chairs, the brown linoleum
scraped to licorice at the door and around each table. A jukebox
with red plastic filigree sat against the wall opposite the door,
and above the jukebox hung a calendar with a picture of a Kenworth loaded with old-growth logs. A large-breasted blonde
in a red sweater leaned against the cab of the truck and smiled
as if she knew a secret about the big machine. At the end of the
counter nearest the kitchen, the cash register sat next to a rack
of postcards. Above the postcards with their pictures of
meadows and peaks and black bears, a sign read, "Welcome
to Forks—Gateway to the North Cascades." On the wall behind
the counter hung two more signs, one saying "No Shirt, No
Shoes, No Service," and the other "You Don't Have to Be Crazy
to Work Here, But." The bottom half of the sign had been torn
off. On the torn edge someone had written in red pen, "Does
a bear shit in the woods?"

The customer revolved on his chrome-edged stool, and Tom
recognized J. D. Hill. The man who owned most of the valley
stood up and walked to the jukebox and, without looking at
the list of selections, pushed two coins into the machine and
punched two buttons. As he walked back to the stool, the jukebox sang, "We don't grow our hair long in Muskogee. . . ." J. D.
plicked a piece of lint from his brown sportcoat and smiled at
Tom, the slight overbite giving him the grin of a fox.

Tom nodded, noting that J. D. still wore Levis and western
boots with the sportcoat, and that there didn't seem to be any
gray in his hair. The blue eyes had an unfocused intensity.

"How's college treating you?" J. D. asked, adding quickly,
"This valley must seem kinda small after you've been all the
way to the University of California."

"Okay," he replied before he turned to watch a drama
unfolding in the pie case. In the case on the wall across the

counter, a fly buzzed erratically against the glass until it fell dazed into the froth of a lemon-meringue pie. "How's Buddy?" he asked the fly as it settled in for the duration.

"Buddy's doing good. I guess you haven't heard the latest news."

Karen reappeared from the kitchen. She stopped, the pyrex coffee pot held out before her like an offering. She turned awkwardly and gestured with the pot toward J. D.

"No thank you, Karen," he said, rising from the stool. "I better get to gettin."

J. D. carefully placed two folded bills under the edge of his saucer. "We'll be seeing you Sunday," he said to Karen. Smiling toward Tom as he headed for the door, he added, "Welcome home, Tom, good to see you." As he pulled a raincoat from the rack and opened the door, he said, "Buddy's a lucky boy, if you ask me."

Karen set the pot on the counter and leaned back against the pie case, her arms straight at her side. "I'm sorry about your uncle," she said.

Tom shrugged. He'd never realized how long and smooth her neck was. She'd never worn her hair up before. Gold circle hung from her earlobes, setting off the dark hair, and he remembered a time when they had swum together in the Stillaguamish. The rare sun had glanced like fire off stones in the clear water, and Karen had seemed to glow with light.

"I came by when I first got back," he said, "but you weren't here."

"I must have been off. I only work part-time now. Your hair's longer. You look like an Indian."

"Must have been all that sunshine." He attempted a grin and gave up. "How come you stopped writing? I kept writing but you didn't answer."

She reached up to tuck a wisp of hair behind her ear. He heard the faint buzz of the fly as she said, "I guess I just couldn't think of anything to say after a while."

"I don't understand."

"No, I guess not." She moved the coffee pot from the counter to a hotplate next to the pie rack and leaned back again, shoving her hands into the pockets of the white uniform dress. "I kept getting those letters from you, telling me how great it was. Like you were Christopher Columbus or somebody. Telling me how pretty it was, how you could swim in the ocean between classes, how great the teachers were. What could I write back? I was supposed to sit here in this valley and serve pie and coffee and wait for the hero to come home?"

"But . . . ."

"No," she went on. "Let me tell you how it was. What could I say? Dear Tommy, I'm glad you're having a fine time on the beach. I'm having fun going nowhere and doing nothing. Well, you could have gone to school right here in Mount Vernon and stayed in Forks, but you didn't."

"That's a junior college," he said. "I had a chance to go to the University of California."

"Well, I didn't have to wait." She pushed another stray strand of hair back into place. "You were having your fun down there, and I figured I had a right to the same, even if it was just in Forks."

He looked at his folded hands on the counter. "I made up a lot of that stuff, so you would think it was okay there. It wasn't. They built that campus on top of an old Indian burial ground. Sacred ground. Nobody else seemed to notice it, but I could feel those people there all the time. They didn't want anybody there, and they made people ill. People were sick all the time there, and they didn't understand why. I'm not going back."

"How could I know you made it up? I just thought nothing back here mattered much to you any more." For the first time she looked directly at him. "The valley's different. Everything's different. You should know that before you decide to stay."

Before she could go on, the cafe door opened and two loggers came in, fallers with big pads of foam rubber on their right shoulders where they balanced chainsaws all day.

"Can you get Jimmy's truck?" she said quickly.

When he nodded, she said, "Pick me up at eleven." Then she walked quickly toward the two customers.

He slipped his jacket on as he heard the door close behind him, hoping Jimmy was back from the Red Dog or that he'd left the keys to the pickup at home. He didn't notice the silhouette at the base of the fir tree until it stepped in front of him. "Too bad about Jim."

He recognized the voice and stopped.

J. D. stepped closer, smiling in the near-dark. "You may not know it," he said, "but people here in the valley were proud when you got that scholarship. Nobody ever did that before, especially none of your people. I wanted you to know how proud we all are."

The taller man pushed hair back from his forehead and added, "You know, I was kind of hoping back then that Buddy would get himself a football scholarship to one of the universities, but I guess their scouts don't pay much attention to a two-bit school like Forks."

When Tom didn't reply, J. D. said, "You played with him. He was good enough, wasn't he?" Tom nodded. "Buddy was good enough." Buddy Hill was a natural, an athlete who didn't even have to think about what he was doing.

"That's what I always thought. I wish to hell I'd made him go to school in Everett, any place a kid could get noticed. I tried like hell to get him to play for Mount Vernon. They wanted him so bad they couldn't see straight, and he could have transfered to a university once the scouts saw him. But he wanted to make big money logging."

Tom clenched his hands in the pockets of his jeans and waited, remembering the high school games, the excitement and mud, always mud.

"When you heading back to school?"

Tom shrugged. "I don't know."

J. D. cocked his head. "I waited out here for two reasons. One was to tell you that I heard you might not be going back to school, and to try to change your mind. This valley has only one future, and that isn't logging. The timber's about gone, and already people are heading up to Canada and even Alaska. Logging's hardly much more than a tax write-off for those of us still doing it."

Tom started to speak, but J. D. held up a hand. "I don't know why you might be quitting school, but if you need money I'd like to loan it to you. Interest free. You can pay me back after you're a big Indian lawyer or something." J. D. folded his arms across his chest and cocked his head even further, reminding Tom of a magpie. "You're not only the first boy from Forks to get a scholarship to a university, you're an Indian. We all know that your people have been stewed and screwed for a long time in these parts, hell, everywhere. I'd like to help make up for that. You go back to school, and you can do a lot more to help your people than you can without an education."

Tom looked at Buddy's father in amazement. Finally he said, "That's a fine offer. I appreciate it, but money is not a problem. I just have to think about what I want to do."

J. D. ran a hand through his hair and let out a long breath. "You got to do what you got to do. A man's got to scratch where he itches. But you think about it carefully. When I got started in this valley a guy could work his way up from setting chokers to owning his own outfit, but that's not the way it is anymore. I did it because I was smarter than everybody else. But now I'm on top and nobody's smarter than me. Buddy's going to take over my business someday, but a guy like you doesn't have that option."

"I'll think about it," Tom said, glancing across the road toward home.

"Well, let me give you something else to chew on. If you feel you have to stay here and not go on with school, I can offer you a job With even a year of college you're way ahead of most of these yahoos, and you're smart. Right now I have the contract to put the road in to the new mine, but there's going to be one hell of a lot of development around here, and I plan to get my share of those contracts. More than my share. That mine's going to be operating for twenty-thirty years at least, and there's a future in it. A guy like you that's Indian could be invaluable for a operation like this. You could symbolize the future for Indian people, progress. You and Buddy almost took a lousy football team to the championship; you can go to the top of this thing together."

Tom watched a small shadow disengage from the vines across the road and scurry to the other side toward the river. "Why do you want to do this for me?"

J. D. looked up as a heavy car lumbered along the road past the cafe, the car's three-quarter cam throbbing rhythmically and the headlights cutting for a moment across Tom Joseph's angular face.

"Why not? Name me another guy as smart as you, and one who knows this country as well as you do" They were both silent for a moment then J. D. added, "I feel bad about your uncle, and, believe it or not, I feel a little bad about cutting that road into the wilderness area. But it's going to happen whether we like it or not, and I'm going to make sure that the multinational company doesn't just come in here and take everything. I'm going to see to it that some of that money stays in this valley."

Tom let out a deep breath and looked at the scudding clouds. "I appreciate your offer, and I'll think about it."

The moon slipped from the clouds for an instant and silvered the glacier on Whitehorse, and then the clouds slid back across the moon in quick shadows.

"The mine isn't going to be stopped," J. D. said softly. "The valley's changing, and you can be part of that change." He paused for an instant before going on. "One other thing. I don't know if Karen told you, but she and Buddy are getting married. I thought you ought to know that right now if that's one of the reasons you decided to stay."

J. D. turned and walked toward his pickup, and Tom started across the road toward home, feeling like a man walking in water, his legs and arms suddenly heavy, his breathing liquid and difficult. Across the pavement, he looked back. Karen was moving behind the counter, and on Gold Hill above town a hunting dog complained bitterly. Along the river a night heron squawked, and the clouds moved more quickly toward the east.

6

When he pulled up in the truck, she hurried out of the cafe and climbed in, wearing a faded denim jacket with the collar turned up over her uniform.

"It sure seems cold for summer," she said. "Boy, I remember this old truck." She patted the metal dashboard affectionately.

"A couple of times lately it's seemed like I never left," he said. "But then I hear a sound, like the river, or smell something, and it seems like I was gone ten years."

"You were gone a hundred years, Tom." She rubbed her palm across the passenger's window and looked out through the swath she'd made in the condensation. "A thousand, million years."

The truck moved out of the shallow light from the cafe and onto the road. "J. D. told me," he said, maneuvering the wobbly spine of the stickshift into third and hearing the engine settle into a steady low-speed whine.

Karen watched the church slip past in its small clearing. The spears of second-growth seemed especially tall and menacing around the little church. "I wanted to tell you. You know, at first I used to ask Jimmy about you every time I saw him in town or in the cafe, but after a while he acted sort of embarrassed, so I quit asking."

He glanced at the abcess in the dashboard where the radio had been. A couple of wires hung down toward the floor, the copper strands of the bare ends catching what little light there was. A nighthawk swooped low in the headlights and arced back into the sky.

"You couldn't wait?"

"There's more to it. Our driveway is just around that corner."

The pickup eased across a silver bridge, and they passed the silence of a big creek. He stared hard at the timber, looking unsuccessfully for landmarks, a bearing of some kind.

"Just beyond the split hemlock, remember?" she said, and all at once he remembered and slowed the pickup to make the turn.

In the driveway in front of the dark house, he leaned both arms on the steering wheel.

"Can you come in?" she said. "My parents aren't home. After the funeral they went to Camano Island for a couple of days. Buddy's in Seattle."

She opened the pickup door and jumped out, and he got out and followed her past her father's truck with the mismatched fenders. She unlocked the door and went inside, holding the door open for him.

The house was comfortable. In the metal insert in the fireplace at one end of the room, a pair of firedogs looked sturdy and warm. On the mantle a black-tasseled graduation picture of Karen stood beneath one of the old, discolored whipsaws that Leroy Brant had used as a kid, the curved teeth of the saw menacing the girl in the picture. The furniture was overstuffed and soft-looking, and on the longest wall of the room hung a crude painting of a white mountain, the paint laid on in an impulse of thick, childish strokes, the mountain and surrounding peaks out of proportion to one another.

"Why don't you build a fire while I change?" Karen said as she left the room.

He found the kindling and newspaper in a willow Indian basket beside the fireplace, and he piled the kindling rip-rap style over wadded-up paper. The matches were on the mantle, and by the time she returned he had laid the split maple across the kindling and sat back on the couch, watching the yellow flames begin to lick up over the wood.

"Would you like some wine?" She had changed into faded jeans and a blue teeshirt. Her nipples stood out through the thin shirt.

When he looked surprised, she said, "Oh, Leroy won't let me drink yet, but Mom doesn't care. So we don't tell him."

After a year away, it surprised him to hear her call her father by his first name. Indians often did that, but not white kids. Maybe, he thought, it was because Leroy looked so much like a Leroy that even his wife and daughter had to admit it.

She came back with the wine in two water glasses and handed one to him before settling on the far end of the couch.

"J. D. told you about me and Buddy?"

He nodded.

"We're supposed to get married in September." She swirled the wine and looked through her glass toward the fire.

"I used to lie in my room at first and cuss you out for going off to school. I felt like you'd just abandoned me. For a while, I'd look everytime somebody came into the cafe, thinking it might be you. I even thought about coming down to see you at Christmas, surprising you. But I was afraid."

"So Buddy?"

"Buddy kept coming into the cafe and asking me to go out with him. Finally I said yes."

He took a drink of the sour red wine.

"I was lonely," she said. "I thought you were down there having fun and forgetting me. What was I supposed to do? You know, there's a dream I have. It comes to me sometimes when there's a wind over the valley, and I don't know what the connection is. I'm in a cave and it's dark sometimes and I sleep like an angel. But sometimes it's light, and then I sit and think, or write things down. I never have to talk, because the bears in the cave read my mind. I don't have to read theirs because they have no thoughts for me. They just want to take care of me. I think that there are five bears most of the time—four adults and one cub. The bears in this lovely cave I'm with are dream bears. They smell like cedar, and their coats are soft and clean. They are well-groomed bears. And they groom me. They comb my hair gently with their claws, and they bathe me with their tongues, sometimes the way a mother cat bathes a tiny kitten and sometimes differently so that their tongues are drawn up my legs and over my belly and breasts, warm and wet and soft and finally exciting me in a wonderful way. I'm always naked, but I'm never cold. The cave isn't damp. The ceiling, walls, and floors are the color and texture of red cedar. I'm never hungry, so I never have to eat anything. But everytime I wake up, one of the bears serves me a delicious cup of coffee. All I do is sleep, drink coffee, read, write, and enjoy the bears." She sipped the wine and then added, "But they expect something from me. I know there's something important I'm supposed to do, but I can't figure out what it is."

She looked at him and laughed softly. "Funny, isn't it? I always connected it to you somehow."

He let out his breath. Bears. A bear dream that must have been drawn from those long-ago Cherokee ancestors across all this time and space. He imagined dream bears soaring through the dark on those nights of wind, coming to her from that distant place to the south and east. It would have been a dream to discuss with his uncle. A singer like his uncle might have understood such a dream.

He thought of the girls McBride had introduced him to. Rana and the others.

"I thought about you all the time," he said, and it was true. Just like he thought of the rivers, the forests, the high lakes no one ever saw. "Do you remember the other dream we used to talk about? The house?" They had sat alongside rivers and planned a dream home, a log house at the edge of a meadow. Behind the house, old-growth timber would rise up toward rock and ice, while in front of it spotted horses would graze in a valley divided by a salmon river. They would be self-sufficient, and they would need no one.

"I thought you were gone. Your letters seemed like they

were from somebody I'd never see again."

"Are you in love with him?"

She sipped the wine and pulled her knees up to her chest on the couch. She looked past him at the fire. "No, I guess not. I'm in love with my dream bears, can't you tell? Someday I'll know what it is I'm supposed to do." She looked at him. "For a while I thought I was in love. I guess I wanted to be. To be something, at least."

He thought about how hard she'd argued against his going. They could have gotten married. She would have worked while he went to junior college. They would have lived a familiar story.

"You know, down there in Santa Barbara I used to think about this valley, and I'd get mad. But I never could figure out what I was mad at, or about. I didn't fit in down there. It was like I was too dark—inside, not outside—like maybe I'd been in this valley so long I couldn't stand that much light." His dreams there had been of darkness, of valleys where the air flowed like water through and above the old-growth, of dream salmon slanting through the falls. And on the deepest nights, of wolves. But a bear dream was something else, almost too powerful to even think about. He looked at her with wonder.

She moved closer and set her hand on his leg. "You should go back to school, Tom. There's nothing left for you here."

"J. D. offered me a job with his mining business," he said. "He told me that Buddy and I could go to the top together if I stay."

She reached up and brushed his long hair back behind one ear. "In the first place, you won't do that. In the second place, you know why J. D. wants you. It's because of what your uncle was doing. J. D. doesn't give a damn about you, but if he can't get rid of you he might at least get you on his side. If he got a full-blooded Stehemish on his side, nobody could stop him."

"Can anybody stop him now?"

She shook her head, and then she bent to set her wine on

the floor, and when she arose she moved closer and kissed him. She stood and took his hand and pulled him from the couch.

In the bedroom she unbuttoned his shirt and slipped it over his shoulders and spread her hands down his chest to his sides. She stepped back and lifted the teeshirt over her head and dropped it to the floor. Her breasts were larger than he remembered, muscular looking.

She knelt to unlace his shoes and then reached up toward his belt. When they were both naked, she began to kiss him, beginning with his nipples and moving down the flatness of his belly with a sureness that surprised him.

When she made love to him, everything was new. The contours of her body, like the terrain of a strange country, was full of surprises, little shocks. Against the white sheets her darkness stood out like a shadow on a snowbank. Her long legs and full hips swept up to the firm breasts with their dark nipples and to wide, strong shoulders. And now she made love confidently, reaching for him, teasing him, turning inward to herself once he was inside so that he felt lost, alone in a land he didn't know. She drew him deeper, her breathing sharp and her green eyes closed.

Afterwards, he watched as she slipped his shirt over her shoulders and left the room. When she returned with the two glasses of wine, he watched her breasts move beneath the shirt and noted that there was something new, something more solid about her body.

She sat beside him on the bed. When he started to speak, she placed a hand against his mouth. "Not yet," she said.

He shifted his leg to feel the smoothness of hers. Setting the wine on the stand beside the bed, he reached to touch one of the nipples until it hardened and he heard her breath deepen. Gently, she pushed him back on the bed, her lips and tongue again playing across his chest and down his abdomen to his thighs and up again to his center. As he hardened, she caressed him with her hands and tongue and he imagined himself in a dimly lit cave in the heart of the mountains, his body given over to the vision bears and her mouth touching him all over like rain.

He moved with the arcing rain and slid his hand down until he felt her dampness, and then he rose above her. The second time they made love, she held him tightly to her, pulling him in and clutching him with her arms and legs so that he felt a strange sense of panic, and then she arched her back and came with a single sharp cry that reminded him of a hunting hawk. She rolled away and lay with her back to him.

After long minutes of silence, he said, "What about Buddy?"

"Leroy doesn't like him," she answered.

"You can't marry him."

"You don't know anything, Tom. You came back to this valley thinking everything would be the same just because you wanted it that way—the rivers and mountains and me and everything. But things have to change." She rolled onto her back and looked up at him as he leaned on one arm. "You like my breasts better now, but you don't see why." Her eyes caught a spear of light from the lamp. "My breasts have changed because I'm pregnant. I fucked Buddy to get even with you, and now I'm pregnant."

When he reached home, Jimmy was asleep on the couch, wearing his jeans and plaid shirt and gray wool socks with the army blanket lying half over him and half on the floor. A bottle shot green sparks from the floor when Tom flipped the light switch.

He stretched the blanket over his brother, tucking it around Jimmy's shoulders and chin, smelling the heavy wine. Then he turned off the light and felt his way through the doorway at the back of the room.

"Tommy."

He stopped and felt a dim light come on behind him. When he turned he saw his mother standing wrapped in a star quilt at the door to her room, outlined in a faint illumination so that her face and the hall before her were in shadow.

"Come and talk," she said.

He followed her into the little room. The same bare bulb hung in the middle of the room, but this one hid partially behind a torn paper shade like a parasol. Through the jagged tears in the paper, the light shone like odd-shaped stars. She lowered herself to the edge of the large bed and let the quilt slide from her shoulders as he sat on the wooden chair close to her. On the night stand beside the bed lay a bible with an eagle feather protruding from the closed pages. Her unbraided hair flowed over her shoulders to her waist.

"We're tired," she said. She smiled and he glanced at the glass on the night stand where her teeth were soaking.

He began to speak, but she held up a hand. "I waited until tonight to tell you that you must go back to school. This place isn't good for you now. My brother was not crazy like they say, like even Jimmy thinks. But he didn't understand the way things are now."

"Why was he shooting at them?" he asked.

She rubbed one dark, smooth hand over the other. "It was simple. He didn't want them to build that road, or to put that mine in, so he shot their machines. He knew that that was all he could do, shoot at the machines. It's what Indians have always done." She paused and seemed to turn inward for a moment. "You know, in some ways Indian women are stronger than Indian men these days. We don't break, you know. We just go on because that's always been our job. Men, they know the stories, too, but they remember and have dreams about what it used to be, and then they want all that back again. Even if they don't know that's what they want. They get to wanting it so bad, like my brother, they forget things get to always change. Like the salmon, you know."

She reached to touch his shoulder and looked past him toward the doorway. "And sometimes I been thinking that maybe the spirits forget, too. Maybe they come to people and make them want the old ways back because this ain't a good world for spirits no more, the way a ghost wants so bad to stay where its life was and has to be told to go away. This here world is for the live ones, them ones who just keep changing when that's all there is to do."

She brushed her hand down one side of his straight hair and smiled as he sat amazed at the flood of words. "You know, when I was a little girl I used to dream about all the white people going away and leaving just us Indians here like it used to be. I'd get sad because that meant some of my white friends would have to go away. But I thought that maybe if they left this country to us Indians we could fix it again. Indians used to know how to live so's we didn't destroy our mother earth. We had to live that way because we knew we would always be here. I think white people treat the earth like they do because they think they'll only be here a little while. They believe Jesus Christ, our Lord, is going to come and fix everything and take them all away, so they don't take care of things." She folded her hands in her lap and smiled. "My brother used to say that Jesus is what messed everything up, that it was Jesus-sickness. But Jesus was a good man, he was a singer, too."

He waited for her to build to her point, methodically, moving around the real point carefully like an animal skirting a camp at night.

"There were things he couldn't teach you because they were lost to him just like they are lost to me and the others," she said. "Things you would have to know now to stay in this valley." She reached for the Bible and set it in her lap. Her fingers, dry and smooth looking as the skin of a rattlesnake, stroked the smooth eagle feather where it protruded.

"What things?"

"Things no one can teach you now." She caressed the feather. "It's too late. The changes are too much. There are things no one knows any longer. My brother knew some of them, but if he had known enough he would not have shot at machines."

He watched her fingers on the feather and waited.

"That's why you have to go back to that school now. Wait until a better time to come back. Wait until you're stronger and the time is more correct."

She set the Bible back on the nightstand and stood. Stepping close to where he sat, she pressed his head against her side. "Go to bed now. You've come a long way, and you must go a long way back to find out who you are." She paused and smiled. "You smell of a woman. Now go to sleep."

When he entered his uncle's room again, shadows leaped at him across the darkness before he pulled the string for the light. He undressed and turned the blanket back on the bed and lay on the sheet for a moment before reaching up to turn out the light. Once again, knowing how dangerous such an act might be, he opened himself up to his uncle's presence. Again he felt only the old house and the trees and the river beyond the trees and the black mountains cutting the valley off from the world. His thoughts moved against the current of the rivers up the drainages and into the high country. A thin white man with a beard and long hair came dancing down a mountain trail, wearing a white gown, a rattle in one hand and eagle feather in the other, lifting each foot high and prancing like a deer. The man's eyes were clear pools, without centers, and they looked beyond everything. Tom stood frozen on the dark trail until the dancer approached and passed through, their bodies one for an instant, the white man's blue-water eyes fixed on the distance.

He awoke thinking of the mountains. This time of year the high meadows and ridges would be white, the mountains huge and white and empty for a thousand miles south and north. He pulled the string above his head, and the light blinked on. He went to his uncle's pack, taking it from its place against the wall and leaning it next to the door.

7

A line of dumptrucks, graders, and caterpillars huddled alongside the new road and in the gravel parking lot where the old trailhead had been.

"They've been working since the snow melted down here," Jimmy said as he stopped the truck.

Tom looked around at the flattened platform cut out of the hillside. At one edge a pile of stumps smoldered, lacing the air with the raw scent of burnt cedar. In the background the river smashed its way down the drainage, and when he looked down the slope he saw the white rapids.

"Thanks, Jimmy." He got out and went to the back of the pickup. When he swung the pack on, the thin straps cut into his shoulders. Jimmy turned the truck around and headed back toward the town, and Tom walked between gunmetal tractor blades and dumptruck tires as high as his head. Two neat holes the size of quarters pierced the hood of one truck. A windshield radiated a spiderweb of cracks, the delicate intricacy of connections telling a story. He looked at the thick-timbered slope above.

An iron-pipe gate blocked the trailhead, and a metal sign on the gate warned against trespassing. In the lower left corner, the sign said, "Honeycutt Copper." Someone had dotted the first 'o' with a large-caliber rifle.

He climbed over the gate and looked again toward the timbered ridge. The mountains had been taken from Indian people by white invaders and had been taken from the invaders by the invaders' government and made an official wilderness area by government act. He'd read the words of the law. "In perpetuity," it said, to be "untrammeled." A half-million acres, just a small place. "This is a good thing they did," Uncle Jim had said, "because now maybe they won't cut all the trees and build roads. But if you think about it, it's pretty funny. When our people lived here long ago, before the white folks came, there wasn't any wilderness and there wasn't any wild animals. There was only the mountains and river, two-leggeds and four-leggeds and underwater people and all the rest. It took white people to make the country and the animals wild. Now they got to make a law saying it's wild so's they can protect it from themselves."

Uncle Jim had started to grin, but the grin bent into a rare frown. "You know, it's like they made a treaty with these mountains and trees and rivers. They say it's set aside forever, but that's just like in all them treaties with Indian peoples where they said 'long as the grass grows,' and stuff like that. They busted every one of them treaties, and someday they're gonna bust this one, too. And then maybe this wilderness is going to have to go on the warpath." With the last words his uncle had laughed out loud.

He thought of the way his uncle liked to describe Columbus's discovery of America. "That's like when you need a new radio, so you go in the back window of your neighbor's house when he ain't home and discover his radio. Then you say, 'Oh, look at this wonderful radio I have discovered.'"

His uncle had shown him some of the ruins of Indian cabins further down the river, where the Stehemish people had built finally in retreat on the nearly uninhabitable slopes between the vertical ridges and the white river. Then they had all moved away to mill towns, the cedar fences had fallen into the salal and ferns, and the cabins tumbled until the hand-split cedar was covered by living earth. Now the lower stretches belonged to the national forest and were almost all second-growth, while the upper reaches of the river were in the wilderness area.

The ground was wet. Beyond the gate, the trees lay with their tops downhill toward the river, and stumps leaned where they'd sprawled against trees when the bulldozers shoved them over the side of the lengthening road. He picked his way through stumps still embedded in the ground and ridges of tractored earth and debris until he reached the end of the clearing a quarter-mile from the gate.

Here the old trail began again, paralleling the river through timber so thick and tall that it shut out the sun. The trail swung in a wide, uneven circle around the great mountain in the center of the wilderness, throwing off side trails, meeting and joining the Pacific Crest Trail for miles north and south, rising and falling over ridges and shoulders of the mother mountain, crossing streams and rivers on stones, logs, split-cedar bridges. With his uncle, he'd walked all of it, every trail and the places where there were no trails, searching out the remote ridges and hidden basins.

He filled his lungs until they strained against his chest. He'd come to the wilderness first as a boy, stepping in the bootprints of his uncle, and the wilderness had been an enormous, boundless world of meadows and waterfalls, silver lakes, granite and ice. But as he'd grown, the wilderness had shrunk, and he'd come, finally, to know the smallness, the delicacy of the place, a fragment of what had once been, with everything connected so carefully like the strands of a spider's web across a path at sunrise.

The lug soles of his boots left waffle tracks in the mud as he threaded his way between patches of hard spring snow made gray and brown by the fir and hemlock needles. He thought of the moccasins the old ones had worn, and he was glad for his heavy boots.

Off the trail, where low branches protected it from the thin, infrequent sun, the snow lay in a solid sheet, broken only by the trunks of trees and by the bowed backs of young evergreens and maples locked to the earth by winter. As he watched, one of the saplings broke free and leaped upright.

The loggers called those "nutcrackers." You never made the mistake of stepping over one twice.

The forest was in flux, fern and salal and bunchberry pushing up through the humus or thin crust of snow around the trunks or where the sun had struck, logs lying half-buried in snow and gouged and crumbled by prying roots. A tall hemlock stood with roots wrapped around a granite boulder left by the flooding river. The smaller roots had discovered a crack in the rock and were reaching toward the center. Along the back of a cedar log six-feet through grew a row of small firs, each about two feet high, marching in file along the nurselog toward the enormous rootwad. There was no demarcation, no place where he could say, "This is alive, this is not."

Reaching behind him with both hands, he lifted the pack and shrugged to shift the straps off pinched nerves. His uncle had carried the pack for days with fifty-pound loads, but now, with half that weight, his back ached and he longed for the missing Kelty with its wide, soft straps and waist-belt.

After two miles the trail disappeared under snow, and he walked on the hard crust, climbing in and out of suncups and stepping over embedded blow-downs. He'd been up the long, straight trail so often that he paid little attention to the Forest Service blazes cut into trees every hundred yards. Following what he knew was the same trail the old ones had followed across the mountains a thousand years before, he tried to imagine himself as one of them. An image of a plains warrior padding silently through the forest came to him and he smiled. Books and movies seldom showed Indians who looked like the Salish people of these mountains. Short, dark people dressed in woven cedar bark weren't as exciting as Sioux warriors in eagle-feather headdresses on horseback, the sun always setting behind them.

He edged around a suspicious-looking snowbridge that arched over a stream, and he listened to the hollow rush of water beneath the snow. Every few hundred yards, another stream crossed the trail, sometimes only a ribbon of sound under the snow, and sometimes a blue and green froth that appeared and disappeared in shadow beneath the ice. In the stillness the sound of rushing water rose and fell, blended and split against the background of the river a few hundred feet below. Except for the mumbling water, silence lay like steel across the snow.

At ten miles a waterfall dropped from the trail to splinter against rock in a chasm across the trail. A cedar bridge spanned the twenty-foot gap in the trail at what the Forest Service called Devil's Elbow, a bridge now heaped with snow and laced with ice where the water splashed. He stopped midway on the bridge, slipped the pack to the snow, and looked up to where the water gleamed into sight in threads that split and joined and shattered on ledges and fell to a pool below the bridge before sliding over the edge toward the river.

He dragged the pack to the end of the bridge where the mist did not reach, kicked the snow off one of the railings, and sat on the bare, wet cedar. Opening the top of the pack, he dug until he found a can of peaches. With his pocketknife he levered the can open and speared the slices, taking each slice off the tip of the knife with his teeth. The snow lay deep on both sides of the bridge, shrouding logs and making deep bowls around the trees.

Halfway through the peaches, he was looking at the thick forest and thinking about his ancestors. They hadn't had cans of peaches, so they had made some kind of traveling food out of the inner bark of trees. He wished he'd paid more attention when his uncle had explained it. You scraped the soft pulp from inside the bark and mashed it up and leached it or something before baking it in coals. They'd baked it all night, or maybe for a couple of days. And they'd made some kind of dry powder from salmon and dried chokecherries and stuff like that.

He noticed a movement at the far end of the bridge. First one forefoot carefully and then the other, and the long neck extended. and he could see the antlers, three points on each side. The black nose twitched, and the black eyes flitted around the area before the bridge. There was no other way across without climbing the steep ridge, but the buck sensed the difference in the woods and stepped into the clearing with muscles tensed. And then the nose widered and the deer half turned, balanced perfectly.

He watched the play of muscle on the gaunt hind-quarter, the dampness in the eyes, and he remembered the first deer he'd killed. Lung-shot, the two-point buck had fallen to its knees and sobbed. He'd finished it with the Krag and then thrown up until his uncle told him to field-dress it. And when the deer was hanging from a tree branch, his uncle had told him about the spirit. "This is the way it has to be," he'd explained. "The deer understands that sometimes it isn't easy." They'd fleshed out the buck and then sunk the bones and hide and antlers in an eddy of the fast river so that the deer would return once more. As they made the offering, his uncle sang softly in a language Tom couldn't understand.

They'd climbed the high ridges in the mornings when the clouds rose up from the valley bottoms, tangling in the huckleberry brush and small trees, and in the evenings when the meadowed ridges lost their sharpness and ascended toward the mountains and the distant moon. And as he listened to the stories he came to understand that the power of a singer was a subtle thing, deep and unswerving, a complex web that drew upon all the forces of the mountains and brought them to a single focus like perfect silence. And he learned that a spirit was a difficult thing that might wander away a year and leave its possessor stumbling in darkness only to swoop suddenly down upon the man so that a spirit dance would have to be held for healing. A spirit might come to a song or to a need, and it might leave abruptly for someone with greater need. There were many spirits and many ways and times to find one.

It was at the lake they called Image now that the wolf had come to his uncle. A boy, Uncle Jim had gone to the lake and fasted for three days, making a rope of cedar bark he'd carried up from the drainage bottom. After three days he brushed himself with hemlock branches the way he was supposed to, tied the rope to a big rock, and waded into the lake. When he was waist deep, he threw the rock as far as he could with two hands and then swam and pulled himself down toward the bottom until the light was weak and distant. And then out of the dark the man who seemed all light beckoned, and when he swam close the man was the wolf and spoke, teaching him the song. "You will be afraid of nothing and you will hunt like the wolf," the figure said before turning and trotting along a narrow trail into a forest. After that, the wolf had been his helper.

"Only three things you got to have," Uncle Jim had said. "You got to search for it, and you got to need it." He pushed a thick rope of hair back behind his ear. "And you got to not be scared."

Tom watched the deer frozen at the end of the bridge, remembering when, finally, he'd asked, "When can I do this, when can I go on a spirit quest?"

Uncle Jim had looked away. "Things are different now. People don't do this very much now."

"But I want to," he'd pleaded. "You can teach me how." Again his uncle had looked at the ground. "Already I told you things I shouldn't tell. Besides, your mother is a good Christian lady. She'd be mad as hell, you know."

"Then we won't tell her."

His uncle had smiled then but said, "It can be dangerous, this thing. Sometimes it doesn't go right and nothing happens. Sometimes bad things can happen and you don't even know it for a long time, even years."

A few weeks later he'd climbed the ridge to the north of Fish Creek until he came to a small lake his uncle had described. The lake sat in a tight basin in a wrinkle on the long, meadowed ridge. Above the lake the ridge rose to a crest of dark granite and ice. There was no trail, and the lake was on no map.

For three days he fasted and slept on the brittle heather beside the lake, not even building a fire for the cool summer nights or a shelter from the nearly constant drizzle. By night coyotes howled up and down the ridge, warning one another of the intruder at the lake, talking him over, while icy stars spun great circles through the clouds. During the day, bears stumbled into the basin looking for blueberries. When they smelled him, they galloped off toward more remote places. Ravens swooped laughing over his place by the lake, mocking him as they flapped to the high rocks. Further up the ridge, the marmots sat on their scree slopes and whistled his solitary presence to their relations.

He flinched at the memory that came next. It was on the fourth day, after the sun came over the peak and touched the edge of the shallow lake. He took off his clothes and smeared the stone he'd chosen with saliva the way his uncle had said he should, and then he'd waded into the water, feeling the cold cut into his groin and chest, excited and terrified. And when the water closed over his head, he held to the stone and struggled to stay upright, waiting for the vision he knew would come. But instead of the spirit, he met only blank and total fear as the water sealed him from the sky and gripped him like a fist. Dropping the stone, he fought for the edge of the lake.

He lay in the sun that day for a long time, hearing the buzz of mosquitoes and being vaguely aware of the sharp points of the heather. That night he collected wood and built a fire while the coyotes explained his failure in exquisite detail to the world. The next morning he had gone home, and his uncle had looked at him and required no explanation.

The worst part was not believing. He knew that nothing had happened because he hadn't really believed. And afterwards it would always be worse, for now the one thing he could truly believe in was the fear itself. That had been real.

The deer began to browse on bare stems that stuck through the snow. He watched it, musing on his uncle. He had learned early not to repeat the old stories. When he'd told kids in first grade that Dakobed, the great mother mountain, had moved to its present location from over in eastern Washington, they'd laughed and hooted, asking if it had taken a train or backpacked. After that he'd told no one, not even Jimmy.

He shifted one leg and the deer spun and vanished, leaving a sense of neither sound nor motion. He finished the peaches and smashed the can against the puncheon with his boot before putting it in the pack. His uncle's eyes had become still when he'd told him about the scholarship engineered by the teacher in school. That day Uncle Jim had walked away without speaking, but the next day he'd come up while Tom was splitting kindling and said, "It's fine, this school. You'll go there and then you'll come back. It won't be like it used to be. Nothing will change." He'd propped one foot on the chopping block and leaned his hands on his knee. "At first I thought it might be bad, like it was in the old days when they stole us kids. I thought you might forget who you were. That's what they always want. But I thought about it, and it's okay. For Jimmy it would be bad, and for a lot of the other kids in the valley, not just Indian kids neither, it wouldn't be too good. But for you it'll be fine. When you come back we'll go for a long walk. When you come back we'll walk clear over the mountains to Lake Chelan the way the old ones did, and I'll tell you all the stories. Maybe we'll walk all the way to Canada, and I'll teach you all them things you ain't learned yet."

And that had been the last time his uncle had talked with him until he waved through the window of the bus pulling out of Everett for California.

A light wind moved up the creek and swept beneath the bridge, and he raised the mackinaw collar and pulled the wool cap lower over his ears. Thirty minutes later a trail broke from the blazes and climbed the ridge to his left through thick stands of white pine and fir. He climbed in a vertical line, kicking steps up the steep snow. Now it was simply a matter of getting to the top of the ridge, six miles by the buried trail but much closer by the direct snow route.

In an hour he stopped, listening to his heart drumming against his chest and feeling the cramps working their way through his thighs and calves. The light thinned toward dusk in the timber, and the air grew colder as the shadows lengthened between the trees. The high, shrill piping of a thrush glanced off the snow and faded into the still air. He regretted not leaving the trailhead by daylight. Now he'd have to camp somewhere on the side of the ridge

Angling across the snow to the bowl of a big hemlock, he dropped the pack into the depression around the trunk of the tree. As he stepped down and sat on the edge of the pack, he breathed deeply and felt the fine, cutting edge of the air, an edge that might grow painful later. The big hemlock was a freak of nature here near treeline. Around it the silver fir and mountaim hemlock were smaller and thinner, giving way in places to the twisted alpine fir. The narrow trunks cast angular black lines on the snow with the last of the light, and as he watched a host of shadows came out from the timber and crept up the snow around him. The wind moved the bare branches of brush that stabbed through the thinner patches of snow, and the branches waved like sparse skeletons. The shadows rose and lengthened, unfurled long arms up the trunks and rippled across pockets of snow to merge and bring on the first wave of evening.

He pulled the collar tighter. On a similar evening, when they'd camped at Blue Lakes, his uncle had watched the shadows crowding close and said, "Sometimes I like to think I see the people in these shadows, that maybe all the people are coming back." At the time, he'd thought it wasn't good for his uncle to keep looking for things in the shadows, but he'd said nothing.

He dragged the pack up to the snowbank and began looking around in the thin timber. A few yards from the hemlock he found a hollow large enough to stretch out in and sheltered from the up-slope breeze by a wall of snow and narrow trunks.

Working quickly, he tied parachute cord between two trees and stretched the plastic over it, anchoring the corners to other trees to create a low, gabled shelter. The second sheet of plastic went on the ground beneath the blankets, and he sat on this and ate a can of beans and the porkchop Jimmy had fried that morning. He threw the bone into the trees downhill from the den and rolled in the blankets, using his jacket as a pillow. Overhead through the sparse timber he watched as constellations came out to slowly fill the four quarters of the night sky until finally the heavens seemed to flow like a glacial river.

As he slept, a shadow disengaged itself from the darkness and moved heavily across the snow, criss-crossing the slope between the trees. A few yards below the sleeper, the shadow stopped and sat back on its haunches. A fleck of light glinted in narrow yellow eyes that gazed unbroken at the den in which Tom Joseph lay. The wind swept over the ridge and flowed across the sleeper, and the lips of the shadow curled back and then the shadow turned and vanished, as enormous as a mountain, leaving no sign on the hard-packed snow.

During the night the moon rose and silvered the dark peaks and set again, and it did not rain or snow. He awoke in the morning to light leaping off the snow outside his shelter. His legs ached and the bad shoulder shivered with pain when he moved it. The grayed plastic gave the light pouring through the appearance of thunderheads, and when he shoved his head up out of the hole he was slashed by the bright sun.

He shook himself free of the blankets and crawled out of

the depression, squinting tightly as he rose. He pulled a plastic water bottle from the pack and drank half the contents and then, scraping the top layer of debris from the snow, he dug clean snow to stuff into the bottle. Then he fished a nylon stuffsack from the pack and slipped its knot. From the bag he removed a cherry poptart which he began to eat as he strolled away from the hemlock.

Once outside the clump of trees, he looked out over the timber that thickened toward the river. Stretched below him was the upper reach of the Stehemish drainage, a wide vee of timber that covered the Great Fill where the glaciers had ground down the mountain and silted a deep plateau across the valley. Runouts cut from several glaciers on this side of the big mountain and formed sharp ridges crumbling into gray streams. Then the streams came together and carved a deep trench out of the Great Fill, and that was the Stehemish River which began in ash-gray froth and the waste of the mountain and whitened on its way down the valley toward Forks more than forty miles away. Tall, old-growth timber tilted and fell off the crumbling edges of the fill and slid down to the streams to form logjams that flushed out with each spring's runoff and became the battered, polished logs that lined the banks and made new impasses as far down as the meeting between Sauk and Stehemish.

Only the tops of the glaciers showed above the ridges the glaciers had carved, the uppermost regions of the living ice sheets rising together toward the summit of the mountain that erupted in white light over the drainage. Dakobed, which the Stehemish called the mother mountain and the whites called Glacier Peak, towered above everything on the horizon, the mountain under whose ice Coyote had loved Goat Woman and brought the roof of the world tumbling in. On the slopes below him the timber grew even thicker as it climbed the sides of Miners' Creek, the creek named for the men who'd been prying and tapping like burglars at the ridge for half a century.

His eyes burned and teared and he swallowed the last of the pastry and returned to the pack. He found his uncle's goggles in a side pocket and slipped them on, wondering as he did so what the old ones had done about the sun that came off the snow like a flint knife. Maybe they'd used wood with narrow slits like he'd seen in photos of Eskimos. It occurred to him that there must be books that would tell him about his ancestors.

He loaded the pack and swung it onto his back, working the stiff shoulder to soothe the cramped nerve. Climbing again, he passed fewer of the little, twisted trees blasted by winters and hardened by growing seasons as brief as a heartbeat. He edged his boots into the hard snow, working to keep his balance, careful not to lean too close to the slope. The trees thinned and dropped away, and the ridge became a burning line of white against the blue sky. He timed his breathing to his steps, one breath one step, and kept a steady pace up the ridge, feeling more secure as the snow softened under the growing sun.

Just below the sharp edge of the ridgetop he stopped and turned, kicking deep steps to balance himself. Looking down the fifty-degree slope, he wished for his iceaxe; something else Jimmy must have traded or sold. With the axe he could stop any slide, but without it he might not stop bouncing until he hit the trees a long way below.

Across the valley, the mountain had grown. The slumplines of covered crevasses stood out, and the white blocks from recent icefalls made shadows like oddly tilting houses on the glaciers. The Teeth, distinct twin spires of rock, stood snow-whitened near the summit, and the icewall above the Teeth was only a softly rounded angle of white this early in the season. Later, the snow would melt away and lay bare twenty feet of vertical ice to block that route up the mountain.

He stared at the white mountain, the center, the great mother, and tried to feel what it had meant to his tribe. They had woven it over thousands of years into their stories, telling themselves who they were and would always be in relation to the beautiful peak. Through their relationship with the mountain, they knew they were significant, a people to be reckoned with upon the earth. Away in four directions the world streamed, and Dakobed was the center, a reference point for existence. One look, and a person would always know where he was. This much his uncle's stories, and his mother's stories, had made clear.

The loggers—growing more and more desperate—cursed the mountain for having spawned a wilderness around itself, a barrier between saws and timber. The miners looked at the mountain and thought of copper and molybdenum and more.

The old ones hadn't climbed the mother mountain, and loggers and miners didn't climb it, but Tom Joseph had climbed it. Without ropes or crampons, icescrews or carabiners—all those things he had seen the serious mountaineers bring through Forks—he'd followed his uncle up the Ptarmigan Glacier through the Teeth and, with a hatchet to cut steps, over the icewall to the summit. The shadow of the cedar pole his uncle had cut on the Great Fill had leaped against the icewall, pointing the way.

When he breathed, the air had lost its cutting edge, and the day came streaming together where he stood. In a land of rain such a day was a gift, a thing to be prayed for. He wished he knew such a prayer, something in the old language, but he was inarticulate before such beauty, his tongue a heavy, dead thing.

By the time he rounded the line of the ridgetop, his legs ached and his head pounded with each breath. The Forest Service lookout tower stood a quartermile away at the end of the ridge, balanced on spindly legs over the long drainage. At the other end, the ridge dropped into a bowl strewn with small trees and then climbed again to the sharp summit of the little mountain they called Plummer. Hidden in the bowl was Image Lake.

He stood for a moment with his hands in the packstraps, hearing the drumming of a grouse in the timber just off the far side of the ridge and recognizing the peaks that lifted into view on all sides. The closest was Fortress, a blunt barrier of rock, snow and ice. Behind Fortress, Formidable and Eldorado crowded in. On the opposite side of the horizon Dome and Spider and Blue gathered together in spires of black granite and white glacier. Far to the south the white cloud of Mount Rainier floated, and above everything loomed Dakobed just across the valley. As he watched the scores of peaks that stalked away in all directions he wondered what the old, real names were for those mountains. His uncle must have not known either, for he had never mentioned any of those names. And without them he must have felt mute, without the proper language of prayer.

Settling the pack more comfortably, he began to move away from the lookout, half walking and half sliding down the ridge toward the basin. The snow had blown up a cornice where the ridge narrowed, and he balanced just back from the lip, skiing down the dips and kicking his way back up again.

A halfmile from the lookout he entered the clumps of stunted timber around the lake. On the deep snow he was as tall as many of the silver trees, and he looked over and through them for a glimpse of the lake. In its place he saw a flat expanse of white at the bottom of the basin, and he laughed, realizing that he'd expected to see the white mountain floating in the indigo lake, imaged in the water. But even the outlet stream lay buried under snow, bursting free only at the instant that it toppled off the edge of Miners' Ridge toward the creek two thousand feet below.

Once again he turned to look at the big mountain and then around in a full circle at the wilderness that stretched in a chaos of white and broken granite for more miles than he could see. A shrill *kree* cut the air over the basin and he looked up to see a golden eagle breaking over the white line of the ridge leading up ᴅ Plummer, breaking almost black as it swooped low over the snow. The eagle rode the updraft off the ridge for a momen searching for marmots and then soared toward the peak anc out of sight, the bird's shadow knifing across the ridge like a da ker brother.

8

Ab Masingale, the inventor, sat in a chair away from the bar so that his legs in their stiff twin casts could jut out before him. Traffic in the Red Dog eddied and swirled around the logjam of the legs as Ab poked the air and pounded the round oak table. Long-torsoed and lanky, Ab dominated his corner of the tavern with his wispy white hair, broad shoulders, and pale blue eyes in a face covered with a week's whiskers. New teeth flashed when he talked. His jeans, split to accomodate the casts, were held up by red suspenders on a blue-striped hickory shirt.

"Mistake was them tin blades," Ab said loudly. "Too damned thin. Damned things got to going around." He flailed a circle with one arm, and a portly old man with a bowler hat shoved his chair back with a mild look of alarm. "Got to going around and started bending ever which way till they come off and took to flying by theirselves."

Ab's long, delicate-looking hands were incongruously scarred and twisted, with thick nails and gnarled knuckles. The index finger on his left hand ended at the first joint, the skin puckered and white where it came together.

A circle of loggers balanced mugs of beer and watched as Ab showed how the tin blades flew away, his arms flapping in opposite directions like drunken crows. In a lighted sign above the horseshoe bar a man in a canoe paddled endless circles on a sparkling blue lake. A jukebox warned about somebody who "shot a man in Reno, just to watch him die." From the back of the room came the clatter of a pool table. The wall opposite the bar held pictorial history: tree stumps big enough to support a dozen loggers posed with crosscut saws, doublebit axes and a mule; steam-donkeys so big that it took a fourth of the timber cut just to keep the engines burning;

undercuts high and wide enough for loggers to stand in the wedges with handlebar mustaches and baggy suits. Newer pictures showed a topfaller perched like a bug in the clouds topping a spar tree with a chainsaw, the last twenty feet of the limbless tree frozen in an arc toward the earth, and logtrucks taking the last of the massive old-growth out of the valley. Above the photos one of the old crosscuts hung on the wall like a shark's maw. There were no women in the bar.

"Just about took my goddamned head off," Ab Masingale said, letting the arms crash to the table like broken wings. Tilted too far back in the chair, Ab was forced to suddenly swing his legs in a violent half-circle to right himself. "Next time, by God, I'll use a heavier metal. Next time I'm going to make them blades out of the hoods off that pair of Chevies I got in the pasture. There ain't no stronger metal than them old Chevies."

"Hell, Ab, you can't make heelicopter blades out'n car hoods," said the man in the bowler hat.

Ab turned on the little man. "What the hell you know about flying, Floyd, you water-soaked rat. I was you I'd quit thinking about heelicopters and start worrying about J. D. Hill taking my waterworks away from me."

Floyd lifted the hat from his head and began turning it in his stubby hands.

"J. D. can't do that," Leroy Brant said from a stool at the bar. "He ain't got enough votes."

"Well, I wouldn't be so sure, the way things is going in this town," Ab replied. "Hell, don't he own practically every god-damned thing in the valley? Don't you work for him, Leroy?"

Before Leroy could respond a figure appeared in the tavern doorway, and the crowd turned to watch Floyd's dark twin step into the room.

Sam Gravey dropped solidly into a chair between Ab and Floyd. "Beer," he said happily. Gray underwear showed at the neck of his red wool shirt, and graying hair grew thick on the sides of his head, thinning into a halo near the back.

The bartender brought a beer, and Sam drank half of it before looking from Ab to Floyd. Teeth showed white through the foam-flecked mustache.

"Well now we got the three oldest bastards in the valley in one spot," Leroy said, grinning at the old prospector.

"Yeah, now we can hear us some stories about how men used to be men and Wobblies had balls big as a bullmoose's," Dinker said from the next stool.

Ab looked around him with scorn. "Shit," he said. "Dinker, you wouldn't a been man enough to carry a Wobbly's asswipe. Hell," Ab looked at the men, "these shittails they call loggers today don't know what real logging was. In them days a rookie choker-setter had a life spectancy of about three weeks, ain't that right, Sam?"

Before Sam could nod into his beer again a loud voice came from the direction of the pool table. "Sure Ab, and the woods was full of injuns just dying to lift your hair, ain't that right? The way you old farts tell it, the whole valley was full of Paul Bunyans and woods niggers back then."

"Woods niggers, huh? Remember Splitlip Jim?" Ab looked from Floyd to Sam. "Splitlip Jim would've eat Jake on toast for breakfast, wouldn't he?"

Sam nodded into his beer, and Floyd said, "An Splitlip Jim was an injun. The toughest goddamned. . . ."

"Too bad about Jim Joseph," Sam said suddenly.

Unnoticed, Jimmy slipped from his stool at the end of the bar near the door and left the Red Dog.

In the back of the bar, Amel Barstow lined up the cueball for a combination on the four and five in the corner.

"You going to sink that, are you?" The speaker held his cuestick in both hands and leaned his head around it, grinning. "I guess those old farts don't want to talk about woods niggers, huh?"

"Am I going to sink it?" Amel said. "Does a bear shit in the woods?"

Amel stroked the cue smoothly and the balls caromed erratically off the bumper.

"Does a chicken got teeth?" his opponent said. "Too bad. You oughtn't try to listen to Ab's bullshit and play pool at the same time."

Amel watched him line up his cuestick, crouched over the table like a coiled spring. Jake Tobin was a short, broad man with a blunt head and brown hair cut close to the scalp. His belly protruded against his suspenders and his biceps inside the rolled-up denim shirt were nearly as big as his large head. Amel stared with fascination as the muscle swelled with the movement of the cuestick. Jake's big, oval face squinted around gray eyes, the muscled cheeks and double chin stippled with a coarse beard.

"Say, Jake, you heard that Tom Joseph's back?"

The cueball caught its target a fraction off center and spilled it into the cluster of balls in the middle of the table. Out of the covey the black ball rolled slowly and fatefully toward a corner pocket, hung on the lip, and dropped out of sight, rolling away with a sound like faint thunder.

Jake swung toward Amel, holding the stick like a club. "Pretty fucking smart," he said. "For a shit-for-brains like you."

Amel grinned. "Hope I didn't disturb your shot."

"What the fuck you mean, he's back? He ain't never gone nowhere that I know of. I seen him swilling beer in here today."

"That's Jimmy, the older one. I'm talking about Tom, the young one who went off to college. I gave him a ride in from Arlington the other day."

Jake twisted chalk onto the end of his cue. "Rack 'em," he said, motioning toward the table with the stick. "So what's that supposed to mean to me? Why should I give a good goddamned?"

"Looser racks," Amel said.

Jake stood with both hands on the tip of his cuestick, leaning slightly toward Amel and glaring.

Amel shrugged and picked up the rack.

Jake reached with the end of his stick to push a couple of balls toward where Amel had placed the rack. "Something the way Jim Joseph went nuts, wasn't it?" Jake said in a friendly tone. "Sam hadn't brung him in when he did, they was folks around here ready to go injun hunting with deer rifles. I always knew that family had nuts blood in it."

Amel looked up from placing the balls in the rack. "You and me both knew Jim Joseph a long time," he said. "He never did nothing crazy in his whole life before. Hell, you worked with him. He was one of the best buckers in the woods till he got stove up."

"Maybe, but I always thought he was a oddball. Whole family is, even that fat one. This is about the first time I ain't seen him in here. Sits over at that bar drinking and never saying diddlysquat to nobody. Like he's too goddamned good to talk to a white man."

Amel walked to the other end of the table. "Tom was down at the University of California. They gave him a scholarship. He's smart."

"No shit? One of them Josephs went all the way to Califuckinfornia to get hisself educated? Schools around here ain't good enough, I guess. College education, huh?"

"Tom's a good kid. He was the best damned fullback this town ever had." Amel set the white ball up for the break and chalked his cuestick.

"J. D. says they're just pissin their pants to get injuns and niggers and chinks and any other damned foreigner they can in them colleges. Turning away American boys to do it. Like Buddy. He was the quarterback, and quarterbackin takes brains. Ever notice how you don't see nigger quarterbacks in the pros? But Buddy didn't go off to Califuckinfornia for college."

Amel twisted the stick in a cube of chalk. "If brains was gunpowder Buddy couldn't blow his nose. You ought to know that." Amel sank two solids on the break and grinned up at Jake Tobin.

"Shit," Jake said. "You know how to get a squaw pregnant? Come on her feet and let the flies do the rest."

Amel lined up his next shot and said as he bent over the table, "I heard that one forty years ago, Jake, and the way I heard it was Polacks." He looked up. "You ain't Polack, are you Jake?"

9

They left Leroy's car hidden in a turnout at the end of the spur road, and Karen followed him through the blowdown maze of the trail, crawling under logs and climbing over jackpots of trunks and rootwads on this trail the Forest Service had abandoned. The three miles switchbacked steeply, the way a child might trace a zigzag fingerline down through the thick timber, and then the trail swung parallel to the ridge and climbed through slide alder and huckbrush and snowmelt to the wide granite saddle of Squire Creek Pass.

Tom let her move ahead for the last mile and watched the brittle huckleberry limbs brush off her jeans as she climbed easily. When they left the timber, he spotted the sawtooth end of the ridge outlined against the shallow sky, gray cutting into blue. Below, the Squire Creek drainage plunged to a sharp vee and rose again to the exfoliated gray walls that became Whitehorse and Three Fingers. He remembered another day with Jimmy, finding the old trapline just below this saddle and following it down into the timber, collecting the rusted traps. And Jimmy using his boot to spread the jaws of the one not rusted open and releasing the marten leg, scraping away the splintered gray bone and bits of rotten fur.

The marmots had seen Karen and began whistling across the wide flat of ridgetop, sitting on boulders, brows furrowed, forelegs held daintily, then diving into the snow-lined scree.

They'd used the traps that same winter, oiling away the rust and moving them further up the drainage to take marten and fox and an occasional ermine. Remembering the deep snow along the trapline, he remembered the drumming cold of the frozen woods just after daybreak and the breadth of his brother's back, even at twelve, moving ahead between the trees, clumsy in the snow.

"You lost back there?" She grinned at him from fifteen yards ahead, arms folded and hair in twin dark braids over her white shirt. Behind her the twisted trunk of a solitary mountain hemlock with thick, gnarled branches stitched the flat of the ridge to the empty sky.

"Sorry." He quickened his pace and caught up with her. "I was thinking about coming up here with Jimmy when we were kids. We found an old trapline." His voice disturbed him on the silent mountain. The traps had been set in little shelves cut in tree trunks above snowline by a trapper who had probably gotten drunk and died down in Forks or some other town. "That old marten probably got along swell with three legs," Jimmy had said when he'd seen Tom's eyes watching the splinter of bone.

"Well?" Karen looked at him curiously, still smiling.

When they reached the hemlock he kicked remnants of snow off the granite and spread the blanket over the rock. Karen sat on the blanket, legs folded, and watched him as he looked out over the valley where the two big rivers came together.

"I shouldn't have let you talk me into this," she said. "Buddy will go crazy if he finds out."

"Who cares about Buddy." He looked across the slab granite to where the ridge dropped away to Squire Creek. On the other side was the deeper cleft of Clear Creek. On either side of the ridge, the towers of Three Fingers and Devil's Thumb faced each other blankly. Several feet of frozen drift, pitted by the sun, lay up against the teeth of the ridge above them. From the jagged granite on the horizon, a long-abandoned prospecting trail led down to the remote backcountry behind Three Fingers and Whitehorse, country he'd heard his uncle describe but that he'd never seen.

"Tom, you have to get it through your head that I'm still engaged to Buddy. We can't do this again."

He turned to look at her. *'Probably didn't even hurt when he chewed it off,' Jimmy had said. 'Like this.'* Jimmy had pretended to gnaw at his knee and then he pretended to run around on two feet and one hand. Jimmy carried the killing club when they checked the traps, and Tom trailed behind with the twenty-two so that his older brother would not see his eyes again.

"When he gets back you can tell him you're not going to marry him," he said. And then he added, "You know, I was just remembering again. One of those traps we found had a marten's leg in it. He'd chewed it off to get away, I guess. I used to dream about that trap, and sometimes in the dream it would start getting bigger and would keep growing until it seemed like it was the whole valley and I'd start screaming and wake up just before the mountains sprang shut on me."

He looked away, embarrassed. How could he tell the horror of the gray bone in a dream, a bone not just his but him? How could he explain mountains closing with a sound like steel?

"You're getting to be real serious," she said. "Like the Indians they always show in those old movies." She was smiling at him as she pulled sandwiches out of her daypack.

He looked carefully at the angles of her cheeks, the brown hair and dark skin, not as dark as some of the tans in Santa Barbara, but a dark that stood out amidst the pale complexions of the valley.

"You're an Indian, too," he said. "You don't have to be a full-blood to be Indian. It just matters how you feel, what you think. Your dreams."

She looked away from him at the range of peaks, and he added, "You know, it sounds funny, but I used to wonder if that marten ever came back to visit his leg. Just maybe to remember what it had been like before."

Above them a marmot whistled and was answered from the scree to the north of the ridge. Two lone clouds trailed past the Thumb and slipped by the stairstepped black granite across the valley. Below, the timber shredded the cloud shadows and seemed to grow darker.

"My uncle knew a whole lot that he tried to teach me," he said. "But I never really listened. I mean, I never listened like it would really make any difference. And now I think about all the questions I should have asked." He picked up a chip of rock and tossed it into the snow and then accepted one of the sandwiches she handed him.

"Buddy comes back from Vancouver tomorrow," she said.

He lay back to watch as a pair of clouds sailed beyond the valley, alone in a sky with no sign of rain.

"I told Leroy we were coming up here," Karen said as she unscrewed the thermos cap. "He told me to warn you that J. D. and some others have been talking about you being opposed to the mine like your uncle was. Leroy says he thinks J. D. is trying to stir people up for some reason." She tapped him on the shoulder and he looked around at her. "Are you against the mine like your uncle was?"

"I think I saw a wolf," he said. "The first night I was back. I'm almost sure it was a wolf." He reached to touch her neck and then he kissed each eyelid slowly and carefully, moving his hand to the softness of her neck beneath the long hair and then down over her breasts to the barely perceptible swell of her belly.

"If you went with me, I could leave the valley," he whispered as she lay back and pulled him over her.

She looked up at him with a near smile, and he felt her hips moving very slightly and rhythmically. "Let's just think about right now."

One of the fragments of cloud trailed an edge over the sun and he saw the cloud's shadow in her eyes. He imagined himself a shadow, insubstantial and dark above her, and he thought of his uncle alone in the forest. Even the singers—the men and women with power—must have wondered at times which was the shadow and which the spirit, which world dreamed the other. Did the fire make the shadows dance up the cedar walls, or did the shadows dream of fire?

She dropped him at the end of the gravel road, and he walked to the house, scuffling his boots to hear the sound. The ripening summer brought out the sweet sharp pitch of the trees and the sour distant stench of the mill. Deerflies hovered in the slanting sunlight at the edge of the forest, and on the far ridges above town fires were burning. The Forest Service would keep the slash fires burning somewhere in the mountains until the fall snows came.

He breathed in the sweat of the trees and the cool, clean smell of the rivers that joined nearby, and it began to feel good to be home. The graveyard along the river was far away, and his thoughts drifted from Karen to the stone with his name and higher up to the shadows of the ice caves. Suddenly he wanted to see the caves, to climb down inside them.

When he stepped into the yard he saw the group on the porch. Bayard Taylor sat on the top step talking up to their mother in her chair. And on the next step sat a thin, redheaded figure in a Forest Service uniform.

Bayard saw him and rose, stepping off the porch in one stride and holding out his hand. The skin hugged his thin face with a healthy, parchment shine, and his brown eyes were wide and bright.

"Tom," Bayard said in a nasal voice that was almost a shout. "Amel told me you were back, but I had to see it myself. You look educated as all get out."

As they shook hands Tom grinned at the old surveyor. "Hi, Bayard," he said.

Bayard jerked his thumb back toward the porch. "Tom, this here's Martin Grider."

The redhead stood and held out a long, bony arm, and they clasped hands for a moment. Feeling a surprising wiry strength, Tom looked in Grider's face.

"Bayard told me that you know more about these mountains than any man alive," Grider said.

Tom looked sharply from Martin Grider to Bayard, and Bayard said quickly, "Tom's uncle was the man that knew this country, every rock and root of it." Turning to Tom, he said, "I'm real sorry. I was telling Sara, I would've come to the funeral but I was over in the Okanogan and never heard in time."

Tom nodded. The soft evening light shone on Bayard's nearly bald head and on the close-cropped hair above his large ears.

"Martin's the new wilderness stranger up the Stehemish and over in the Northlakes area," Bayard said. "He asked me the best way into the Snowking Lakes and I had to admit I ain't never been up there. I told him that if anybody around here knew it was you."

"There's no trail in there, and I'd hate to waste a whole day or more bushwhacking if I don't have to," the ranger said.

Tom sat on the porch beside his mother's chair, and Bayard and the ranger sat on the porch to his right with their feet dangling. The screen door banged and Jimmy appeared with a handful of green beer cans. When Sara Joseph waved one away, Jimmy handed three out to the other men and sat back against the house with two cans on his lap.

"If I remember right, you'll have to do some bushwhacking no matter how you go," Tom said. "Did you bring a topo map?"

Martin Grider pulled a pair of maps out of his back pocket and unfolded them on the porch. Tom and Bayard and the ranger knelt over the contour maps, while Tom traced the logging road Grider would have to drive in on and the switchback where he should park the truck and leave the road on foot.

"There's an old burn right here that's pretty tough to get through," Tom said, "all grown over and full of logs you can't see because of the slide alder and berries. But if you work your way along the south edge here you can get onto the ridge and then it's a piece of cake. There's an old trail that runs right along the ridge." He showed Grider how far to follow the ridge and where to drop off to hit the first lake basin.

"The best camping is right at the outlet," Tom went on, feeling strangely reassured by his own voice. "And when you head up to the other lakes, stay on the north side or you'll run into some mean rock faces. To get up to Hurricane Lake you have to climb up beside this waterfall." He pointed to a sharp vee on the map. "It'll probably take you one long day to get in and another to get out, but once you're in it's easy."

The lakes were clustered around the peak they called Snowking, a jagged rock sticking up like shrapnel with a glacier down the north side that crumbled into the lake named for the peak. Snowking Lake was a milky green, and he'd pulled slow, pale green and pink trout from the thick water. At night the deep lake basin had felt heavy, haunted, the black air weighted with something. "You feel it?" his uncle had asked when they were camped near the outlet. "Some places are friendlier than others. This lake is never happy when people visit. But once in a while I have to come here to remind myself that there are such places as this, too." They'd lain in their blankets under the plastic tarp listening to the glacier calving in the lake with small, almost inaudible surges, and the next morning they'd climbed the waterfall and gone beyond Hurricane Lake to fish a small tarn near the shoulder of the mountain. Out of the absolutely clear water they'd taken ancient trout with enormous heads and teeth and small, starved bodies.

"Most of the year this little pond is covered with snow and ice," his uncle had said. "These skinny guys live in darkness, waiting for a just few weeks of light and air each year. You could say they're like some people, only I can't think of who right now. Maybe later I'll make a story out of it, or maybe you can think about it and make a story for me." Uncle Jim had chuckled and slipped his trout back into the tarn, watching it slash toward the center. "I ought to just kill this fish, you know. It's too skinny and tough to eat, and there's too many of them guys in that lake so they ain't enough food to go around. A white man would probably kill it because that's best for all the fish together. But I figure that the creator's handling this situation, and those trout elders got a right to live and suffer and eat each other. They must be wise by now, cause it's hard things that makes us wise."

"Have you ever considered working for the Forest Service?" Martin Grider asked as he refolded the maps. "We could use somebody who knows the country like you do."

Tom shook his head. "I don't think so."

"Tom doesn't trust the forest circus," Bayard said. "And I can't say as I blame him. I may work for 'em but I don't trust 'em either."

The chair creaked and they looked up to see Sara Joseph standing.

"Come and have coffee," she said turning toward the house.

Bayard sprang up. "Sounds wonderful."

Grider slipped the maps into his pocket. "I'd like to, but I have to get my equipment sorted out if I'm going into those lakes tomorrow." He held out a hand to Tom. "I appreciate your help," he said. "I'd like to talk to you some more about this country, when we get a chance."

They shook hands, and the ranger started across the yard toward the rusted railroad tracks and the ranger station.

As they drank the coffee Tom said, "How are the ice caves this year, Bayard? I thought I might take a look at them before dark."

Bayard pulled on an earlobe. "Just fine. Bigger than ever. That's a real good idea, because you could drop me off on your way out there. My old lady took the pickup into Everett to stock up on shotgun shells. Since you left she's took up skeet shootin'."

Tom looked up in surprise when Jimmy said, "Mind if I ride along?"

Jimmy drove with Tom straddling the stickshift and Bayard

leaning his head out the passenger window. Above the road, Whitehorse rose gleaming, the granite face a wall and every line of the glacier etched in the late sunlight. A brown and white hound slinked across the road ahead of them, its nose low and tail between its legs.

"You still have all your dogs?" Tom asked.

Bayard shook his head. "I only got two left, Bascomb and Molly, them two blueticks. I gave the rest to my cousin over in Rockport a couple weeks ago. Couldn't put up with all them hounds all over the place anymore, and since I gave up hunting it seemed ridiculous."

"You could've sold those dogs for a good price," Jimmy said as he peered after the disappearing hound.

"I suppose so, but Regal wanted 'em pretty bad, and he'll take good care of 'em. Regal ain't the kind of guy that'll be shoving six dogs in a little box in the back of his truck like some of these fellas."

Jimmy turned the truck onto a gravel road next to a small wooden gas station and store. The rear of the truck fishtailed, and Jimmy accelerated out of the slide and bounced through a wide puddle.

"Whoa, there," Bayard said. "My house is just around the corner."

When the pickup stopped in front of an isolated house deep in the trees, Bayard looked at Tom. "I heard J. D. offered you a job and you turned him down. J. D. ain't the talkative kind, you know, so he ain't told no more'n two or three hundred people. J. D.'s making it sound like it's because of the mine and that you're too much like your uncle. You know how J. D. works, he don't come right out and say too much."

Bayard climbed out and stood for a moment. "I wouldn't worry too much about J. D.," he said. "But I'd keep my eyes open, because he's got something in mind. J. D. didn't get to own most of this valley by being a nice fella."

Bayard walked toward the house, and two writhing hounds appeared around a corner of the log building and slammed into his legs so hard he nearly fell.

"You never told me about J. D. offering you a job," Jimmy said as the truck pulled away. "He offers me one, by god, I'll take it. Jobs don't grow on trees around here."

"They used to."

"What?" Jimmy couldn't take his eyes off the strip of tortured road through the trees.

"Jobs used to grow on trees around here," Tom said as the truck tunneled through low-hanging branches and brushed vines back from the sides of the road. Water stood in dark pools every few feet.

At the bottom of a boulder-strewn gully, they got out of the truck and began to climb up through the rocks, picking their way around and across a milky stream. On one side of the gully the dark stone of the peak was a broken wall rising a thousand feet, and on the other the ridge sloped into the gully in a tangle of brush. Blackflies hung in the cool air and moved aside to let them pass.

Two hundred yards from the pickup, a ceiling of ice arched over the stream and the narrowed gully, the ice climbing from the slope on one side to freeze against the granite on the other. Beneath the white arch, the ice caves were tunnels of shadow out of which the little stream twisted. Side-by-side, the two caves looked like the pale green eyes of the mountain.

Tom climbed into the cave on the right, the one that spawned the larger tributary of the stream. The floor was a jumble of broken ice and brown rock, and the arching walls were smooth, a scattering of blue and black shadows darkening to where the ice closed with the mountain a hundred feet back.

He walked to the back of the cave and sat on a flattened rock, feeling the sharpness of the air. Jimmy followed and chose a rock close by. Together they sat and watched the greenish-white water come out of the ice and move toward the light further down the mountain.

Jimmy looked from the stream to his brother. "It's funny," he said. "Once when you were gone I came out here. But I sat in the pickup and looked up here and thought I saw faces. I got scared and left. What was funny, though, was that what I was scared of was that I'd recognize them. That's when I figured I'd been spending too much time at the Red Dog."

Jimmy laughed, and the hollow air of the cave swallowed the sound so suddenly that they both looked up with a start.

"You really turn J. D. down?"

Tom didn't look at his brother. "You think I could help put in that mine after what our uncle did, after what happened to him?"

"Our uncle wasn't thinking straight," Jimmy said. "He was too old and stuck in ways you and me can't even understand. I don't care how many stories he told you. He never saw that we have to live here, the way it is right now. Jesus, I couldn't even go get a beer when he was out there without somebody giving me hell. They wanted me to go get him and make him stop, but he never would listen to me."

He was silent for a moment and then went on. "He didn't understand that Indian don't matter no more. What matters is that we're people and we have to live here, with other people like J. D. and all the rest. Hell, I don't even know what Indian means, and neither do you. All I know is there won't be any logging here pretty soon, and then what'll we do?"

"We'll do something else," Tom said quietly. "Our people lived here a thousand years without logging. Even if everybody has to leave, every one of us, that's better than an open-pit mine." He picked up a piece of ice and snapped it. "Nobody seems to realize that a mine like that won't last forever. Twenty, even fifty years, and it'll be dead, and then there'll be nothing here except a bunch of junk and a road to a hole in the middle of what used to be wilderness."

"You're preaching. Even he didn't preach," Jimmy said, adding, "All I can say is we need jobs. I got a job now but we both know Vern Reese ain't going to last much longer. J. D.'ll get him, too, or else he'll just go bankrupt, and then what?"

The sun was moving to the west behind Gold Hill across the valley, and the last light spun into the cave and touched the ice. Then the shadows seemed to advance like a wall from the back of the cave. Tom looked toward his brother and saw only a black outline against the final light of the valley below them. For the first time he realized how absolutely alone his brother was in the valley. He thought of the photograph of their dark father, and the incredible possibility came to him that the names were wrong, that there had been a mistake, a crucial error on the stone. The light thinned and the cave turned black. They sat together in silence, and the pulse of the stream flowed outward, away from them.

"You ought to get a haircut," Jimmy said. "There's a town meeting tomorrow."

10

Dan Kellar nosed his new Dodge up against the Fir Tree and sat for a moment admiring the rain glimmering on the blue hood of the car. The company provided decent cars. Nothing snazzy, but he liked the automatic stick shift in this one, and the black naugahyde bucket seats.

He got out and looked around and then locked the door. On one side of the cafe was a big tree. On the other side was a tiny state-licensed liquor store, an empty lot, and a store with work boots and Ben Davis pants advertised in the window. He'd already passed a store selling chainsaws and a Texaco gas station, and that seemed to be the town. The whole damned town.

Above all, he was aware of the mountains that ringed the town. He had the feeling that the timber had crept ever closer to the small cluster of buildings until it stood poised for some kind of dark revenge. Attack of the second-growth. The second-growth from hell. He grinned, but the grin vanished quickly. The peaks cut off escape with a wall like jagged metal, and two fast, green rivers slid through the town like time itself.

"Poor bastards," he thought, breathing in the cold air. He knew a lot about the people of the valley because that was his job. He knew about the past and a lot more about the future of the people in the valley than the people themselves did. He'd seen the figures and projections and knew that the timber remaining outside the wilderness boundary wouldn't sustain a logging industry big enough to support the town. The loggers had cut and trucked their futures right out of the valley to the big mills in Everett and on to Japan. The only thing that could save the desolate little town now was Honeycutt Copper. When the mine got into full swing there would be jobs for the loggers. They'd take to the work because they were used to hard, dangerous work—a lot more dangerous than running machines in a mine, as far as that went. Those who didn't want to mine could move to Alaska, and even then they'd find that logging wasn't what it used to be because of all the federal regulations, environmental impact reports and all that. Logger. It was a funny word. He was proud of the fact that he didn't have a racist bone in his body, but still the word "logger" kept reminding him of the word "nigger." Logger-nigger, nogger-ligger. He grinned again and then shook his head.

"I must be tired," he said aloud.

It would be a big thing for the little town. There'd even been talk of the company investing in a resort right in town, at the foot of Whitehorse. They said the mountain had the lowest glacier in the continental U. S., and there couldn't be a more beautiful setting in the country, though he doubted if the spot got enough good snow for a ski resort. He made a mental note to mention the resort in his talk. And the wilderness. He knew the loggers had been pissed off for a long time at how the wilderness had locked up prime timber. Well, they couldn't cut the timber, but the mine would allow them to tear a living out of the guts of the wilderness anyway. They'd like that. "What good is a wilderness," he mused as he entered the dingy cafe, "if people can't eat?" That was a good line, and even though the environmental battle was over, he might as well work that one into the talk also.

Tom sat drinking creamy coffee near the register. Karen wrote out a young choker-setter's order and the logger and Indian looked at each other, Tom noting that the choker-setter's hair was longer than his own and pulled back in a ponytail. There was a small gold stud in one ear. He thought about what he would look like with a little earring like that. At ceremonies, especially, a lot of Indian guys wore earrings. And sunglasses. Indians always had those sunglasses on. He nodded, and the logger looked at him blankly before leaving the cafe.

He watched Karen move toward the kitchen. Tonight there

was a sense of distance in the way she looked at him and in her voice. Buddy had come back that morning. When the man in the gray suit came into the cafe, the knot in Tom's stomach tightened, and he watched covertly as the man took the logger's place at the counter.

The suit looked expensive, and the man had a good haircut that came down just a little over his ears, each hair looking as if it had been carefully laid in place. The man's face looked friendly, with eyes that didn't appear to shift and a mouth that looked like it was always about to smile. It was like a face carefully created to inspire trust. Tom's stomach twisted more tightly and he stirred his coffee, watching the cream swirl.

He thought of the mine and J. D.'s offer. Jimmy knew quite a bit about the mine. The road would cut all the way to Image Lake, and they'd build houses down in the flat of Miners' Creek fifteen miles inside the wilderness. There'd be a concentrator in there and a clearcut near the river to dump waste. Jimmy had a pamphlet that explained it in detail, especially the part about jobs and money. There was a picture of an alpine lake. That was what the mine would look like when the operation was abandoned and the pit filled with water.

He tried to catch Karen's eyes as she set a cup in front of the man and poured coffee. When she didn't look up, he went and stood in front of the register. As she pushed the buttons on the register she said, "We have to talk. It's important. Are you going to the meeting tonight?"

He nodded.

She pretended to study the bill and said, without looking up, "Can you come over and pick me up at the house afterwards?" He shook his head once up and down as she handed him the change.

Dan Kellar watched the Indian and the girl. Their attempt to be discreet was amusing. The girl was cute. More than cute, she was pretty sexy, especially the way her breasts strained at the buttons of the uniform dress and the way the dress moved when she walked toward the kitchen. It was kind of unusual that she'd be involved with an Indian, especially such a dark one. But in a town like this the selection must be limited. He remembered a joke he'd heard an Indian make about what great lovers Indians were. "We're the only people in the world that need an agency to manage their affairs," the Indian had said. He glanced at the boy as he left the cafe, and then his mind shifted back to the upcoming meeting. It wasn't usual for Honeycutt to send just one man out to address a gathering, but Porter, his partner, had been sick and this wasn't any big deal.

"What good's a wilderness when kids don't have shoes on their feet?" He spoke the words in his mind with just the right amount of indignation. "What's the good of. . ." No, that wouldn't work. Despite the piss-poor condition of the town, the loggers might get mad if you said something like that. Besides, the decisions had all been made and there wasn't any need to stir things up any more. "What good is a wilderness when decent men can't find jobs, when families have to go on welfare so people from Seattle and California can go backpacking?" That was better, but still there wasn't really any point in it. In a way it was too bad there wasn't any need for some rabble-rousing. Rousing rabble could be fun, especially if he'd had Porter with him so they could laugh about it over drinks later. And then there was J. D. Hill. Hill was damned serious about the whole thing, and he couldn't tell how Hill would react to statements like that. Honeycutt was being generous as hell with the small-town entrepreneur, more than they really needed to be with a small fish.

The land was patented, as good as owned, and Honeycutt could do anything they wanted with it, even if it was in the middle of a wilderness area. And once the road was in, even the diehard environmentalists would give up and go look for a cause that wasn't already lost. It was legal and allowed for right in the

Wilderness Act, and it was for the good of everybody. All he had to do was a little p.r. for the company tonight.

Kellar stirred his coffee and watched the curve of the waitress's breasts as she made a new pot of coffee. If the situation was a little different, he knew he could take her out, buy her a fancy dinner at one of the oyster places on Chuckanutt Drive, and be in her pants in a couple of hours. She looked like the intense kind. He'd had fun in some of the small towns Honeycutt sent him to.

"Excuse me, miss, but could I get some more coffee?" He smiled.

Karen looked up and felt herself grow warm. With Tom in the restaurant she hadn't realized how handsome the stranger was. And he seemed nice.

11

Jimmy wore his good cowboy shirt with the beige bulldoggers and imitation pearl snaps. He sat in the ratty overstuffed chair next to the couch, a sixteen-ounce Oly balanced on the chair arm and his belly hiding most of the Mac Truck buckle on his wide belt. His Levis were new and dark, and his boots shone with mink oil.

"Ain't you going to get ready for the meeting?" he asked when his brother came out of the back room.

"I am ready." Tom looked at his own faded jeans, washed nearly white and ravelled where they came down over his work-boots. He lifted the Lee jacket off the back of a kitchen chair and slipped it on over his denim shirt.

"Mom coming?"

Jimmy shook his head. "She's not feeling too good. She said she wanted to lay down for a while. I don't think she ever really came back from that pneumonia last winter."

"You didn't tell me about that," Tom said. "You should have written me."

Jimmy shrugged. "She went to the IHS hospital in Seattle for a week, and she got better."

When they were in the pickup Jimmy said, "You ought to pay attention tonight. You'll see that this mine ain't so bad." He lifted the beercan from the seat between his legs and took a drink. "Besides, this mine's going to be the only show in town pretty soon."

"You're still logging," Tom said.

"Sure. Like I said before, how long you think Vern's going to last? A gyppo logger ain't got a chance anymore. Look around, how much timber you see to cut? Christ, we're high-leading slopes already that'd turn a cat over and ain't got hardly any timber worth cutting. They're doing helicopter logging over at Sultan. Three or four years and even if J. D. doesn't squeeze him out Vern won't be able to land a logging contract within a hundred miles of here. Forest Service's giving it all to the big guys, what's left of it."

"You ever think about what it was like a hundred, three hundred, a thousand years ago? This used to be Stehemish land, Indian land. He said that country was sacred up there. You ever think about that?"

Jimmy finished the beer and rolled the window down and hooked the can into the bed of the truck, then he turned the pickup onto the pavement and said without looking at Tom, "What's that going to get me? You stop to think about how many of our people are left around here? You ever look around? They're gone, Tom. The whole goddamn tribe. You want me to polish up the Krag and move out to the woods so I can start blowing holes in machines? Maybe somebody'll pay me to do that, huh?"

"So instead you want to help them dig a big fucking hole in the middle of the last country around here that isn't clear-cut. So a few people can go another ten or twenty years swilling beer and buying four-wheel-drives."

"Who's got a four-wheel-drive?"

Tom shook his head as they neared the school. "It'll take two hundred years for the timber to come back like it was around here. You just don't understand why he was doing it, do you?"

"You go off to college and then you want to come back here and wander around that so-called wilderness pretending you're an honest-to-goodness Indian talking about mother earth. That's great, but who's going to buy the porkchops you take on your backpack trips? How're people going to support their kids in this town?"

They turned into the gravel parking lot in front of the high school gym. Built by the loggers one winter with lumber they'd cut and milled themselves, the gym looked like a Viking barn, with huge logs crossing the ceiling inside and framing the walls.

Wooden beams, wooden walls paneled with fir, wooden basketball court of varnished alder.

Tom was startled at the crowd filling the wooden bleacher
seats. The whole valley was there, loggers old and broken and
young and tough, loggers' wives wrung out from kids and
winters and booze or young and pretty and fading fast from
kids and winters and the early discovery of the solace of Olympia
beer, Rainier Ale and Jack Daniels. Winters were cold and the
men stayed home when snow covered the mountains. Wives
gave birth in the early fall or late summer. Now these children
scrambled under the bleachers and climbed the metal frame-
work and chased each other.

The glass backboards were folded close to the ceiling, and
a platform and lectern were set up at the far end of the gym.
In front of the platform was a small, noisy crowd in folding
chairs, with the rest of the audience in the bleachers.

The two brothers climbed through the crowd and sat in the
top row far back from the front of the gym. Across the room,
Tom saw Karen sitting with her father and mother on one side
and Buddy Hill on the other. From the way Karen was staring
away from him toward the front of the room he knew she had
seen them come in.

He looked over the crowd. He knew stories about most of
them, and they all knew more stories than he did. They met
in the Red Dog or in homes during the long winters and slan-
dered one another in rich detail, following ritualized patterns
almost the way the Stehemish had once come together in the
winters to tell the stories that told them who they were and
where they came from, stories of Raven, Coyote, and Fox. For
several generations now these intruders had gathered under
the unvarying shadow of winter rain and snow to remind each
other of their existences, and their signposts were the same
mountains, rivers, and forests the Stehemish and Stillaguamish
and Skagit had known. The map was the same but the signs

pointed in different directions, toward different destinies. Jimmy, he knew, was following a different compass now, and wasn't that really why he'd gone all the way to Santa Barbara?

After several winters in Forks, the weaker minds closed like dark fists and looked out at the world through suspicious eyes. It was easy to spot these. One of them was Jake Tobin, the logger who had a trophy declaring him the strongest man in the valley. Jake sat beside Amel Barstow a few feet from Buddy Hill, surveying the crowd.

In the front row of chairs sat the mayor and the sheriff, Will Baker. A tall, serious man, Will Baker had replaced Tex, who'd been from Arkansas but wore riding boots, checkered pants, cowboy shirts and a Stetson. Tex had been run out of town by Ma Coulter when he'd started shooting up the ceiling of Ma's cafe with his twin Colts one night. In the time between Tex and Will, the mayor, Harve, had hired an escapee from the mental hospital at Cedro Wooley to be Forks' sheriff. No one found out that the new sheriff was an escaped pyromaniac until he'd burned down the only movie theater the town ever had and torched Ma's cafe as well. Now people felt lucky to have Will, who'd grown up in the town, wearing the badge. Will was even a long sight better than Molly, who'd taken the job for a few weeks before Will was hired. Molly set chokers for her father's gyppo logging operation and had fourteen-inch biceps. Molly had worn jeans and an untucked white teeshirt with her gun strapped over the shirt. Eyes hidden behind mirrored sunglases, Molly had cruised like fate through the little town with her enormous arm and those mirrored shades showing over the patrolcar window. The valley had sighed when Will took over and Molly went back to logging and winning bowling trophies.

Ab Masingale sat at the front of the folding chairs with his legs forward. Floyd sat at Ab's right, waving his short arms and stamping a heavy boot on the basketball court. On Ab's left sat Sam Gravey in dignified silence, arms folded and face focused serenely on the platform a few feet away. Only Ab heard the soft snores emanating from Sam's beard.

Ab let Floyd rage on and looked over at Sam. Ab was worried. The old prospector was slowing down. Since he'd brought Jim Joseph's body in he'd aged, spending more and more time in town and forgetting recent events while remembering only the distant past In Sam, Ab saw the unwinding of a generation, his and Sam's and Floyd's, and it worried him. It had seemed that they would go on forever, digging holes in the streets, building flying machines, searching the mountains for fools' gold. But Sam was the clock, and the clock was running down.

Ab turned to watch J. D. Hill and the mayor who were up on the platform now, and then he turned to look at the flatlanders behind him, a dozen nervous men and women. One of the bearded men smiled at him and he turned quickly back toward the front. He knew the kind. Sierra Clubbers. Environmentalists, the kind who'd built their summer cabins last year and didn't want any more built this year, who'd built their fancy Seattle houses out of cedar and redwood and bragged about their woodburning stoves and then pissed and moaned about how terrible logging was. Doctors and rich bastards from the cities. "I'd like to lock one of them Sahara Clubbers in a room for a week with no toilet paper and see how he liked logging," he'd said more than once in the Red Dog.

Floyd was talking about J. D. Hill's attempts to get control of the water company the old man had built, and Ab listened to his friend and wondered how long it would take J. D. It was time Floyd let go. Everything was different now. The environmentalists behind him didn't belong there; they weren't welcome. But it didn't really matter. The mountains were logged. There wasn't much left. Maybe the mine would help some people for a while and maybe that was good, but what people like him and Sam and Floyd had come to the valley for was gone. Somehow the loss seemed connected to the dead Indian, Jim

Joseph, but he couldn't figure out how. He thought of the old saying about the only good Indian, and he remembered drinking by a campfire with Jim Joseph.

A shrill metallic sound stabbed through the room, and people abruptly stopped talking. On the platform the mayor was fooling with the microphone. He blew into the device and the crowd stirred, then he tapped it with his knuckles, and then he said, "Good evening. I'm glad so many people could make it tonight because tonight we're going to hear all about the mine that's going in. The one Honeycutt Copper's putting in. And I don't have to tell you what that means for Forks."

"So let's get at it," someone shouted from the crowd.

Harve smiled nervously. "We got a representative of Honeycutt who's going to explain everything and answer any questions you might have."

As he sat on the platform listening to the mayor, Dan Kellar looked out over the crowd and felt good. He was selling something that had obviously already been purchased. Not paid for, perhaps, but bought. The down payment made really when the first two-man crosscut took a wedge out of the first cedar to fall for money in the valley.

Kellar rose and stepped to the microphone, feeling smooth and accomplished in the midst of the loggers, a long wingtipped step above them but still, he reminded himself, genuinely concerned about their futures. In the first row below him a lanky old man with casts on both legs was vigorously scratching his crotch while a shorter, squat old codger stared up at the microphone with hostile beagle eyes. In his college days when he was freelancing for extra cash he might have written a colorful piece about the folk in the valley. Something light for the Sunday supplement.

He moved into his memorized talk with casual ease. To the women he confided the good news. To the men he offered no-nonsense, sound advice about their futures without seeming to lecture. He could feel himself being manly one moment while his voice warbled confidingly the next. He heard the honesty in his own voice, saw the frankness sway them.

He reminded them that some men were already working on the road and even at the mine site in spite of the snow left up in the high country. He stood erect, and the loggers measured the width of his shoulders and admitted reluctantly that he looked like he could take care of himself. For thirty minutes he gave them the facts and the expectations and he finished by declaring, "Honeycutt will provide the jobs to keep this town alive, and Honeycutt will be dependent upon all of you to make our mine work. I'm here tonight to thank you for your support during the last few years, and to tell you that the court battles are over and the special-interest groups that opposed this resource development have lost. When the snow melts enough we'll swing into full operation up there."

The audience clapped and shouted and boots beat the floor. For an instant he was mesmerized by the image of a man a few rows back spitting accurately from six inches away into the hole of an empty beer can. When he asked for questions, a wiry, balding man stood up in the middle of the bleachers on one side of the room. His nasal voice cut across the room, and the crowd swung toward him.

"I know these here jobs'll come in handy and all," Bayard Taylor half-shouted across the big room. "But if you go and put that mine in, what you plan to do up there when the copper and all the rest is gone? You gonna leave that big hole and all that junk up there?"

Bayard remained standing, a serious expression on his narrow face, and Dan Kellar smiled at him. "I'm glad you asked that question. No, I'm happy to say that we're not going to leave it like that. When resource extraction is completed, and that will be many, many years from now, Honeycutt will remove all traces of the operation, close off the road, and reforest the sites that have been cleared. The pit will naturally fill with water, and in a few years the only difference will be a new alpine lake up there. In fifty years you'll hardly be able to tell we were there."

Someone seated behind Ab laughed sarcastically. Bayard sat down, and one of the outsiders stood up and said, "Isn't it true that you're cutting many of the oldest and largest cedars left in the continental United States just to put the road in? At a time when there are almost no old-growth cedars left?"

Kellar held up a hand to quiet the catcalls. "Let's allow this gentleman to speak," he said. "After all, I'm sure he's come from a long way outside the valley to be here tonight." He fought back a smile and then held up a hand again to quiet the crowd. "We've all heard these arguments before, and they're based on legitimate concerns," he said. "It's true we'll be forced to harvest some of the old-growth—what knowledgeable foresters often call over-ripe timber—and in fact, as some of you know, we are already doing so, but what alternative is there? How else can we build the road? Some people, including the gentleman who just spoke, have legitimate and admirable concerns about the minimal and temporary impact on this particular wilderness area, but we're thinking of the future of the people in this valley, of the people in this country, and of the people in the entire world. Let's face it, copper is essential to modern industry."

"Let's cut all them trees and be done with it," someone shouted.

"Go back to Seattle," came another shout from further back.

Tom saw Bayard shake his head and he watched the group of environmentalists draw together. They were the kind who wore mountaineering boots to classes at the university and carried their books in rucksacks. They had romantic ideas about Indians. They were the kind who said, "How come you don't have an Indian name if you're an Indian?" They wanted all Indians to have names like Sonny Sixkiller. Some of the students in the Native American Students Association, he knew, had changed their names. There was a pretty part-Cherokee girl named Lone Deer whose name, according to McBride, was really Twyla Green. "But, hey," McBride had said with a grin, "it's traditional for Indians to change their names whenever they want. Maybe Twyla counted coup and changed her name. As a matter of fact, I personally know Twyla counted coup."

There was a contest among the urban mixedbloods to see who could be more Indian. The skin cream called "Tanfastic" helped, and there was a lot of unnaturally black hair. There was a famous Indian actor they said had been in two hundred movies who dressed in fringed buckskin and wore a black braided wig. He'd show up at the pow wows, and you could see his thinning gray hair under the wig, and the Indians would joke among themselves that he wasn't Indian at all. "There's that Italian guy," they'd say. But he was rich and important, so they only said that when he wasn't around. He wrote a column for the local Indian newspaper and had starred in an environmental commercial. He looked like an Indian was supposed to look, and he was famous, and he helped Indian orphans, and maybe he really was Indian. And at the urban pow wows would be guys like the kid from Laguna Pueblo who sang and drummed and, between songs, listened to heavy metal on his earphones. That was what real Indians were like. And he was a good singer and part of a family that was in demand for all the pow wows. McBride always liked to point out the white hobbyists who'd be at the dances, out on the floor doing a high plains traditional or a fancy dance with outfits that were more authentic and impressive than the real Indians who'd come all the way from North Dakota or Oklahoma. "You know," McBride said once with a grin, "in Switzerland there are hobbyists who speak Lakota and do beadwork that museums can't tell from the real thing. They're really screwing up Indian collectors, messing up the commodity." To McBride it was all funny.

Tom watched the environmentalists and wondered what

they would make of Jimmy, and he wanted to stand up and shout at the man he'd seen in the Red Dog, to say something eloquent about the land being special or sacred or something. But no words came to him.

When he looked up again, the mayor was at the microphone and people were beginning to leave, talking and laughing as they milled toward the big doors. The environmentalists were heading toward the doors in a small, frightened knot. Across the room Karen was staring at him, and he wasn't sure but it looked like she was shaking her head. Then she disappeared behind Leroy's bulk. Somebody farted close to him and he looked at his brother.

"Jesus Christ, Tommy, let's get out of here," Jimmy said with a frown. "Somebody farted."

He glanced toward where Karen had sat and saw Buddy Hill and Jake Tobin looking at him and talking near the base of the bleachers, and then he was swept toward the doors with the rest of the crowd.

As they approached Jimmy's pickup the crowd thinned and Jimmy farted loudly. "Damn," he said, "must be catching."

They climbed into the cold shell of the pickup, and Jimmy pushed the starter. Neither spoke as the truck edged through the crowd and turned onto the asphalt road that took them past the scattering of houses near the high school. When the truck swung onto the gravel lane toward home and the front tires found the familiar potholes, Tom felt himself relax.

The night carried the odor of pulp from the mill on damp air waiting for rain to fall. Sounds were muted, and smells lingered thick on the air. Jimmy held both hands over the cracked steeringwheel and stared into the scope of the headlights. Tom adjusted his wool cap and leaned out the window to gulp the damp air. Above the valley new clouds had moved in out of the southwest, and as he watched a blade of lightning descended upon the granite crest of Whitehorse. Thunderbird began to beat his wings over the valley, scattering fire like jagged flint to split trees and warn the people. Tom wondered if Thunderbird knew that most of the people who spoke his language were gone, vanished.

He thought about Karen, hearing Thunder beating across the peaks. The chill of the pickup door penetrated his jacket and shoulder and he shifted away from the metal.

"Mind if I borrow the pickup when we get home?" he asked, not looking at his brother.

"No problem," Jimmy said.

They were beside the plum orchard when they saw the truck, a black rectangle stretching from the railroad tracks on one side almost to the vines and tumbled-down fence on the other. Four dark figures leaned against the truck, outlined in the dim headlights. The clouds rattled again but still the rain held off.

"Goddamn," Jimmy said softly, braking the truck and letting the motor idle.

Jake Tobin stood in the middle. It was impossible to mistake the huge arms and the blunt head that rested on heavy shoulders without the apparent need of a neck. Next to Jake, Buddy Hill leaned against a front fender, his hands in his pockets. On the other side, Tom recognized a logger named Raymond Dent, a man he'd known slightly when he'd set chokers the summer before going off to school. Dent had been a chaser then, working the landing. The fourth man was a stranger.

"We could back up, maybe," Jimmy said. "But that's our friggin home."

Tom nodded and let out a deep breath. He got out and walked toward the group, hearing the pickup motor die and Jimmy's door open and close behind him. He stopped a few feet from Jake, and Jimmy came up beside him.

"Evening, Jake." Jimmy said, nodding at the other three as he spoke.

"Hello Jimmy," Jake replied. Turning to Tom, he said, "Heard you went to college down there in California." He watched the brothers and waited as if he felt he had said something very profound.

Tom glanced from Buddy to Jake. Jake Tobin had a bad reputation as far away as Everett. He'd hurt a couple of men over his wife, and a few more just for fun. Tom had heard Leroy say that Jake's wife liked to play with her husband the way a cat plays with a bug. "Jake's so dumb he thinks that's shinola he wipes off his ass," Leroy had said. But being dumb hadn't kept Jake from picking fights on a regular basis in the Red Dog.

"All the way to Califuckinfornia to learn to be an Indian, huh?" Buddy added.

The brothers remained silent, and Tom saw the stranger, a tall, skinny man who looked to be in his thirties, shift nervously.

"Indians don't talk, I guess," Raymond Dent said, stepping closer to Jake. "You think maybe they just grunt?"

"We can't get home," Jimmy said. "Your truck's in the way."

The stranger laughed thinly, and Jake snorted. "Say something educated," he said. "Talk California."

Jake laughed at his joke, and Tom measured the odds, feeling a rising nausea combined with a familiar excitement. He knew that his brother didn't like to fight. But if you lived in the valley you grew up fighting, and nobody had ever beaten Jimmy. Jimmy was strong and astonishingly fast, as the white kids in the valley had learned to their dismay. But Jimmy had never fought Jake Tobin, and Tom knew that neither of them was a match for Jake.

"Why'd you come back, Joseph?" Buddy straightened up from the truck fender and took his hands out of his pockets. "Nobody wants you here. We have enough trash already." No one spoke for a few seconds and Buddy added, "Stay away from my girl."

"We don't want woods niggers bothering white girls," Jake added.

Tom watched the ex-quarterback. In grammar school and again in high school he'd beaten Buddy in fist fights without hardly trying. Buddy was easy to beat because he was always scared and therefore swung without thought or control. Tom had learned at once to step inside Buddy's reach and hurt him with a couple of quick punches. When he felt pain, Buddy would quit.

"Can you still talk like a duck?" he asked Buddy.

Jimmy was staring at the ground, but Tom could see that his brother's concentration was on Jake Tobin. Jake shifted his stance slightly, and there was a general shuffle among the four men facing them.

Jimmy raised his eyes. "We have to get home. Our mother's not feeling well."

"Ah," Jake said. "Poor babies. Your mama can wait a few more minutes for her injun boys can't she. Old Sara's probably got herself a bottle to keep her company, don't she, a little firewater?"

Buddy shifted nervously, and Jake was still grinning when Jimmy hit him. Jake arched against the hood of the truck, his head making a hard metallic sound. Jimmy hit him again before he could straighten up, and then Jimmy had Jake by the collar and was pounding his head against the truck as the others watched in amazement. Raymond Dent's foot was drawn back to take Jimmy from behind when Tom hit the logger on the side of the head and saw him collapse beside the truck. Tom grabbed his hand and winced, and then pain exploded in the back of his head. He felt himself stumble back and hit the bumper of Jimmy's pickup, and then he saw the boot that swung black and slow toward his stomach. He rolled, the gravel digging into his face, and he was back on his feet as a fist glanced off his ear. There was a blocky shadow of a man in front of him, and he brought his foot up fast into the crotch of the shadow and saw it fall. Buddy Hill writhed on the ground making what sounded like small bird calls, and then Tom turned toward a strange, empty sound behind him to see Dent and the stranger holding Jimmy while Jake hit him in the face. There was a sound like a mallet in soft cedar, and Jimmy was lifted off the ground and collapsed into the arms of the men, reaching back for them as if to draw them close. Tom jumped and Jake turned in time to catch Tom's fist flush on his nose. Tom felt the cartilege melt and saw Jake sag, and then his legs were kicked from under him. As he fell he saw a boot drawn back again, and he struggled to remain conscious as the impact rolled him against the tire of the pickup. He rolled again and shuffled on all fours around the bed of the truck oddly conscious of how absurd he must look.

A voice from somewhere far up in the mountains thundered "Kick the motherfucker in the head this time," and he grabbed the bumper of the truck and pulled himself up just as another dark figure came around the end of the pickup. Out of one unfocussed eye he saw Jimmy's breaker-bar in the bed of the Ford, a long piece of steel pipe. He grabbed the pipe as a hand grasped his shoulder and spun him, and he came around with the pipe and swung it hard into the bulk of the shadow. There was a dull impact, and the shadow grunted and fell back, holding its side.

Tom shook his head and staggered back around the truck, remembering once when he'd run a trail too hard and tasted blood in his lungs. The image of the weeping deer rose in front of him. Thunder shook his wings over the valley again, sending the peaks crashing toward the valley floor. His uncle was telling stories about the way it had been and the way it really was, and his lungs felt as if they would burst and he knew he'd have to rise to the surface soon and the vision would be lost.

Jimmy lay near the front tire of Jake's pickup, his face bleeding shadows into the gravel. The stranger saw the pipe in Tom's hand and turned to run, jumping over Buddy who lay on his side moaning, the sound reminding Tom now of a sad mallard. Jake's huge boot was drawn back to kick Jimmy again when Tom brought the pipe down with two hands across Jake's wrist. The arm snapped and Jake looked at it in amazement. The wrist bent at a strange angle, and dark fluid leaped toward the gravel.

Jake screamed and fell back against the truck as Tom raised the pipe again. And then Tom spun toward a scrabbling noise in the gravel and saw Buddy dragging himself sideways on the dark road. And suddenly Buddy was illuminated, his horrified face thrust upward by bright light and his eyes glowing like a deer's. A car skidded on the gravel as the brakes locked and a door leaped open.

Leroy Brant towered over the car.

"That you, Tom?"

"Over here," Tom said.

Tom stepped into the headlight, the pipe dangling.

"Jesus H. Christ." Leroy looked down at Buddy curled up now and crying openly, and then he looked at Jake framed in the headlights where he sat against the truck bumper holding his wrist in his lap with an incredulous expression. In the light a little fountain of blood was springing from between Jake's fingers.

Leroy stooped over Buddy for a moment and then looked at Jake. He glanced at the pipe in Tom's hand and then stripped off his jacket and flannel shirt, ripping the shirt and wrapping Jake's wrist while Jake stared like a surprised infant. When the wrist was wrapped, Leroy pressed his fingers across Jake's arm higher up.

"We don't keep pressure on this, he's going to bleed to death," Leroy said.

Tom knelt beside his brother. In the headlights Jimmy's face made strange angles, and bloody bubbles formed when he breathed. Tom folded his jacket and placed it under Jimmy's head and saw, out of the corner of his eye, that Buddy was sitting up, crosslegged. Oddly, he thought of a picture he'd seen once of either Crazy Horse or Gall.

"Buddy, shut up and get over here," Leroy said.

Buddy rose to the voice and limped toward Leroy.

"Can you use your hands?"

Buddy nodded.

"Okay. Clamp down on this artery, right here, direct pressure. Don't let up or old Jake's going to be compost by morning."

Leroy turned to Tom. "Good job. Both bones sticking out, and you got the artery." He stooped to look at Jimmy's face and listen to the breathing which rattled like gravel in water.

"I'm going to get Jake and Buddy in to Arlington," Leroy said. "I think you better do the same for Jimmy." He looked at Tom and shook his head. "Goddamn," he said. "You don't look any great shakes yourself. Hospital's gonna get a lot of logging accidents tonight."

"How'd you know about this?" Tom asked.

Leroy placed his hands behind Jimmy's shoulders. "You take the feet and we'll lift him into the truck," he said. "Karen heard Buddy talking to his old man. That sonofabitch."

Tom put the jacket under Jimmy's head again and then took the blanket from the truck seat and tucked it under and over his brother.

Leroy got Buddy and Jake into the back seat of Leroy's car, and Tom watched Leroy back up toward the pavement and then heard the car disappear.

Tom swung Jimmy's truck onto the highway leading out of the valley. Overhead, another splinter of lightning touched one of the peaks and shot the black rock into relief against the flaming sky. A drop of rain broke on the windshield, and then a flurry swept down across the pickup, touching lightly upon Jimmy's face and glistening on the dark hair.

12

The old pickup rattled up the bent-wire switchbacks, dust rising behind it in the morning sunlight and settling quickly. Jimmy drove, watching the switchbacks above for the crucial dust cloud that would signal a log truck.

"Remember," Jimmy was saying, "Reese is a good man to work for as long as you don't screw up. He doesn't ask more than a guy can do, and he pays as good as J.D. Soon's I can, I'll be back out here."

Tom looked at his brother. Beneath the right eye, a wide purple seam crossed the cheekbone, the stitches reminding him of crevasses in late summer. During the past three weeks, the punctured lung had healed well. Lucky thing he didn't lose any teeth, he thought, watching Jimmy's absent-minded smile through the corners of the still swollen mouth.

The dust settled on the windshield and caught the sunlight and mirrored the truck's interior, and Tom looked at the dark face that faded and then grew sharp before him. He'd been lucky, too. No scars, and the smashed cheekbone was doing okay without surgery. Too bad Jimmy had gotten the scar instead of him, he thought. Another mark on his face wouldn't have made much difference. The slanting light darkened his profile in the glass and cast a brighter, shining reflection of his brother at an angle toward the left corner of the windshield. As the truck climbed and turned, both reflections rippled and faded as the sun left them to reappear on the next switchback. He thought of Jake coming out of the cafe as they'd driven past that morning. Jake's arm was still in the cast, hanging from the thick neck by a piece of knotted flannel, and a metal splint still covered the bridge of his nose. They said that Jake had a double compound fracture and that the chances of it healing fully were not good. Already the doctors in Seattle had had to re-open it and put a second set of pins in.

"Priorities, Tom." Karen had hugged her knees and stared down at the water where the Northfork fell a hundred feet. The granite shelf was smooth and cool, the gorge of the falls sheltered and shaded by hemlock and big maples on both sides.

"Leroy talked about priorities."

Tom waited, watching the distant slow flap of a bald eagle moving downstream in search of spawning salmon. Along the river below them, a dozen or more of the white-headed eagles balanced in tall snags and watched the waters. The sun came and went with sluggish clouds, and occasionally a fat dolly varden trout surged clumsily against the bottom of the falls, a failed synapse giving false cues, nervous system forgetting the barrier that had always been there so that the fat speckled trout drifted finally exhausted in the pool near the white water.

It had been a week after the fight, when Jimmy was already back home and Sara Joseph was boiling venison into thick brown liquid for him. They'd driven to the falls like they had before he'd left for California, because she had something to tell him. She wore a bulky sweater and loose sweatpants, and her hair alternately gleamed and sank into shadow.

"After the fight he seemed sort of tired and sad. He came into my room when I got home from the cafe."

A pair of ravens settled in the top of a tattered hemlock and began to mock and scold, flapping a few feet into the air and settling again with jagged laughs. Far down the twisting drainage toward town, he could see the crest of Whitehorse, the galloping horse of the glacier etched clearly just below the slow-moving clouds.

"He said that we all went through a lot of things in life and that sometimes we want one thing that makes another thing impossible. I don't remember exactly how he said it, but he said we all have to make choices."

He stared down at the white water. Waterfalls unmake themselves, he thought. They are their own cancellation. The dolly varden finning stupidly down there might not really be wrong. In the long run that the trout's genes yearned toward, the waterfall didn't really exist, had ceased to exist in the same instant it had begun. The ravens barked again, and he felt in some strange way that the message was for him if only he knew the language.

"Leroy knows I'm pregnant, and he knows it's Buddy's."

The ravens lurched off the hemlock and swung in jerky circles above them rising toward the ridge on the far side, their caws settling into the timber in thin echoes.

"It doesn't matter," he said. "We could go away, leave the valley. We could get married."

She settled her chin on her knees and looked down to where the river swept out of sight between the trees. "No. That's what Leroy was talking about. I made a choice. Buddy and I are getting married. Leroy said you didn't belong here anymore, that you'll have to leave. I thought about it and decided Leroy's right. I love this valley. I can't leave it and you'll have to."

"I thought Leroy liked me," he said. "I thought he didn't like Buddy or J. D."

"He does like you. He liked your uncle a lot, too. But he's right. Jimmy can stay here because nobody really ever notices Jimmy. But not you."

"I'm not leaving."

"What?" Jimmy wrenched the pickup onto a turnout that hung over the valley, and they watched a loaded log truck swing past.

He looked at his brother in surprise. "Nothing. Just daydreaming, I guess."

Far below, between the patchwork of houses and scattered farms, large areas of scrub alder and maple, mixed with thin second and third-growth fir, covered the valley floor. The valley timber had gone first, back in the eighties and nineties when

Swedes and Norskies had stood on springboards wedged into the trunks and felled the giants. Now they were two thousand feet out of the valley, driving the pickup toward another logging operation. The Wobblies had done their part, too, burning a third of the valley just after the turn of the century.

Where the ridgetop curved back toward the jumble of peaks beyond the valley, the fallers and buckers had come and gone, and a hundred acres of limbless logs three and four feet through lay pointing down the steep slope, the limbs and brush dragged to a yumpile at the base of the unit. Near the pile, on a level landing gouged out of the ridge, stood a tall yellow tower, fixed in position by a spray of guylines.

At the bottom of the tower, the yarder's diesel engine farted out noise and fumes, while in a cage above the engine a man grabbed levers and caused a steel cable to run in a wide triangle from the top of the tower to the tailhold stump at the highest point in the unit and back down to the base of the tower. The mainline cable ran up the slope thirty feet from the ground and passed through a block at the tailhold and angled off to a second stump before sliding back down to the tower, and from the mainline hung two choker cables which two men were frantically wrapping around a pair of logs, the men's shiny hardhats bobbing and sinking out of sight in the tangle of fallen trees. Finally the two jumped free, scrambling out of the narrowing vee of the cable triangle that the loggers called the jaws of death and leaping behind a stump just as a third figure shrilled three short blasts on a whistle and the man in the cage jerked levers to start the haulback. The two logs jumped into the air, throwing debris across the logging unit, and swung ponderously down the hillside.

When the logs reached the landing in front of the tower, the cable slackened and they dropped to the ground where the chaser ran to unhook the chokerbells and stumble back out of the way. As the little man scrambled for safety, a huge machine with pincers like a great yellow beetle approached with jerky motions, poked and lifted the logs and set them on a waiting truck. Two whistles blared across the clearcut, and the mainline shivered taut and reeled back up the slope with the chokerbells flying free and deadly from the ends of their cables. At a single quick whistle the mainline stopped, and the choker-setters scurried over the rubble to loop the cables around two more logs while the loaded truck started off the mountain with a great whine and another truck took its place to be loaded.

Through the open window Tom listened to the shouts and whistles and grating splinter and howl of machinery and grinding gears and belching air brakes. And through it all he heard the keening shriek of a redtail hawk. When he looked up, he saw the hawk like a bent staple high over the ridge.

Jimmy swerved the pickup to the edge of the landing as the outgoing truck moved past, and they came to a stop fifty feet from the tower.

"They ought to break for lunch pretty soon," Jimmy said.

Tom watched the small men in the unit wrestle with the forest. There was something heroic in those puny figures working to move trees, and something disastrously out of proportion. His uncle had told of the Wobblies, the bitter men who camped in the woods in 1917 demanding food they could eat in the lumber camps, an eight-hour day, and a wage above what they called the deadline, the line below which a man could not live. His uncle had watched those timber beasts—the Swedes and Norwegians and Danes who looked upon Indians as strange creatures like the trolls in old stories. Those men, who could not speak English, walked miles through rain to put in a twelve-hour day with crosscut saw and axe and then walked back through the rain to food they could not eat and wooden beds without mattresses or blankets. The Indian boy had watched those men wear out and break down, wondering at the strange man-machines and watching their places fill up with others just like them. What brought these violent men so far from their own kind to work and die, the boy had wondered.

The ones they called Wobblies had stuck lists of demands on trees around the little town, and to each list they had added a little wooden propeller that turned in the slightest breeze to draw the eye. The Indian boy had slipped from tree to tree collecting the propellers for himself and Sara, his little sister. And he watched from the edge of the trees when the men with shotguns and axehandles came into the valley on the train, and he learned to spook through the woods so that he would stumble upon the Wobbly camps where they would give him coffee and tell stories. That way he'd heard of what the Wobblies called the Everett Massacre. He tried to imagine two hundred and fifty loggers on the deck of a little boat caught in a crossfire from Sheriff McCrae's five hundred deputies. The dead, the men said, piled up on the deck and filled the water of the dirty harbor. And so he became aware that they killed everyone, these whites, not only Indians but everyone, each other. He had pondered upon that.

When they told him they would burn the valley he just looked at them, tasting their bitter coffee close to the warmth of their campfires and wondering how a man could do such a thing. These good, desperate men were the enemy too, he realized, men who would destroy their mother earth. He blew on one of the propellers held on its nail between his fingers, and he watched the men. Had no one ever taught them the danger of what they were planning to do? Were all white men so ignorant?

"Some people called them 'I won't works,'" Uncle Jim had said. Looking off across the valley he had told of the fire-whistle that sounded that day like a horrible bird and of the smoke that rose at once in every corner of the valley.

"Reese is the rigging-slinger," Jimmy said, pointing toward the third man out in the unit. "He's running the show."

Tom saw the rigging-slinger like a statue on top of a big stump, gesturing. Tom had set chokers a couple of summers during high school. It was a job intent on destroying you, ripping your hands off with jaggers of frayed cable or flaying you with the electric lash of a broken mainline or snapping your spine with a winging chokerbell or splintered log. You could tell old loggers by missing fingers or hands, twisted legs, backs crumpled or branded with the white flash of a recoiling cable. The loggers won the war, but the mountains won the battles.

A pair of logs slammed into the landing. A sharp whistle sounded and the noise stopped. The choker-setters and rigging slinger crawled out of the logs and stumps and worked their way toward the landing, appearing and disappearing in the debris of the clearcut.

He followed Jimmy out of the pickup and leaned next to him against the front fender. The diesel fumes settled, and the mountain air reasserted itself. On Whitehorse across the valley, an indigo sky met the glacier at High Pass. Below, the Stillaguamish wound the length of the valley, blue in the wide places and pale in the narrow. A fine breeze came up, and the burr of a stream at the edge of the clearcut rode over the quiet voices of the men.

The loggers headed for the crummy, a sad-looking green van. The chaser and loader operator, closest to Tom and Jimmy, looked at them and turned away. The men grabbed lunchpails from the crummy and headed toward the stream.

Watching the men, Tom realized how little he knew the people of the valley. He recognized one of the choker-setters and the chaser; he'd gone to school with both. But he didn't know them. Then he saw the heavy, gray-haired man walking slowly toward the pickup.

"Morning, Jimmy." Verne Reese's voice was friendly, but his eyes were hooded and skeptical. "The pieces coming together like they're supposed to?" He squinted into the light of the valley and the raw, red face softened.

Jimmy held out his hand.

"If the glue holds," Jimmy said.

"I hear Elmer's works best on you wooden Indians." Reese's lips formed something that might have been described as a grin.

Tom looked on and wondered. It was obvious that Vern Reese liked his brother.

"This is my brother, Tom. You probably never met him."

"Sure. I remember Tom. Toughest goddamn fullback this town ever had. I still remember that game against Rockport." They shook hands, Tom carefully trying to shake in the white way with a firm grip.

"Heard you went off to college," Reese said.

Tom nodded.

"When you head back? You didn't graduate already, did you?"

"No, I didn't graduate. I'm not sure when I'll go back."

Reese looked at Jimmy's cheek. "You don't look like you're ready to start setting chokers today," he said. "And that's too bad because we need another setter. That damned greenhorn from New Jersey walked into a chokerbell yesterday. He's going to be hearing echoes all the way back to Jersey."

Reese looked at Tom. "Saw Jake Tobin in town yesterday. Seems like one of his wings is kind've outa whack."

"It was four against two," Jimmy said quickly. "We tried to talk those guys out of it."

"Well, Jimmy, you never were much of a talker," Reese said. "Hell, if it was me I'd put Jake's head in a cast and not even mess with that puny little arm of his. Jake's been cruisin for a bruisin for a long time."

Jimmy started to speak, but the old man went on. "I was you two boys, I'd keep my eyes open. I've knowed Jake a long time, and I never knowed him not to get even." He took a deep breath. "Okay, Jimmy, what's up? You got back pay coming?"

"Wish I did. We came up to see if Tom could take my place

for a while. He's set chokers before, for McDaniels before J. D. bought him out."

Reese looked at Tom intently for the first time. "You want to log?"

Tom nodded.

"Well, I don't care a bugfart for no smartass college kids, but you're starting to look one hell of a lot like your uncle, and he was a real logger once. You can have a shot at it."

"Thanks, Vern," Jimmy said, and the old man waved his hand again.

"Breaking Jake Tobin's arm is something in your favor, at least," Reese said. "The crummy'll be at the Red Dog five sharp tomorrow morning."

"I'll be there," Tom said, looking past Reese at the silent logging unit.

"One more thing. Some of these boys probably don't feel the same way about Jake that I do, so you better keep an eye peeled."

They headed back down the mountain. The sun angled more sharply and refracted on the dust of the windshield. Across the valley the huckleberry and vine maple were turning red and gold. In another month the clearcuts would be a deep scarlet.

"I'm not going to see you anymore," she'd said. "You ought to go back."

Down there where the rivers came together and split again, it wasn't his home anymore, not earth-blood and rock, cedar red like blood, rivers cutting at the old ones beneath their stones, a pulse through the moutains like the heartbeat drum at one of the spirit dances.

13

In the Thunder Creek drainage behind Whitehorse, Sam Gravey dropped his pack and stooped to pick up a sparkling piece of quartz. A dull gold line ran through the transluscent rock and shimmered in the afternoon sunlight. Close to the spiked tops of the tall firs, a pigeon hawk ducked and swooped after small game, a dodging flutter of gray in the green of the timber. Higher up, a golden eagle rode the air currents off the ridge from Whitehorse and soared lazily against the rare blue sky.

Sam heard the eagle cry, and then the sounds of the creek were sharp and clear as it tumbled down the rock. The light hit the pools and shattered into silver splinters that spun off down the canyon just as Sam felt the first stabbing pain. When he fell, the quartz dropped and glanced off a piece of darker rock and bounced into the pool, settling to the bottom and taking its place amidst a flood of stones. The eagle screamed again as Sam's face entered the shallow pool and the tight fist of pain clenched around his heart. The splash sent diamonds of light against the gray granite, and Sam rolled free of the stream and lay still.

The curious ground squirrel made the mistake of pausing for a moment to look over its shoulder at the shadow in the trees, and the pigeon hawk fell from the green branches and struck. The squirrel's cry was lost in the voices of the stream and the loud whisper in the tops of the trees.

14

Salmon that had escaped the hooks of the commercial trollers and sportsmen and dodged the gillnets of the Indians beat their way up the Skagit, Sauk, Stillaguamish, and Stehemish. Backs humped, jaws distended and red, tails and fins ragged, sides and backs scarred and raw, they smashed their way across gravelbars and through rapids toward the high stretches where the journey had begun. None would make the return trip, yet the next year the same fish would fill the rivers.

15

Tom stood at the edge of the road listening to the picks rattling the asphalt and watching her move behind the counter of the cafe. The logging boots with their spikes hung over his shoulder, and he held a black lunchpail in one hand. The other hand, with a trickle of blood frozen across the back, dangled an aluminum hardhat against his knee. He shifted the hardhat to the same hand that held the lunchpail and reached to brush a loose strand of hair back toward the ponytail that reached past his shoulders.

Behind him he heard the old man giving directions to the boys. They had put a new pipe through so the houses on that side of town would have water, but now they were digging close to the intersection again. With darkness coming up from the rivers, however, the picks clattered into the back of the old man's truck. Without looking, he heard the truck start and he knew that Floyd had set a sign near the hole and was driving the boys toward their dinners.

He waited for a black Firebird to pass and then crossed to the home lane. A few yards up the graying road, he came to the bulky shadow of a car parked at the side, part way in the vines. He stopped, feeling his chest tighten, and then he walked more carefully, his eyes shifting from the car to the shadows that pooled around the bulk and flooded into the vines on one side and the trees on the other.

"Canst thou draw out Leviathan with a fishhook?" The dry voice came from the edge of the trees, and an angular shadow emerged and stood in front of him.

In the darkness Mad John seemed stripped as bare as the winter skeletons of blackberry vines, his face mere angles, eyes shrouded and black. His arms hung straight at his sides.

"Who causeth it to rain on a land where no man is, on the

wilderness wherein there is no man?" Mad John took a step forward and Tom retreated a step.

"Hath the rain a father, Tom Joseph? Out of whose womb comes the ice?" His eyes glinted, and Tom controlled an urge to run. Mad John's cheekbones drew sharp lines down his face.

"Hello John." He felt the hairs stirring at the back of his neck, and he remembered the eyes of the man in the clearing.

"Demons, Tom. Be wary of 'em." The voice fell to a whisper, and the old man looked at the trees beside them and then back. "It was demons got your uncle, and now they're calling you. I hear 'em ever night, howling out there in that desert waste." He waved an arm toward the darkened mountains, his crewcut giving his head a strange abruptness.

"Now I told you. I waited for you and told you and done what I was called to do. A man can't do no more than that." He turned and walked to the car and stopped with his hand on the door.

"Be careful, Tom Joseph. I hear 'em howling for you ever night. Out there a'calling your name."

Tom stepped around the car and walked quickly toward home. Behind him, Mad John's car erupted into unmuffled life and roared away, and he saw the light of his mother's window through the trees.

Jimmy came around the corner of the house to meet him, wiping his hands on an old teeshirt.

"Anymore of those beers left?" Tom asked.

Jimmy tossed the teeshirt on the porch and went into the house, returning with two beers. "This is bock beer," he said. "It's the special thick stuff that's left in the bottom of the vats when they're all through. On sale at the Serve-U."

Tom tasted the bitter, overdone beer and then sat down on the top step of the porch. Jimmy sat beside him, and they watched Gold Hill disappear in shadow. A coyote began yodeling somewhere above the town.

"Old Man's singing again tonight," Jimmy said. "I love to listen to that. Come on, let me show you that new carb I got."

He followed his brother around the house to where a trouble light hung from the open hood of the pickup. He was relieved not to have to go into the house right away. He thought of Mad John and listened to the coyote.

16

Tom watched the stone strike the pool and ripple before it wobbled to the bottom. His legs and arms ached, and his hands were cut and raw despite the gloves that lay beside his lunchpail. Nobody ever got in shape for setting chokers, he thought. You got stronger and harder, but mainly you just hurt all the time.

His faded black Ben Davis pants ended three inches above the ankles, stagged off and hemmed so they wouldn't snag out in the unit where anyone who couldn't move might die. Sunlight glinted off the nails on the bottoms of his boots, and he looked at the shiny spikes and wondered why the boots were called "corks" but spelled "caulks." He'd wondered that for years but he couldn't think of anyone who might know the answer. He'd asked his uncle once, but Uncle Jim had just laughed and said, "Either these white people are all the time tricking their language or their language is always tricking them. I ain't figured it out yet."

He stretched down to the creek and filled his tin cup with water so cold it hurt his teeth when he drank it. Blue sky touched the tops of the trees along the creek, and a light wind followed the water as it tumbled down the ridge. Twenty yards away, the scarred face of the clearcut shone brown and red and gray through the timber. The cool air and tumbling water soothed him after the howl of logging. He eased his back against the roots of a hemlock and settled into the tree, sipping the water.

Vern Reese leaned against the trunk of a cedar a couple of yards downstream, his feet propped on rocks at the stream's edge and his hardhat tilted so that it cupped his head against the stringy bark of the tree. Further downstream the rest of the loggers lounged, and he heard fragments of talk about the chances of snagging a few silvers out of the Sauk without being caught by the fish and game people or the Skagit Indian patrol. One raised his voice to tell a story about being surprised by one of the Indian wardens.

"Sonofabitch had his whole fucking truck covered with brush, and him standing there quiet as a snake. I threw that fish up the bank, and when I went to get it the first thing I saw was these huge fucking boots."

Vern held a sandwich in one fist, contemplated the white bread and tuna, and ate half the sandwich in one bite. He chewed, watching the water slide over rocks and gravel.

Tom watched his boss. The gray hair, stiff with sweat, stuck out from the angle of the hardhat. He couldn't figure the old man out. That morning he'd stopped the crummy to point out a bear cub in a clearcut, and everyday he raced to get up the mountain in time to see the alpenglow on the glacier across the valley. He hated Sierra Clubbers, but he'd told Jimmy that he'd once hiked two hours just to look at one of the old, giant cedars inside the wilderness boundary. The old man loved nature and was deadly efficient at stripping it bare.

Tom looked down at the other loggers. They'd kept their distance. Nobody liked Jake Tobin much, and some hated him, but Jake had been a good faller, and now everybody knew Jake's arm would never be any good again. Even Tom could feel that there was a terrible, fundamental wrong in the fact. "You Josephs been a goddamn lot of trouble lately," the chaser had told him. So he did his work and concentrated on staying alive in the tangle of the logging unit.

"Quent Masingale claims he heard a wolf the other night up the Northfork." Reese seemed to address his words to the stream. "Says he heard one howling up near Red Creek."

Tom looked at Reese. The rigger took a hard-boiled egg from his lunchpail, crushed it to fracture the shell, and began peeling the white fragments and dropping them back into the lunchpail.

"You think it's true?" Tom asked.

"Can't say as I do. Wish I did, but I think old Quent's been spending too much time around Arn Cain's still. There ain't been no wolves in this country in longer'n you been alive." The old man removed a bit of film from the egg and stuffed the whole egg in his mouth, chewing thoughtfully.

"In thirty-nine I saw five of 'em up the Whitechuck," Reese said. "Three little females and two big black males." He had swallowed the egg and was looking directly at Tom now.

"Running on the snow along my trapline. Just before the war. Gray ones, the big males almost black. I come out of a patch of alder with a marten and there they were, standing in the open and watching me like I was the circus and they'd bought tickets. I had my ought-six and could've dropped one of 'em easy as pie. We looked at each other for a hell of a long time, till I got the shivers, and then they kind of sauntered away pretty as you please."

Tom picked up a fir cone and pitched it into the stream, watching it spin in the froth of a small waterfall.

"My uncle used to tell me about wolves he'd seen in this country."

"Sure. Jim would've seen 'em if they were here. But that was a long time ago." He pulled a muffin from the lunchpail and delicately removed the paper. "You ain't exactly winning any popularity contests around here, are you?"

Tom didn't say anything.

"I see how the boys act. It's too bad, but hell, they're pissed off about Jake. Even though he ain't worth the gunpowder it'd take to blow him a new asshole." He ate half the muffin, swallowing once. "You're kind've an outsider now. It's funny when a guy thinks about it. Your people been in this valley a thousand years maybe."

He finished the muffin and picked up the paper cup, folding it into neatly creased triangles and dropping it in the lunchpail.

Then he fished a banana from within the box and began to peel it.

"You ain't a real logger and you ain't a white man, and the only kind of men in this valley is loggers and white men. If you were at least one of those two it'd probably be okay." He paused and offered one of his faint grins. "You know, about the only color of Indian I ain't never seen is a red one."

Tom regarded the stream at his feet. "If I'm not a logger what do you call what I've been doing for the last month?"

"Oh, that don't matter. You could be a goddamned good logger. As good as Jimmy, maybe as good as your Uncle Jim. But your heart just ain't in it. The fact is Jimmy fits in and you don't." He laid the banana back in the lunchpail. "I knew your old man before he got killed. He didn't fit in neither. Made people nervous. He was always heading off somewheres and coming back again and then leaving. Spent a lot of time out in the woods by hisself, too. Not hunting and fishing or running a trapline the way guys do, but just spooking around out there. Guys out hunting or trapping would run into him, and he wouldn't say nothing, just take off. He wasn't the kind of guy you could get comfortable around.

"And you kind've remind me of Jim, too. He was a good logger, but he never made too many friends neither. Maybe because he took things too damned serious."

"Uncle Jim had friends," he said.

"Folks liked Jim, but how many went to his funeral, a man that was born and spent his whole life here?"

"That was because we buried him in the Indian graveyard."

"Maybe, but that's kind of what I mean right there. Hell, I liked Jim but I didn't go to that funeral, and I can't even say why." He picked up the banana and finished it in two bites.

Tom thought of his uncle out there along the Stehemish, aiming the Krag.

"You can work for me as long as things don't get too bad

out in the unit, but you'd be nuts to. You ought to go on back to school. Get a college education before you bash out those brains with a chokerbell or start drinking 'em to mush like the rest of these yahoos. And watch yourself. A guy's got to be careful if the guys he works with don't look out for him, and some of these boys ain't going to be looking out for you any too much."

Tom listened to Reese's voice trail away and then looked at the group down the hill. When they rose to return to work, he heard the redtail scream again and looked up to see its tail flame as it banked and slid into the sun.

17

When he got home that evening his mother was sitting on the porch. The rainclouds had held off all day, and August brought the smells of the river and timber to a rich peak about the house, the thick smell of fir resin mixed with the stench of the mill.

He waded through the weeds in the yard and watched her face come into focus over the knitting. A lot of time had passed for her in the last two months, the joints growing more stiff and raw as the days warmed, and the tight, introspective face of pain more constant.

His boot caught on the hidden transmission housing, and he stumbled. His mother looked up. Jimmy talked about cutting the weeds, but like others that chore would fall to the frosts of autumn. Salmonberry and blackberry vines now reached over the tops of the junked cars in a blanket of green leaves and red and purple berries, and the vines shot green tendrils up the sides of the house. The porch leaned further toward the yard, and as he walked toward it he imagined the house folding, settling into the hungry vines. Already the front door had the air of an entrance to a den: inside would be damp earth and old bones.

He settled onto a log-section stool that Jimmy had placed on the porch and began unlacing his corks.

Sara Joseph smiled toothlessly. "Now you look like your father."

He thought of the photograph and the gravestone as he set the boots beside the door and slipped the moccasins over his wool socks.

"How's logging?" Jimmy opened the screendoor and came out to the porch. "You keeping my job warm for me?" He leaned against the upright pole, and the porch creaked so menacingly that he jumped away with a laugh.

"Got to fix that post," he said. His face was flushed, and Tom could smell the thick wine.

"Some mail for you." Jimmy held out a greasy envelope.

Tom saw the return address and folded the envelope and put it in his pocket. It was from the registrar at school and would say something about the finals he'd missed and the classes he'd failed because of that. They'd want him back because of affirmative action, so they'd give him another chance.

"Just registration stuff," he said when he saw his mother and brother watching him. "It's not important."

To Jimmy he said, "How about giving me a ride to the Stehemish trailhead in a while?"

Jimmy looked surprised as he stifled a belch. "Sure. Have to get some gas though."

Tom picked up the corks as he rose from the stool. "I thought I'd take a walk up the river."

As Jimmy went into the house, Tom felt his mother's hand on his arm. "Take Jimmy with you," she said.

He lowered his voice. "He wouldn't like it." When her hand remained on his arm he added, "I'll be careful. I just want to see the high country."

18

Two weeks of almost constant sun had swelled the river into a gray and brown rage of melting snow and ice. As the truck shivered on the washboard road, Tom watched the trees for glimpses of the rapids. Every inch of the river cracked in dull angles that broke on logjams and boulders. Trees and rootwads rolled and staggered in the current, and the water ate at the banks, gulping trees and rocks and spewing them out miles away. At the road's end the yellow machines again sat idle, the workday over. A pile of cedar logs five and six feet through lay to one side and a pincered loader squatted beside the logs. The steel gate still closed off the path, but now the road on the other side of the gate was graveled and hard, the stumps gone.

They sat together and looked through the dirty windshield.

"Holy shit," Jimmy said. "I didn't know they were this far along. I'm going to talk to Leroy about getting on out here, see if he can put in a word for me."

"You remember who Leroy works for?" Tom asked.

Jimmy's excitement faded. "Well, J. D. can't control everything. He's just putting the road in. They're going to need a lot of men to get that mine going."

"Sure." Tom looked at the loader and thought of a giant insect he'd seen in a movie. There'd been a radiation problem, and things had gotten big. A cop was about to walk around the corner of a little cafe way out in the desert, and just around the corner was an insect that looked like the loader. It was one of those times you think, 'Don't go in there, you fool.' But in the movies they always did.

"I might as well have a job as somebody else," Jimmy said. "I doubt Vern's going to last another season. Somebody's going to have to bring in some money when you take off."

"Didn't I tell you I wasn't going back to school?" He tried

to peer into the depths of the new road that vanished in a quickly darkening vee in the timber.

"I kind of figured Karen had changed your mind," Jimmy said. "Now that she married Buddy."

Ida had told Sara about the wedding. The dress had flounced and ruffled enough to hide Karen's swelling belly, and most of the town had gone to the wedding in Everett.

"You ought to take a hike in here with me sometime," Tom said. "It could be like when we were kids." He remembered Jimmy in the berry-house clearing, the fire changing shapes as Uncle Jim talked and Jimmy looked off beyond the circle of light as though his mind wandered toward possibilities in the shadows.

"Not me. I never was crazy about walking around in the woods without a reason. When they get this road through I can drive on over."

Tom opened the door. "Do you know where they're living?"

"Karen? I heard Buddy bought the Nations place out on the Prairie, where those old Stehemish longhouses used to be. Bayard said he's already had the whole house remodeled. He had that old camas patch plowed under, Bayard said."

Tom grabbed the pack from the bed of the truck and put it on. Jimmy climbed out and stood watching, his hands in his pockets.

"I got to bleed my lizard," Jimmy said, turning to urinate beside the truck. "You just going to walk that road? You want to see if we can bust that lock and drive up a ways?"

"No thanks," he replied. "The road has to end sometime. They can't be too far."

"Not much fun walking a gravel road, is it? I got a crowbar in the truck. That's the white man's road you'll be walking." Jimmy grinned a little as he buttoned his pants.

Tom settled the pack and tightened the waistbelt that didn't take any weight off his shoulders. "No," he said finally. "Not much fun, I guess."

"Up there's where Sam found him." Jimmy pointed with his lips in the direction of the upper drainage.

"How about picking me up Sunday about this time?" Tom asked.

"No problem. The Stehemish taxi company is at your service." Jimmy leaned against the door of the truck, his hands back in his pockets. "Don't get any ideas about this stuff the way he did. There ain't nothin you can do about it."

Tom shrugged to settle the packstraps. "I just want to get away from a choker cable for a couple of days. And maybe see what they've done in there. And I figure the lake's probably open by now."

He walked toward the gate and Jimmy followed. When he slid around the steel post, Jimmy stayed on the other side. For a moment they faced each other across the bars.

"Take it easy up there."

"Sure." He turned and took a couple of steps and then looked back. "Thanks."

Jimmy waved the thanks away and pivoted toward the truck, and in a moment Tom heard the motor turn over.

Above the road, the sharp tips of the trees no longer closed out the sky. Light, cooling and darkening that late in the day, streamed onto the road and lapped at the edges of the undergrowth. But directly ahead the road vanished in angled shadow.

Before he'd walked a hundred yards a high, thin cloud trailed across the sky above the roadcut, and within minutes other clouds had sailed into place beside the first, high transparent clouds that joined and began to fan across the strip of sky. He felt the air change. The wind picked up high above the trees and swept in from the southwest, the direction of storms. He hurried his pace. In August, darkness came more quickly in the forest.

Within half an hour the sky had sealed. He increased his pace, stepping along a gravel road where earlier in the sum-

mer he'd walked a narrow trail. He passed Three-Mile Camp.
The builders had pushed stumps and debris into the level camp-
site, and the stream near the camp now ran through a culvert
pipe below the road and emptied into a sludge of gravel and
mud ten feet down the slope.

The first drop plopped heavily onto the back of his hand,
and he looked up to see the points falling. He left the road and
slipped under a big hemlock. For five minutes he watched the
rain and hunched under the shadow of the big tree, and then
he left the shelter and began paralleling the river. In a few
minutes he found a shallow furrow between two enormous trees
with interlocking branches. Inside the cave of the downswept
branches no rain had yet penetrated. Not even the wind could
reach him there, and there was no sign of the road above him.

He rigged the sheltering tarp and laid the other one on the
ground, throwing the blankets on the plastic. A thrush
announced darkness with a single shrill whistle, and he tried
to pinpoint the hidden bird, but as always the whistle seemed
to come from everywhere at once. The thrush, his uncle had
said, measured the day and called the People home each night.

He wrapped himself in the blankets fully clothed, resting
his head on the folded mackinaw, and listened to the voices in
the nearby river like a low-pitched chant mumbling and rum-
bling their way downstream. He heard his name called softly.
"Tom Joseph" the river sang, "Tom Joseph Tom Joseph." At night
the waters always talked. A strong man could call those spirits.

The shadows probed his wandering thoughts. A spirit of
flame rushed up a tall cedar, the blue-edged fire bright against
the blood of the stringy bark. He ran to embrace the flame, his
boots heavy and tangled in the thick growth, his legs awkward
and stiff, his cry trapped in his throat. The name of that spirit
was two syllables repeated, s's and t's. The man with the cedar
spirit sang his song, "I am not afraid," and Knife and Fire put
fish in the creeks. Souls arced in wailing rainbows over the river,

their cries sucking up trees and rocks, fish and deer and bird till the land was all movement, all flux, a wailing arc from birth to death. Coyote tricked himself and brought the roof of the world tumbling in. The Great Mother Mountain came stalking from the east and gave life and gathered that life back to herself.

The river rumbled its boulders and pulled the cold air over itself like a blanket. He balanced on the precipice of sheer sleep, letting his thoughts drift with the river until they were far down the dark drainage and then laboriously reeling them back to the place in the trees. "Stehemish," he said in his mind. "Stehemish," the river echoed, rolling the vowels and consonants of their identities.

"I've never balled an Indian," she'd said. He lay back on the bed and watched her pull the sweater off over straight blonde hair. L.A. beautiful, with long golden legs and small hips tapering to a smaller waist that rose over taut ribcage to perfect breasts and hair falling over brown nipples. No white to mar the cocoabutter tan but the teeth as white as death angel, *amanita verna*. Blue eyes. And he marvelled at her, this girl he did not know, and at the moment, sensing only when she had drawn him inside herself and was moving under him the way the sea moved, the rivers, clouds, the air, that here was the trap, the danger. A death of spirit in this namelessness. Around them was a world without name. While outside the room the noise of a party moved like thunder over the mountains.

And there had been Rana, a tall, lean Cherokee with light skin, black hair and small hard breasts sharp in the denim shirt. The green-eyed daughter of an Irish father and Cherokee mother, a mixedblood from Muldrow, Oklahoma, talking about the Native American Students Association. She had crooked teeth that pushed at her closed lips, and she corrected him when he said Indian, and she talked of fetal alcohol syndrome and the suicide rate among Native American teenagers. He told her of salmon and of trees that went forever, how waterfalls unmake themselves, and rain like the air you breathed, and she remembered Oklahoma, not the dark and humid North Carolina home of her ancestors. Walking, she explained things, and he thought of his uncle and brother—Indians not Native Americans—and of Karen, while night herons called across the lagoon.

In his dream, a shadow disengaged itself from the gray waters and drifted to where Tom Joseph lay sleeping. It moved noiselessly, with slitted yellow eyes, and as it approached it began to change and rose from four legs to two and looked with gaunt cheeks at the sleeper. "Tom Joseph," it called softly. "Tom . . ." and he woke to hear the river still calling his name in its tangled voices. He shivered and heard the rain falling outside his protected place with a steady patter.

The rain was drumming rythmically on the plastic when he awoke. It had worked its way finally through the thick branches, taking the long night, and outside the den shrouds of fog hung between the trees and the forest dripped. Water fell from downturned ends of leaves and glistened and ran off the white chunks of granite sticking through the brown humus.

He shook his head to clear away the dreams and climbed out of the blankets. He unfolded the mackinaw and pulled it on. The rain would soak through, but the wool would keep him warm. He looked toward the river and thought it strange that on hot days of sun and sky the rivers rose while on days of cold and damp they fell.

He found his breakfast in the pack and climbed with it down toward the river. A swath of shore lay above the water now, exposed by the falling river. Under his boots the bank gave way, and he slid to the boulders six feet below. At an eddy he bent and drank the milky water, feeling the grit between his teeth when he stood up.

He walked onto a log that lay across the river, a big polished fir that rested high on its rootwad and vibrated with the current. He listened to the rocks in the crowded river and sat near the end of the log with his legs hanging over. The rain lightened to a mist, beading on his wool cap and long hair and blowing down the river in banks of fog. The upstream current swirled toward him in waves and whirlpools, the confusion dizzying as he looked up to where the river bent around a rocky curve. Then he followed the water back down to the point where it vanished beneath his boots. The log thrummed like a bowstring.

He swung to face downstream. Here the water sped away, leaping from beneath his feet and sliding to the next bend. Downstream the world was smaller, calmer. He ate his jack cheese and raisins and finished with a black piece of jerked venison just as a harlequin duck shot from beneath the log and bounced away with the current like a blue and gray and gold cork, careening from one pothole to the next, riding the reversals, bobbing and lurching on the edge of a white hole to suddenly disappear and reappear further downstream. His laugh followed the clown duck out of sight.

After five miles the work of the machines and fallers ended, and he took up the trail again. He passed the bridge at Devil's Elbow and climbed the Miners' Ridge switchbacks, bent close to the trail as if in pursuit.

This time Dakobed hid in clouds, and he walked the ridge through blowing particles of gray mist over patches of blue lupines and red paintbrush, alone in this whirling world. Somewhere a grouse drummed in hiding, and the stunted trees were outlined in the moving clouds.

He cut away from the lookout, which would be manned in August, and followed the narrow ridgetop toward the lake, keeping to the rut of the trail and starting a spikehorn buck. The deer plunged across the trail into the mist down the ridge. He jumped back from the animal's suddenness and shook his head. Moisture flew from his cap in a silver aura.

Someone had left a neat stack of wood in the three-sided log shelter near the lake's outlet, and he quickly built a fire. Leaning over the flames, he watched clouds blow across the surface of the small lake and listened to the remote pock of trout on the lake's surface. Before the mackinaw and his pants had stopped steaming, he stabbed a can of beefstew open and set it in the flames.

When the can was empty, he tossed it into the fire and went to the outlet stream, shoving his face into the cold water to drink. Then he angled around the edge of the lake toward Plummer Mountain, climbing the steep slope on heather terraces. At the crest of the ridge rising up the small bare peak, he stopped and stood in the cloud.

On one side, he knew, the Canyon Creek drainage dropped away, narrow and thick with timber, the creek slipping out of the cold, transparent water of Canyon Lake in its white granite basin. On the other side lay the perfect mirror of Image Lake. To the south the peaks fell away in ranks toward the white dome of Mount Rainier, and to the north they clustered toward Canada a two-day hike away. But he could see only the gray mist blowing past and clinging to his clothes and eyelashes so that the world warped and sparkled through the crystals. He felt alone, cut off, a distant speck in the whirling world.

When he awoke in the shelter the sun cut through the silver fir and glinted off the blue water and gray-green heather. The lake basin burned with red and gold blueberry brush, lupines and glacier lilies where the snow had melted.

He rolled out of the blankets and pulled his pants and shirt off and walked naked to the edge of the lake. A cutthroat fingerling spooked in the shallow water, the darting shadow vanishing toward the center. In the middle of the lake the ghost of Dakobed floated cool and distant and perfect, the white image rippling with rising trout. The lake's edge refused to give him back his own reflection.

He waded into the water until the cold cut into his abdomen and snapped him awake. Then he plunged toward the middle, taking a dozen strokes before feeling the cold fully and realizing once again that it was a fist closing around him and crushing the breath from his chest. Then the memory came in full, and he panicked. His feet groped for the bottom, and water as clear as the absolute air closed over his head, and he flailed toward the light. The light blazed above him, so that when he felt the soft bottom he flexed his legs and shoved the heavy body upward. But the body resisted and began, instead, to relax. "This is what it is like to drown," he thought. And then he saw the shadow moving toward him from far away and below, from the deep center of the lake. When his muscles tensed again to fight for the surface, the figure retreated. He turned to look for it and realized then that he did not have to struggle, that one need not fight at all. That, he knew at last, was the key. The secret was to merge with the blue darkness that was lifting him now and moving him in a delicate current toward the center. And out of the depth again the shadow approached, and he tried to call to it, to ask the question, but he knew no language. He began to struggle for the words, and then, suddenly, the light broke over him and his eyes opened.

The shadow bent above him, its face blurred and wavering. "Damn. That was pretty close."

The face began to form and lighten. It had red hair and a swath of freckles and blue eyes. He became aware that he was lying naked beside the lake, and he heard himself gasping for breath. His lungs ached as he gulped the cold air.

"It was a lucky thing I came along or you might've been fish food." The face smiled. He felt a hand resting protectively on his thigh, and then he felt the warmth of the hand go away.

He turned to the side and vomited up clear, sweet-tasting water and then he looked back at the ranger.

"What happened?" he mumbled.

"I came by to check the shelter and saw you out there in twelve feet of water trying to walk on the bottom. You weren't making much headway so I pulled you out. How you feel?"

He remembered the water then and the shadow, and he closed his eyes against the light.

"I could give you a citation for swimming in the lake. That's forbidden. And another one for indecent exposure, I guess."

He opened his eyes and saw the uniform, dark with water, the forest service patch a damp, wet gold.

"You're the ranger, Grider?"

Martin Grider nodded and grinned. "And you're the famous Tom Joseph. Bayard said you knew this country, but he didn't say you tried to walk on water."

Tom shook his head and sat up.

"You better go get some clothes on before one of these horseflies make lunch out of you," Grider said. "If they don't the mosquitoes will, and the noseeums will finish the job."

When he was dressed, he walked back to the where the ranger squatted with a map at the edge of the lake. The sky was higher than it had been all summer, a blue dome over the lake basin, and the shining image of the white mountain across the drainage blocked his attempt to see into the deeper water. Over the far ridgeline a dark falcon appeared abruptly and then winked out of sight. The gold backs of the whistlepigs sunning on the rocks shone dully, and flashes of light caught on the marmot pups playing tag in the heather. A fingerling swam close and rose for a fly, and he glimpsed its silver side as it flipped back toward deeper water.

"Thawed yet?" Grider stood up and folded the map.

"Thanks."

"All in a day's work. It'll look good on my trip report. Lives saved, one." His adam's apple moved as he spoke. "What were you doing out there, anyway?"

Tom looked at the reflection of the mountain. There was

a single cloud lodged against the image of the peak. "I'm not sure. I guess I thought I'd take a morning swim. The water was colder than I thought it would be."

"I patrol this area," Grider said. "The whole Stehemish drainage, Vista Ridge to Fire Creek Pass and on over to Lyman Lake. Lime Ridge High Route thrown in for fun, and Milk Creek on my way out." He jerked his head toward the far side of the lake. "I'm camped in those trees. Came over Cloudy Pass yesterday and headed for Middle Ridge this afternoon."

"You're a busy guy." Tom turned to look at the real mountain on the other side of the river.

"I used to spend more time here at Image, but since they shut off the road and started the mining on the other side of Plummer nobody ever comes up here." He stuck the map in his back pocket. "I just drop by once in a while to make sure they're not over here too."

"Where is that mining?" Tom asked, looking up the slope toward Plummer. Then he noticed a dark line running from the far end of the lake over the shoulder of the mountain, and where the line entered the lake was a platform with a pump attached.

Grider followed his gaze. "That's where it begins. They've been pumping water out of the lake for a week now. Storing it over the hill in a ten-thousand-gallon tank." Grider swatted a mosquito on his forehead and looked at the dead insect and spot of blood on his palm. He wiped the hand on his pants. "You know, I've been mixing jungle juice and Cutter's but nothing keeps these shitheads away."

Tom squinted, followed the pipe up to the horizon with his eyes.

"In another month," Grider said, "I expect the lake to start dropping, once the snowmelt's over."

Tom listened for sounds of machinery. "Have they started digging over there?" he asked.

"Not exactly digging. Mostly just getting ready to dig. To blast the shit out of the place, actually."

The ranger walked to a cluster of alpine fir nearby and returned with a red daypack. "I'm on my way over there. You can come along if you want to see for yourself."

They climbed out of the basin at a slow pace, the ranger shortening his long stride. Halfway up the slope, they stopped and turned to breathe and look out over the valley.

"Nobody's up here today except a guard they leave up on weekends," Grider said. "Kind of a nasty character."

Tom was studying the upper drainage, the deep lines where the glacier streams cut their way to the river. A cloud hung over Dusty Creek.

"Nice, huh?"

He looked at Grider. "My tribe used to call her Dakobed."

"Why do you say 'used to'? Don't you still call her that?"

Tom looked at the ranger with surprise and thought for a moment about the question.

"It means something like the mother or the source, doesn't it?" Grider asked.

Tom nodded. "I thought you just started here this summer."

"That's right. I worked on the Bob Marshall before this."

"So how do you know things like that?"

Grider smiled. "I read books. I went to college like you."

Grider laughed and turned back toward the summit of the little, rounded peak just as the falcon hunted down the crest again, its outsized shadow bringing a shriek of whistles from the marmots. The old boars rocked on their burrows with piercing whistles, while the females and pups plunged into holes. Tom saw small bear faces peering up from the dark burrows into the sunlight.

Grider swung the pack off and pulled a pair of fieldglasses from the top pocket, but the falcon was gone.

"Shit. I've been trying to get my glasses on that bird for two days," he said. "It looks like a peregrine. Notice the pointed wings and quick wingbeat?"

"It's a peregrine, all right," Tom said. "There's always been a couple of them around here."

"Do you realize that if we could prove there was a pair of peregrines nesting up here we could maybe stop this whole goddamn operation? If we couldn't stop it, we could sure cramp their style." As he spoke, Grider was already moving again toward the crest. The sun was over the Cascades and shot the ranger's shadow ahead of him so that it strode in long, wiry leaps up the heather slope. Tom followed, and his own shadow seemed to him to move close to the ground with slow, wary progress.When Tom reached the crest of the ridge below the pyramid summit, the ranger was already there, hands on hips and staring down at the mine site. A hundred feet below them a platform had been gouged out of the hillside, and on the flattened earth sat the black watertank. A line ran into the tank on the uphill side and out of it on the downhill side. A few hundred yards further down the mountain, the ridge shelved into a much wider bench cut the size of three football fields. On the bench, the sun was beginning to feather against yellow machines and silver, corrugated tin buildings. Large piles of rock lay on the far side of the flat, and a handful of bulldozers and frontloaders and other equipment stood between the rockpiles and the cabins.

Grider looked at Tom. "They brought all this stuff in by helicopter, a piece at a time. I'm amazed that falcon is still around with all that air traffic. Now they'll start cutting and blasting till they've worked their way down to the flat, then they'll start the pit, cutting right through to the lake as near as I can figure it. I don't know a hell of a lot about open-pit mines, but I know they'll put a road into Miners' Creek and then switchback the road on up to here, and they'll build a concentrator down on the creek with houses and everything else. A little town down there is what they have in mind. And when they're finished there'll be a fucking highway all the way to Image Lake. You ever see what happened to Railroad Creek?"

Tom nodded, looking southeast toward the creek on the other side of the crest. His uncle had taken him there once just to show him the ugly waste left from mining over there.

"Well that's not even a drop in the old bucket to what they'll do here," Grider said.

Tom imagined his uncle shooting at machines, and he could understand it clearly for the first time. The falcon shrilled from somewhere up the ridge, and Grider started down toward the flat, sliding and scrambling on the loose scree as far as the water-tank. There he turned and waited for Tom.

When Tom arrived, Grider was running his hand over a seam in the big tank and looking carefully at the riprap foundation of rock under it.

"It sure wouldn't take much to knock this baby off the mountain," he said. He grinned at Tom.

Tom stared at the scene below. Over the whole area hung the stinging sulfur smell of blasting powder mixed with the stench of diesel. Fifty-gallon drums were scattered about, leaking diesel and oil, and twisted cables coiled like snakes near the rock piles. The three tin cabins sat on wooden foundations, cold and lonely looking.

He memorized the site and then moved past Grider to slide the remaining distance to the large flat. Immediately he went to the nearest cabin and peered through a window.

"Hey, I wouldn't snoop too much," Grider shouted as he followed Tom down the slope. "You have to remember this is private property."

"I'd take the ranger's advice, asshole."

Tom saw the pistol first, and then the fat hand that held the gun steady on his midsection. And he saw the triggerfinger in detail, red and calloused with a short, clamshell nail black at the end. Then he noticed the other arm in a sling.

"So it's Tom Joseph."

Jake's arm was out of the cast, the hand white and shrivelled where it hung from the sling, the arm shrunk to an icy splinter of itself. Jake smiled crookedly, and his eyes alternately glared and then wavered toward the ranger. The skin of the hand seemed transluscent in the morning light, like a newly molted snake.

"Ever see the hole left by one of these?" Jake was grinning at one end of the question and frowning at the other. A week's stubble moved around the corners of his mouth when he spoke, and Tom saw that his eyes seemed to have retreated further into his skull, the sockets pale and rimmed with shadow. The long barrel of the forty-four magnum was shiny where the blueing had worn away, and it caught and held a thin line of sunlight.

From the side, Grider said, "Good morning, Jake."

Jake kept the gun levelled and didn't look at the ranger. "What the hell you doing snooping around here again? This ain't forest circus property, and there ain't nobody supposed to be here but me when everybody's gone."

"It's my job to check up on this mess, Jake, remember?" Grider came within a few steps of them. "I brought Tom along for company. Now if you don't put the pistol out of sight, I'll have your ass thrown out of this forest and even J. D. Hill won't be able to get you back in again. Check with your boss if you don't think I can."

Tom glanced from the gun to the ranger. Seasonal rangers didn't have that kind of authority, and everybody knew it. They had a hard time writing up a citation for littering.

Jake lowered the gun, and as he followed the motion of the pistol Tom saw that Jake's belly had shrunken so that his hickory shirt fell flabbily over his belt.

"It was Honeycutt hired me to guard this stuff, not J. D.," Jake said, a whine in his voice. "How was I to know this Indian fuck wasn't here to mess things up. Like his uncle did. Besides, he don't work for the Forest Service and he ain't got no right to be here."

"Like I said, he's with me," Grider replied, watching the gun which hung at Jake's side from the good hand. "Now, why don't you put that pistol back in your cabin."

Jake took a half step closer to Tom and raised the arm in the sling an inch, lifting it from the shoulder the way a fish might raise a fin for inspection. "Look at it, Joseph," he hissed. "See what you done. I was the best goddamn faller ever, and now I got to take piddly-ass jobs that a one-armed man can do." He studied his own hand for a moment, his face contorting as if he would start crying, then he said, "Some time I'll find you alone, with no ranger and no lead pipe."

Tom looked at Jake's contorted face and then at the hand. He felt pity but no guilt. Grider shuffled his feet. "I forgot you two already knew each other," he said. "I have to get back to camp for my morning coffee. Care to join us, Jake?"

Jake cocked his head at the ranger like a magpie, almost seeming to appreciate the humor of the invitation, and he remained in that position as they walked away, Tom feeling the weight of the gun in Jake's hand as they left.

At the top of the ridge, Tom turned and saw Jake watching them still. He studied the area around Jake, saw exactly where each cabin and piece of equipment sat.

"Jake's not playing with a full deck," Grider said. "He'd blow your brains out if he could get away with it, and maybe even if he couldn't." He looked up and down the backbone of the ridge and into the air out over the lake basin, shading his eyes with his hand. "Too bad about that arm, though."

Tom looked at the mountain far across the valley and said nothing.

"You feel guilty about Jake?" Grider asked.

Tom shrugged. "No. Some things just happen, I guess. Jake

made it happen. Or he let somebody else make it happen."

The sun had dried the heather and gramma grass, and grasshoppers popped in front of them at each step, shaking the tiny pink and white bells of the heather blossoms. The thick lupine scent rose over the slope, and at the edge of a snowfield in a crease of the mountainside Tom picked an electric-yellow glacier lily with dark green leaves. He held the flower against the light for a moment, and then he ate it, beginning with the blossom and ending with the sweet, whitish stem.

Grider grinned. "They're my favorite flower, too."

In the camp, Tom leaned against a thin-trunked fir while the ranger boiled water on a tiny stove.

"I got out of the habit of building a fire," Grider said. "Don't see any point in burning up any more wood or leaving a fire ring. He handed a cup of instant coffee to Tom and then poured coffee crystals into the water remaining in the pot. He stirred the water with his finger for a second and jerked the finger out. "Shit. That's hot." He wrapped a bandana around the pot and took a sip of the black coffee.

"You thought about what I said at your house that time?" Grider asked, looking at Tom through the steam from the pot.

Tom shook his head. "I guess not. I guess I never thought I'd work for the government."

"Why not? It's a natural for you. The Forest Service could use a guy who knows the country like you do, and you could do a lot of good."

Tom sipped the coffee and said nothing.

"Hell, you could get a degree in forestry or wilderness management. You'd get affirmative action preference for hiring, even. You could stay right here where your tribe's always been and keep people from fucking everything up."

Tom jerked his head toward the pump at the lake's edge. "Could I stop that?"

Grider shrugged. "You can't stop everything, but look over

there." He pointed with his pot of coffee in the direction of the big mountain. "There's a hell of a lot of country left, you know. There's the whole Northlakes area. I go up there, and I never even see a footprint."

"Isn't Georgia Pacific putting in clearcuts up that way?" Tom replied. "Jimmy said something about that."

"Well, yeah, but not in the wilderness or primitive areas. And besides, think about the rest. All the way to Canada there's a million acres of wilderness north of here. You could start walking right here and keep going all the way to the border and be in wilderness all the way. And once you get into Canada you can just keep going all the way to Alaska, and that's where the wilderness really begins. It's a big country. The Bob Marshall Wilderness is a million acres, with places nobody sees in ten years, and there's the Bitterroot and Sawtooth and a lot of other country."

"This is my country, not the Bob Marshall. That's Blackfeet country or Nez Perce or something like that."

Grider licked the rim of the pot to cool it before taking a sip. His breath steamed back up in his face. "I know what you mean, but you also have to figure that it's all your country now, just like it's all mine. White and Indian don't matter, just like tribal boundaries don't matter any more. Your people weren't always here. They came from somewhere, probably the north. You could think of Alaska as home, Mongolia maybe. I talked with a Navajo woman once who had gone to Mongolia with an anthropology class. She said she could understand some of the native language."

When Tom didn't respond, Grider added, "I'm leaving next month, and they'll need somebody to take over. Bayard will put in a word for you, and so will I. You could have this job, and it would give you a chance to keep an eye on things instead of just going around with a grudge."

Tom thought about it. He imagined himself hiking the

switchbacks up from the river wearing a Forest Service uniform, with a badge. He'd have to cut his hair.

Over the line of the ridge, a dark bird swung with rapid wingbeats. Grider jerked the glasses from his pack and watched as the falcon swooped low across the meadow, its shadow racing behind it.

19

In one of the cabins, Jake poured a cup of black coffee and added a shot of McNaughten's whiskey. He sat back in a folding chair and looked at the wall. A *Hustler* magazine lay open on a card table beside the chair. The mountains were too quiet, without even the abrasive barking of ravens. He didn't like staying in the mountains alone. It was better when the others were there and the dozers and loaders were making noise. At night they drank and played cards. The Irish coffee burned across his tongue and down his throat. As soon as he was sure the ranger was gone, he'd go and take a few potshots at the marmots. Next time, he thought, he'd bring a shotgun up and try for the hawk that was hanging around. Then he looked at the hand in the sling and realized he'd have to leave the shotgun at home.

He pulled the pistol from its holster and laid it on the table. He scraped a loose flake of white paint from the handle with his thumbnail and opened the cylinder. A heavy, soft-point shell dropped to the table. He slipped the cartridge back into the chamber and made sure the hammer rested on an empty before sliding the gun into the holster. He thought about Tom Joseph and the ranger, and then his thoughts slipped to his wife at home in the house he'd built. He flexed the biceps of the right arm and then looked at the left. He poured another shot into the coffee and took a long, bitter drink and thought of the trophy at home, the one from the Loggers Rodeo saying he was the strongest man in the valley. He tried to focus his hatred on the Indian again, but Tom Joseph's face blurred into others. He felt the mountains pressing heavily upon the little cabin, and he stood up and went outside to piss.

20

Tom watched from the cluster of alder and maple as Buddy turned his pickup out of the driveway onto the blacktop. It was eight o'clock, and he knew Buddy would be at the Red Dog for at least two hours.

He walked to the front door, careful to avoid the gravel, and silently turned the knob, but the door was locked. Keeping to the grass, he moved around to the garage and went in past the lawnmower and dirtbike and pushed on the door there. The door opened, and he stepped into the kitchen.

Karen was at the table in the dining room in a pale blue bathrobe, her head resting on the arm that lay on the table and her hair spread in a fan across the arm.

When he stepped off the piece of carpet inside the door, her head jerked up from the table with a look of fright, and then she recognized him.

"What are you doing?" she said quietly, and then, "Get out, Tom. Go away."

"Why are you crying?" he asked.

"It's none of your business now. You can't sneak into my house like this." Her eyes, swollen and red, hardened. "What do you want?"

"I wanted to see how you were," he said. "I wanted to talk to you."

She brushed the hair away from her eyes with the back of her hand and said nothing.

"Are you okay?" he asked.

She laughed. "Of course I'm okay. I'm six months pregnant, and I'm married to the richest boy in Forks. I have the biggest house on the prairie, and my husband spends every night at the tavern. I'm fine."

He pulled out the chair beside her and sat down.

"Why don't you have a seat?" she said. "Leroy might come by. Sometimes he comes by when Buddy's gone."

"Could I have some coffee?" he asked, and then he reached out to brush a strand of hair back from her face.

"No." She jerked away. "Don't touch me." She looked fully at him for the first time. "What will you do if Leroy comes?"

"I thought Leroy liked me."

She laughed again and then pulled a handkerchief from the pocket of the robe and blew her nose. "That doesn't matter now, whether Leroy likes you or not. He probably wouldn't like you breaking into his daughter's house while her husband's gone."

"You look good," he lied, looking at her swollen face.

"Well I feel pregnant," she said. "This is stupid. You can't be here."

"We could still go away. You could leave him."

She sat up and leaned back in her chair, her arms crossed above her belly.

"That's funny, Tom. I begged you to stay here but you had to go away for a year. Then you come back and you expect things to just be the same, like nothing ever was supposed to change. But nothing's the same. That's what's wrong with you. You think that because you don't want them to things won't change, or that you can make things go back to what they were just because you want them that way. Well, things change. People get pregnant. People make choices."

She stood up and went to the kitchen counter and picked up a pack of cigarettes. Lighting a cigarette, she leaned against the counter and looked at him through the smoke.

"When did you start smoking?" he asked.

She laughed for a third time. "At least your uncle knew he couldn't change anything. At least he just decided to put a few holes in things instead of going around trying to make everything like it used to be."

"You shouldn't smoke," he said. "It's bad for the baby."

"It's not your baby, so why should you care. It's a white baby, almost a fullblood." She smoked and looked at him through half-closed eyes. "You're selfish, Tom, and you don't even know it, do you? You think you're going around being picked on by the mean old world."

She stubbed the cigarette out in an ashtray on the counter and walked to him, reaching down to touch his hair.

"Your hair's getting long," she said. "Now please go away. There's nothing for you in this valley any more."

"They're putting the mine in," he said. "I was up there. I saw it."

She brushed her hair back from her forehead and looked down at him. "My dream bears are gone, Tom. When the wind blows now, I just lie there and feel the rain. It comes in long black lines like sharpened wire, and it hurts. I'm alone, and I can't find my bear cave." She lowered herself awkwardly into the chair again and stared at the table. "Think of your own dream, Tom. It can be a trap. Like steel."

21

He left the pickup in front of the Red Dog where Jimmy would see it and began walking home, puzzling over the evening. He thought of what Karen had said, and for some reason Mad John's face kept coming to him. A block from the tavern, he heard a vehicle slow beside him and he looked up to see J. D. Hill leaning across the cab to swing the passenger door open.

"I'll give you a ride," J. D. said.

He turned and kept walking, and the truck accelerated past and then stopped. J. D. climbed out of the pickup and stood waiting.

"I wanted to talk to you," J. D. said when Tom reached him.

"What about?"

"I owe you an apology. I didn't know Buddy and Jake and those others were going to pull what they did, and I wanted to tell you I'm sorry about that."

He tried to see the older man's eyes in the vague light but saw only the dark hollows. He remembered his uncle's words about language tricking people, or people tricking language. "I have to get home," he said.

"I just wanted you to know that I feel I didn't do things right. You can tell Jimmy that there's a job waiting for him when he wants it."

Tom looked curiously at the man. "Jimmy'll be happy to hear that," he said. "What are you after, J. D.?" he added.

J. D. Hill laughed a short awkward laugh. "I guess I'd just rather have you working for me."

"I have a job."

J. D. smiled. "For how long?"

Tom stepped around the man, and J. D. said, "You're

going to end up with jackshit, you know. I'm offering you the only job you're going to get offered in this valley."

Tom turned and said, "We've been through this, haven't we, J. D.?" Then he walked away.

"You're a fucking fool," J. D. shouted at his back. "You better wake up."

He passed the cafe without looking in the window. On the gravel lane, the night grew quiet, and he began to hear the sounds from the trees and vines along the road: crickets, frogs, the slap of the river, an owl's hunting call, a creaking tree, the rush of a nighthawk's wings. He shivered and thought of Mad John. What was it he'd said about the rain's father? In an anthro class he'd come across a beautiful Navajo name for the distant sweep of gray drops: the tall walking rain. Hath the rain a father?

He stopped outside the door of his home. From inside came a cadence of low, moaning sounds. When he opened the door and pushed the light switch, he saw his mother in the chair near the dead stove, the star quilt clutched around her. She looked up at him and began the wail again, closing her eyes against the light, and he saw that her silver hair was hacked in an uneven line just below her ears. He stood in the cold house and listened to the mourning and thought of the twisting Oregon highway and the long ride home. Why now, he wondered. What was the old lady mourning?

22

During the hour it took the crummy to reach town, he sat crushed against the door of the back seat and thought about the accident. It could have been no one's fault. The choker cable could have been wrapped by accident so that it flew apart at him whipping the hardhat from his head in a flash of steel that might have crushed his skull like an eggshell. The aluminum hat in his lap had a deep crease across the top, the brim torn and jagged.

The man who was pressed close against him in the crowded van stared straight ahead, and for the first time that summer, no one in the crummy spoke during the hour.

Vern went out of his way to stop the crummy at the lane that led to the Joseph house. When Tom got out no one made a sound, and he listened to the rattling tappets of the disappearing van as he started walking homeward. They hadn't meant to kill him, he knew. It was a warning. It might have killed him, of course, snapping his head off the way a boy might pop the head of a flower off with a rope. But that would have been an accident, not part of the plan.

Musing, he failed to notice the Volkswagen van until he was nearly to the house, and then he looked up in surprise at the wild portrait of Crazy Horse on the van's side.

"Yatahey, bro." Bob McBride jumped up from the steps beside Jimmy and strode across the weeds with his hand out, a can of Rainier Ale in the other.

Tom dropped his hardhat and lunchpail and touched hands with McBride, grinning back at McBride's grin and noticing with surprise that his old roommate was clean shaven and had his hair in twin braids over his shoulder.

"Your brother tells me you're a timber beast now," McBride said. "Damn, you sure look like one."

He shrugged. "It's good to see you," he said. "How'd you find us?"

McBride gestured with his lips toward the town. "I knew what town you lived in, and I figured all I had to do was ask somebody in the tavern where your house was. And I can tell an Indian house when I see one. It's just like home."

McBride's green eyes seemed alive with light as he looked at Tom and beyond, taking in at once his friend, the yard, the trees and even the mountains.

"Man this is one fine valley you got here. No wonder you bored the shit out of us all talking about it."

Tom smiled and wondered if he really had talked about the valley so much down in Santa Barbara. In his memories he never talked at all.

"I was on my way down to Arizona and figured I'd swing by and visit," McBride said. His ribbon shirt was wrinkled and stained under both arms.

"Why don't you both come into the house," Jimmy said from the doorway, and they turned and went in.

Tom set his corks and hardhat inside the door at the end of the couch, and he saw McBride looking at the hat.

"Choker cable came loose," Tom said, glancing at his brother.

McBride picked up the hardhat and turned it, looking at the crease in amazement.

"You ought to find another line of work, bro," McBride said as he set the hat back on top of the boots.

Tom saw his brother studying the hat and frowning, and he looked back at McBride. "I thought you were getting married?"

McBride shrugged. "Well, I was. But when I got back home I found out that she wasn't too interested in that anymore. She was already shacked up with a skin in Missoula. A Gros Ventre guy who's an electrician and makes good money. Fullblood."

McBride took a long pull on the beer. "So I decided I'd head on down to Big Mountain. They're having a Sundance down there where the government's trying to kick the Navajos off their land. It's a chance to pierce and protest at the same time." McBride took another drink and looked directly at Tom. "Thought you might want to come along."

Piercing. Tom looked in wonder at McBride with his brown hair and green eyes, and then he reached out for the beer Jimmy pushed toward him and he settled back in the overstuffed chair.

"Think about it, Tom. I'm swinging on down the coast to San Francisco. We could drop in on Double Saint at the Halfmoon Bay Skin Dip. Of course you don't need the dip, but there'll be some outrageous snagging there. It's not often you can combine women, religion and politics on one trip."

Tom grinned. "I don't think so. I've got this job."

"Well, I'm also making a detour to see some guys I know up in B.C.," McBride said. "Maybe you could come with me up there and think about the Sundance on the way."

"When?" Tom wiped a sleeve across his forehead and felt the grime of the logging unit smear.

"In the morning, man. They're having a sweat tomorrow, and I said I'd be there." He looked at Jimmy at the other end of the couch. "Why don't you come, too? It'll be a good sweat. It's only a couple of hours up there."

Jimmy shook his head. "I don't think so," he said. "I got some things to do around here in the next couple of days."

"You can go, right?" McBride looked hopefully at Tom.

Tom nodded. "Sure. I've got the weekend off. Why not?" He thought about the fact that McBride had been through a lot of ceremonies that he knew nothing about and how funny that was. He was the fullblood, but McBride, who'd grown up on the old Flathead reservation, seemed more Indian in some ways with his seven-eighths white ancestry.

"Great. Now maybe you could get cleaned up and we could all go get some brewskies at that tavern I saw in town. What about it?"

Without looking at Tom, Jimmy said, "Why not?"
What the hell, Tom thought. "I'll wash up," he said.

The Red Dog was crowded on a Friday night, and Tom saw
the loggers and loggers' wives turn to stare at the three Indians
as they entered. The jukebox cast amber reflections on the crowd
and Hank Williams moaned, "I'm so lonesome I could cry." They
found stools at the bar, and McBride looked around happily.

Jimmy ordered a pitcher of beer and poured three mugs
and then buried his face so deeply in his beer that he seemed
to curve into the shiny bar. Tom sat watching while above the
bar the man in the canoe paddled sparkling circles in the land
of sky-blue waters, passing again and again the same tiny pine-
studded island. Tiring of the ceremonial man, he turned to look
quickly at the scene McBride was enjoying.

Around the tables, loggers elbowed one another and bet
in ominous tones on a pool game near the back of the room.
Red beehives floated through the smoke, and sticky, hair-
sprayed blondes lounged and flounced with too little practice,
sagging eyes highlighted by supernaturally long lashes like rays
from a cluster of dark stars. And the men and women swirled
toward the dense center of the bar, a thing collapsing inward
upon itself, the women in tight pants and skirts, smoking and
flirting and laughing, and the husbands in new jeans and flannel
shirts shouting and slapping one another.

At one of the tables, Ab Masingale held forth. "What I'm
saying is it's a danged shame they got to punch a road another
twenty-thirty miles into these mountains and dig a big dog-
danged hole up there. I used to hunt that ridge, and there ain't
a prettier place in the world than that lake with that big old
mountain shining in it. Why I remember when there wasn't no
roads nowhere in these mountains and a man could walk out
of town and trap the best marten and fox you ever saw and be
back before supper. I remember when there was grizzlies in this

country, and wolves even. Shot two wolves myself up the Whitechuck.

"You remember a lot, old man, but what are you getting at?" Buddy Hill stood up behind Ab, holding a mug of beer.

"What I'm getting at is that once this whole valley and all these mountains was the finest darged country a man could lay eyes on. And now most of it's been clearcut and got roads through it and most of the game's gone, and it's a crying shame. And it was fellas like me that done it, me and Floyd and Sam and the rest of you yahoos that made them roads and cut them trees and shot ever last grizzly and wolf below Canada. And you all know it ain't going to stop. There ain't no way it can stop. Now they're digging that open-pit mine up there, and pretty soon there'll be another reason to go a little further. Pretty soon there won't be nothing left."

Ab filled his glass from a pitcher on the table.

"Maybe you're right, Ab." Buddy swayed unsteadily. "Maybe you and all our granddaddies cut most of the trees and shot all the goddamned bears, but that ain't our fault. A man has to work. A man's got a right to make a living."

Ab shook his head. "There it is. A man's got to make a living any way he can. and if cutting trees and digging a hole is the only way, then by god he's got to do it. And it ain't old farts like me and Floyd got to worry about it. It's you young farts going to be round here a long time's got to worry. Hell, someday a man won't be able to breathe anymore."

"You old bastards make me sick. You sitting around here pretending to be some kind of goddamned genius, and that old fool over there digging holes all over town because he don't have the sense to know where he buried pipes."

Leroy Brant reached a hand out from where he sat and touched Buddy on the arm. "Steady there, Buddy," he said in a low voice.

Buddy took a half-step away from Leroy.

"Well, goddamnit, this old buzzard's talking like these mountains are just for flower sniffers. What good's a fucking wilderness to us, the people that practically own it?" Buddy leaned precariously in toward Ab, and the old man shifted his casts to increase his distance.

"Ain't you forgetting some other folks that used to practically own it?" Ab said, nodding toward the bar.

McBride turned carefully and studied his beer, glancing at Tom out of the corner of his eye, while Jimmy lifted the pitcher with great care and filled his own mug again.

"You mean the injuns?" Buddy's voice rose incredulously. "Well goddamn, I hadn't even noticed." He turned toward the bar, and his beer slopped onto the floor. "Hell, that was so long ago nobody even remembers what real injuns looked like. Sides, they weren't doing nothing with it anyway. Ain't that right, Tom?"

Tom turned slightly on his stool and looked at Buddy. When Tom said nothing and his brother and McBride remained facing the bar, Buddy moved around Ab and closer to the bar.

"You injuns don't give a rat's ass what happens to that wilderness, do you?" Buddy said.

Jimmy looked over his shoulder and said, "Nope, not a rat's ass."

The men within earshot laughed.

"Crazy fucking uncle of yours was just nuts, ain't that right?" Buddy stepped closer and leaned toward Jimmy, and then he saw McBride's braids.

"Well, hey, what we got here." He tugged gently on one of the braids and Tom saw McBride stiffen. "Injun or hippy?"

"Take it easy, Buddy." Leroy stood up. "You had too much beer."

Tom felt the bar grow quiet and knew what they all waited for. He turned around to face Buddy. "You're drunk," he said.

From a chair near Leroy, a voice squeaked, "You just cain't hold your firewater, Buddy."

The loggers laughed, and Buddy wheeled to glare at Dinker and then turned back toward Tom.

"You better let this one alone, Buddy," Leroy said. "You're a damned slow learner."

Buddy lurched toward Tom and swung the mug as he rose up on his toes. And just as abruptly Jimmy's hand shot in front of Tom's face and caught the arm, slinging beer across McBride's back so that McBride spun to face the crowd.

Leaning with his shoulder, Jimmy twisted, and Buddy crumpled against the bar. McBride watched fascinated as Buddy screamed once and then writhed against the smooth wood.

Leroy grabbed Buddy by the collar of his shirt and dragged him back to the table.

"Hills never could hold liquor," Ab said. "This one's daddy was worse when he was just a punk."

McBride drained his mug and looked at Tom. "Nice neighbors," he said. Then he led the way as they walked slowly out of the bar.

23

They left early and drove the inland road through Rockport and Cedro Wooley, crossing the border at Sumas, Tom enjoying the wet sweep of the two-lane highway as it twisted up the river valleys.

At Chilliwack they drove through town and out to a scattering of small wooden houses and trailers. They drove past the yards filled with wrecked cars and huge piles of firewood to a square woodframe house where a shirtless Indian in jeans waved at them.

McBride got out and Tom followed.

"Long time," the Indian said with a grin, holding his hand out toward McBride. He wore his waist-length hair loose over his shoulders and chest, with two eagle feathers on one side. "I see you shaved off that white man's pussy hair."

McBride grasped the hand lightly and grinned. "I see you pulled out those two hairs you spent a year growing," he said. Then nodding toward Tom, he said, "This is my good friend, Tom Joseph. Tom, this is Aaron Medicine."

"Welcome," Aaron Medicine said. "You make your friend here look like a white-eye." He reached to shake hands, and Tom saw the Marine Corps tatoo on his biceps and the three puckered scars just above each breast.

McBride slid the door of the van open and brought out an icechest. Handing it to the host he said, "I brought a little venison for the feast."

While Aaron Medicine took the icechest into the house, McBride led Tom into the backyard where a small dome was covered with army-green canvas. In front of the dome an Indian with a thin mustache and straight hair to his shoulders was using a shovel to heap the coals of a big fire into a mound. He nodded and kept up with his task.

"You ever sweated before, Tom?" McBride asked.

When Tom shook his head, McBride pointed to the dome. "That's the sweatlodge. Aaron will run the sweat. He's a pipe-carrier and runs the best sweats in the Northwest. You see those scars on his chest?"

Tom nodded.

"He's pierced three times. And he's got scars on his back too. He's a Lakota who moved up here after his hitch in Vietnam. He was a junkie and now he helps Indians get clean with his sweats." He nodded toward the fire. "That's the fire chief. He's an Isleta from New Mexico."

Tom looked from the short, potbellied fire chief to the painted buffalo skull near the sweatlodge. The feeling was strange and foreign. He knew it was all Indian, but it wasn't familiar. He remembered his uncle's stories about the Indians who would come down from the north before there was a medicine line and raid their tribe. There was a tribe called the Thompsons that would move like death over the high passes. He wondered what the mysterious Thompsons had really been called. Aaron Medicine came out of the back door of the house followed by two women wrapped in towels. One of the women was dark, with long loose hair, and the other was as fair as McBride, with short brown hair and an oriental quality.

In a low voice, McBride said, "Traditionally women aren't allowed in these sweats, but Aaron welcomes everyone—men, women, Indians or whites. These are intertribal sweats, for anybody who needs it."

Aaron Medicine approached and handed each of them a towel. "You ever been in a sweatlodge before?" he asked, and when Tom shook his head, he said, "Bob can explain things."

The pipe-carrier went to talk to the fire chief, and McBride led Tom to the area behind the sweatlodge. When they had stripped down to their underwear and had wrapped the towels around themselves, McBride said, "If it gets too bad in there it's okay to lie down on the ground. People do that sometimes. Or you can pull the towel over your head." He grinned. "Some guys wear huge beach towels so they can wrap themselves. It's only rookies you see with little bitty towels.

"One thing to remember is that when you go in or leave you say *'mitakuye oyasin.'* It's Sioux, I think, and it means something like 'all my relations.' You can say it in English if you want to. It's a blessing. And if it gets too rough, you can ask permission to leave. Everything's okay, as long as you do it with respect."

Tom noticed that a couple of men had joined the group, one of the men obviously Indian with dark skin and braids and a number of tatoos. The other man reminded him of the Chicanos in Santa Barbara, with curly hair and a drooping mustache and thick black hair on his chest. The scars on the insides of both men's arms were obvious even from a distance.

When it was time to enter, he followed McBride on hands and knees, from left to right around the firepit in the center of the lodge until they had circled and sat on the right side near the door.

The fire chief handed three lava rocks on deer antlers one at a time through the open canvas flap, and Aaron Medicine placed them carefully in the pit. The fire chief handed a bucket of water and a gourd through the opening and dropped the flap. Tom strained to see in the almost absolute darkness as Aaron Medicine offered a prayer in a language he couldn't understand, and then the Mexican-looking man near the door sang a long, soothing song in still another Indian language Tom didn't know. The air smelled of sweetgrass and cedar and other things he couldn't identify, and then there was the hiss of water hitting rocks and he felt a cloud of steam rise over his face, searing his nostrils.

From out of the darkness came a prayer he recognized as Spanish. The speaker was one of the two women, and he could tell that she was praying for peace. She spoke of *la familia* repeatedly, and then there was another hiss of water and steam swarmed over him again until he breathed it deep into his lungs.

Twice the flap was opened and they breathed the cooler air, and each time the fire chief brought in additional rocks and the flap closed and the steam rose hotter and more searing. The pipe moved from left to right, and they smoked in turn, and then he recognized the voice of the light-skinned woman as she called upon Grandfather to "make the children strong, the children who are lost in the cities, who seek guidance and love, and the women who suffer and die because they have lost the path." The pipe was passed, and they prayed for all their brothers and sisters and for the world facing nuclear destruction, for those who had succumbed to alcohol or to drugs, and for the four-leggeds and two-leggeds, the underwater people and the above-ground people and as they prayed in Lakota and Navajo and English and Spanish it seemed to him that suddenly he understood it all. And sweetgrass and cedar were offered, and then the water seemed to roar upon the lava rocks and the steam boiled in a thick cloud over him and cut into his nostrils and throat, burning his skin until he wanted to cry out.

Beside him he heard one of the women sob, and he heard the men grunting in voices reinforced by pain. He clenched his fists and eyes against the steam, and then it began to subside. He felt a nudge and heard McBride whisper, "It's your turn to pray."

There was silence as the steam settled and he breathed deeply, feeling a sweetness in his lungs. Someone brushed the hot stones with sweetgrass and the smoke laced the air. "Grandfather," he heard himself say, wishing he could pray in his ancestors' language. "I thank you for the rivers and streams and mountains, for the trees and rocks, for the people of the water and earth and air." It felt awkward, and he wondered if the words were all wrong. He sensed the others' held breaths. And then the tension was suddenly gone, and he breathed deeply and felt, for the first time since childhood, a great sense of peace. When he spoke again his voice was a whisper, barely audible in the thick darkness. "Uncle," he said, "Father of the rain."

"Ho!" came from different voices of the circle, and he recognized Aaron Medicine's as the deepest grunt of approval. After McBride had prayed for all the oppressed peoples of the world, there was a sudden explosion as Aaron Medicine poured the remainder of the bucket directly upon the rocks, and this time the steam came in a scalding flash that swept him back into the canvas in excruciating pain. Covering his mouth and nostrils with his cupped hands, he felt his flesh cook and clenched his jaws as loud grunts and sobs came again from the darkness around him. Beside him McBride let out a low moan, and he felt his friend rock back and forth as the searing pain went on and on. And then the flap was thrown open, and cool air and sunlight flooded into the lodge.

"A good one, huh?" The fire chief leaned into the opening, grinning as the pipe was carefully handed out followed by the bucket and gourd. Then Tom moved with the others back around the circle and into the blinding light where rain had begun to fall in long curving lines out of the southwest.

Outside, they stood singly near the fire without speaking. Tom noticed that both McBride and the man with the drooping mustache were covered with dirt on one side. He felt his pores open to the cleansing rain, and he was happy that he had not lain down during the worst pain.

Later, as they ate the fried venison and other foods people had brought, Aaron Medicine, wearing a black Grateful Dead teeshirt, jeans and flipflops, came to sit on the floor beside Tom. Balancing his plate on his crossed legs, the older man said, "That was a tough sweat. I thought David would open the flap sooner when I dumped all that water on, but he'd gone off to do something and didn't hear me." He chuckled. "That was a good one for your first sweat."

Tom grinned. He was surprised at how good he felt after the pain. He felt clean.

"I liked it," he said.

Aaron Medicine nodded. "We'd like you to come again. We're all trying to live the right way up here, you know. A lot of us have had some problems and now we're trying to help others, mostly Indians but others too. And we're trying to live by Indian values." He grinned. "Don't let all that junk outside fool you. There's a lot more to it."

Tom nodded, unable to think of anything to say.

"Let me show you something."

Tom followed Aaron Medicine to the open door and stepped out into the yard. With his arm, the Sundancer made a sweeping motion toward the thick forest that began a mile away from the houses.

"Those trees are the beginning," he said. "You can go into those trees and start walking and you never have to stop. I always think of that. Things get too bad, that's where I'll go." He looked intense. "Too many Indians don't know shit about nature anymore. They're living in places like L. A. and Vancouver and sticking needles in their arms, and real nature scares the shit out of them. They come out here and see a coyote slinking around and think it's a wolf. One time I had this famous Indian poet out here who's always writing about Raven, all these mystical poems about Raven you know, and I found out he didn't know the difference between a raven and a crow. So many of our people only know the cities now."

He grinned and looked at the clouds and slanting rain. "That's part of all this. We don't mean that an Indian can't watch the superbowl or use a microwave oven if he feels like it, we just want people to find out who they are."

A blue-tick hound came wriggling up and licked his hand, and he pulled on one of its ears while looking toward the mountains to the north. "Sometimes I get pissed off," he said, "and

I want to do something, take action. Sometimes I think we ought to get up a war party and take this country back, all of it that's left. Stop 'em from cutting down all the trees and dumping radioactive trash all over our land. The Russians spewed pieces of a radioactive satellite all over Indian land way up north of here, and the good old U. S. of A. is killing all the lakes with acid rain. Down in New Mexico there's a whole town on one of the pueblo reservations that's contaminated with radiation. They put a uranium mine in and just flushed the tailings out on the pueblo land. Babies are born all messed up and people can't drink the water."

He looked at Tom and his eyes seemed to be fixed on a more distant point. "Sometimes I have a vision of a war party that would make the Little Big Horn look like a cub scout meeting. Everyone of us, man, bloods and breeds and everybody, millions and millions of us just sweeping down from the north on buffalo runners in a huge cloud, and every place we touched would be made like it was, new and clean. Ghost riders in the sky. Ho!"

He turned back to the doorway. Glancing at an upturned washing machine near the porch he said, "I'm going to take the motor out of that and make a go-cart for my wife's son." He added, "We got some peach pie and cool whip for desert." Then he stopped in the doorway and said in a lower voice, "There are grizzlies in those woods, man, realbears. And sometimes at night out there you hear wolves. They don't know it, man, but we're coming back. All of us. Every damned one of us."

24

Squeezed next to the crummy's rattling door, he watched the timber sweep by and thought of the sweatlodge and his friend. McBride had spent one more night at their house trying to convince him and then headed south toward San Francisco and Arizona. They'd stood next to the van in the front yard, and McBride had held the door open while he looked at the mountains.

"One thing I want to ask you, Tom. Where's all your people? Where's your tribe, man, your family?"

Tom shrugged. "Gone," he said. "My aunt's in Rockport, but that's about all. They're just gone."

"Tom Joseph, the one-man tribe," McBride said as he climbed into the van. Then he said, "Take it easy, Tom. There's some mean motherfuckers in this valley."

He'd watched Crazy Horse disappear down the gravel road and wished he could go. And now he wondered when Vern Reese would tell him he was fired. He knew he was a problem on the job. There'd been no fights, nothing too obvious, but little things were happening too frequently. Since the choker cable accident there had been blocks dropped close to his hands and feet, tools tossed carelessly, warnings not given about pinched logs or frayed cables. Little things that crippled and killed, and slowed work.

The crummy moved out over a silver bridge, and he looked down at the scattered water spreading across a stretch of sand and then rushing together over rocks beneath the bridge. He wondered what his brother would be doing at home, if he would still pretend to be busy outside the house to escape their mother.

Vern stopped the crummy next to the tavern, and they all got out, unfolding with grunts of pain. He slung his corks over his shoulder and started home while the others went into the

Red Dog. Under his moccasins the small rocks on the asphalt were hard and sharp.

"Hold on a minute, Tom."

Reese had left the crummy and was walking toward him, his weathered eyes squinting. Tom saw a choker-setter and a chaser look at the rigging slinger and then exchange glances before they disappeared into the tavern.

He waited for his boss to reach him, and they stood together for a moment until Reese said, "I ain't going to bullshit around it, Tom. You and me both know I got to let you go. Either you or the whole bunch of them." He took a deep breath and let it out slowly. "You're going to end up smashed. And we both know them little tricks of theirs is slowing things up out there. Loggers got to look out for each other, and they got to trust each other or it just don't work."

Reese scowled and chewed the corner of his mouth, and Tom shifted the boots to his other shoulder and nodded. "Sure. I just wasn't going to quit to please those bastards." He brushed hair back behind his ear and stared at the old man.

"You can tell Jimmy that if he don't want to work for J. D. he can come back to work for me if he ain't still an invalid." Seeing Tom's expression, Reese added, "It's just you, Tom. That stuff about Jake's an excuse, but it ain't that. Jimmy'll do fine."

Tom looked the old man in the eyes and nodded, thinking for the first time that summer that it would be nice to go into the Red Dog and sit down and have a couple of beers.

"Sorry, Tom." They shook hands and then both turned away, Tom walking homeward and listening to the scrape of his moccasins. A late summer wind herded fat clouds slowly across the sky, and the scent of rain lay heavy on the air. Lightning season, he thought. The black peaks glistened with electric tension.

Bayard Taylor angled toward him from across the road.

"Hello, Tom."

"Hi, Bayard," he answered as they matched strides along the road.

"Thought I'd hike on down to the Fir Tree for some pie and coffee," Bayard said. "How's the life of a choker-setter? You must be pretty good at it seeing as how you still got all your fingers and both feet."

"Not any more. Vern just fired me."

Bayard looked up in surprise. "No shit. I thought you two got along real well. Vern told me you was the best choker-setter he'd ever had."

"Things weren't working out, I guess."

They walked in silence for a while, and then Bayard asked, "You still planning to stay here?"

"I'm staying," Tom said as they approached the cafe.

Bayard bent without missing a stride and picked up a handful of gravel, tossing it in his palm as they walked. "I guess you know what you got to do. How about letting me buy you some pie?"

Tom looked at the front of the cafe and Bayard added, "They got a new girl in Karen's place. The Bryant girl, Lisa."

Bayard held the door open, and Tom went in first. They sat alone at the counter, and as they waited for the waitress to appear from the kitchen Bayard said, "You know, sometimes I wish I'd been born a hundred years ago so I could've been one of them mountainmen. Just roaming around these mountains by yourself, back when it was all like it was before white men came. Wintering up in one of these valleys."

Tom thought, A hundred years ago I would have known who I was.

Bayard spun the postcard rack and looked at the pictures of bears as Ida came out of the kitchen. Seeing them, the lanky waitress nearly smiled.

"Evening, Bayard," Ida said. "How's Sarah, Tom?"

"Okay."

A pretty high school girl came out of the kitchen and smiled at them, her gray eyes flashing at Tom. She carried an empty coffee pot back into the kitchen.

"You remember Lisa, don't you Tom?" Ida asked. "You must've been in school about the same time."

He didn't remember her. "I guess I graduated before she started," he said.

After Bayard ordered, Ida poured two cups of bitter coffee and set a quarter of a blackberry pie in front each of them. Then she, too, disappeared into the kitchen.

Bayard pushed at the pie suspiciously and said, "It ain't none of my business, but what are you going to do now?" Without waiting for a reply he added, "You thought about the forest circus again?"

Tom took a bite of the pie and watched a middle-aged couple in matching plaid shirts, jeans, and hiking boots enter the cafe. The couple sat at one of the tables and looked around nervously.

"You've been talking to Martin Grider," he said.

"Well, yeah, I guess I have. But it makes sense. I think between us me and Martin could swing that job for you."

The couple at the table whispered to one another, and the man cleared his throat loudly and looked toward the kitchen. There was a sound of pans from the back of the cafe.

He thought about it.

"You wouldn't even have to cut your hair," Bayard said with a mouthful of pie. "Hell, the government can't make you do anything like that no more. It's illegal. We got a guy on trailcrew with hair down to his ass, and he ain't even a Indian. Says he's going to be a nurse."

Ida came out from the kitchen and looked at the new customers. "How about some music?" she said to Tom and Bayard. When they didn't answer she rang "No Sale" on the register and shoved a coin into the jukebox. The box sang "When the moon hits your eye like a big pizza pie, that's *amore*."

Tom glanced at the amazed tourists.

"You really think I could get the job?" he asked.

Bayard nodded. "I know you could."

He finished his coffee and got up from the stool. "I appreciate it, Bayard, but I guess I couldn't do it. I'd just get too mad about what they're doing in there."

He reached into his pocket but Bayard put out a hand and said, "On me, remember?"

He picked up his boots and lunchpail and said, "Thanks, Bayard."

The couple at the table were still staring toward the noises in the hidden kitchen, the man's eyes big and disbelieving.

As he crossed the asphalt, a chocolate-brown pickup swung off the road to park in front of the cafe. He stopped and looked back at the big four-wheel-drive and saw J. D. Hill climb down from the new truck. Then he turned toward home, stepping lightly in the moccasins.

Beside the tracks now a wave of ripe blackberries, thimbleberries and salmonberries rode the fence, and he picked one of each to taste the sweet and sour. The tart little caps of the thimbleberries were his favorite, and he slipped half a dozen off and held them on his tongue.

The house sat like a fungus amid the brush and vines and weeds, cold and without life. He stopped a hundred feet away and looked at it and then turned back toward the cafe.

At the counter they watched him through the window.

"That boy smells like trouble," J. D. Hill said as he stirred his coffee. "Just like his uncle."

"Tom won't end up like his uncle or Jimmy," Bayard said. "He's too smart."

"Too smart for his own good." J. D. sipped the coffee and watched Tom Joseph cross the paved road and turn past the Fir Tree toward the state liquor store.

Ida set hamburger plates in front of the tourists and then came to lean against the pie case. "I heard you finally got the waterworks away from Floyd," she said.

"That's right," J. D. answered. "We just couldn't put up with no more maggoty bears in the reservoir, or that old fart spending two weeks digging holes to fix a pipe. The community controls it now and we're going to modernize."

Bayard snorted and got off his stool, moving toward the door as Ida went into the kitchen. J. D. watched Tom cross back in front of the windows with a small paper sack cradled in his arms, and J. D. smiled into his coffee. "I think I'll go take a look at that mine," he said to the pie case. The couple looked up hopefully from their hamburgers and then went back to eating silently when J. D. glared at them.

A hundred yards from the house, Tom cut off the road into the woods. He passed the big cedar stumps from three-quarters of a century before, running his fingers over the notches from the old crosscutters' springboards. The trees now were maple and alder and third-growth hemlock, and the hardwoods wore streaks of yellow and gold through the green. Wild raspberries caught on his jeans, and he knocked down showers of reddish spores from the mass of bracken fern. The sounds of the river lapped up into the vegetation, and he felt the cool shadow of the water.

A big cedar lay across the narrow place in the river, the root-wad resting in a deep hole on the shore and the trunk spearing the gravel on the other side fifty feet away. The log was shiny where it hung over the pool.

He walked out over the little river and sat down. The water sliced by as clear as the gin on the liquor store shelves. He broke the paper and twisted the black cap off the bottle and took a long swallow and gasped and shook his head. His eyes and nostrils stung.

The river swept into the bank in a deep, scimitar pool with

bright stones along the bottom. From the narrow pool, the water fanned out shallow across the gravel with darting schools of minnows in the margin. The steelhead and a few remaining salmon would be resting in the pool, so he tried to penetrate the mirror of moving water for the shadow or flash of silver or flare of red that would give them away. Old Man Salmon hugged the deep bottom, and he felt the second swallow burn its way down, shuddering along his ribs. Then he saw the first one, an old, scarred humpy with bowed back flaming and long, grotesquely distended jaw. It balanced midway down the glassy slope of the water, suspended on the edge of death and waiting for the final push upstream. The current revolved a clear window over the fish for a moment, and he saw distinctly the mosaic of scars along the sides and back. Below the humpy another bowed red back floated into view, and then he saw the other shadows finning cautiously near the bottom. The water swirled into the pool and boiled under the cutbank. A steelhead flashed rainbow sides through the shallow water at the far end of the pool and turned in a manic crash into the drifting salmon. For a moment the fish swam in panicked circles, and then they spread out to drift in place again like arrows in the deep water, waiting for the strength to return.

He raised the bottle and looked through it at the river running away through the trees, now a honey-red river sweeping off between greenish barriers to bank sharply and tumble sixty miles to the ocean. He'd canoed it all the way with his uncle once, struggling in the white water and slipping quietly along in the calm sections, lying on his back and watching the freeway overpass float by many miles away.

He took another swallow and looked at the bottle. He wondered if Sara Joseph would still be mourning. Abruptly he turned the bottle up and watched the liquid ribbon into the stream, sending the heavy shadows darting for the cutbank deep in the pool. He screwed the cap on the bottle and stood up and walked back toward the house.

In the dusk he could see Jimmy standing on the porch with his hands in his pockets. A wave of affection for his older brother struck him.

"Been waiting for you," Jimmy said, his voice tight. "Mama's pretty sick. I called Doc Clemens."

He looked at the junked cars, now nearly covered by vines, and at the thick place in the weeds where the transmission lay, and he tossed the bottle toward the side of the porch. Jimmy followed the arc of the bottle with his eyes and watched him climb the steps.

"Is she in the bedroom?" he asked.

"Uh huh. She's pretty sick," Jimmy said.

In the bedroom she lay with the blankets close around her chin. The ends of her silver hair made a ragged edge on the pillow.

"How do you feel?" He bent over the bed and heard the rattle of her breath as she lay with her eyes closed.

"Jimmy called Doc Clemens," he said. "He'll be right out."

Through the window the moon dripped bits of light from a thin patch of cloud. Still the rain held back.

25

The ambulance was a spot of red in the rain that had begun to fall at last in a steady tempo. He rode beside Jimmy in the pickup, the water breaking the taillights ahead into glistening red beads on the windshield. The raw metal of the pickup roof drummed with the rain and radiated damp cold. He shivered against the door. Jimmy kept the accelerator to the floor, but they quickly lost sight of the ambulance on the twisting road. Then they rode in silence, the slashing of the single wiper and the ripping of the tires backed by the broken muffler and chattering engine. In the headlights the particles of rain loomed larger and more silver as they angled in toward the truck. On either side of the road, the timber stood in an unbroken black wall.

26

He arrived early to dig the hole. Parking the truck at the edge of the graveyard, he took the shovel and pulaski out of the back and began digging halfway between his uncle and father, marking out the rectangle with the shovel and cutting away the top layer of humus with the pulaski. Then he switched to the shovel.

After the first two feet, he began to hit roots too large for the shovel, so he used the pulaski again, chopping the ones under three inches with the adze end and using the axe blade on the larger ones. The roots oozed a purple, watery sap, the ends blood-red where the pulaski went through. Three and a half feet down he hit river gravel and sand and the digging became easier. When he came to the bigger rocks, he pulled them out and rolled them away with his hands. A Canada jay watched and mocked from one of the hemlocks overhead.

He dug rhythmically once he had moved into the deep sand, his mind fixed on the meter of the shovel. Soon he stood waist-deep in the hole, throwing the gravel and sand and occasional rocks out over his shoulder. When he could no longer look out over the top of the grave, he stopped. The light mist of rain felt good on his face, and he imagined the rest of the graveyard. He was at their level now. If what was left of his uncle and father and all of the others who were somehow related to him began to move horizontally, to slide about in that strange kind of dance, they would drop right into his hole. He imagined a game of musical grave, but the bones would not hold together, catching and tangling in roots and rocks.

He looked up toward the moss hanging from shabby hemlocks. The mist would thicken soon, he knew, and it would rain again.

27

When they buried her, clouds swirled down the river and between the trees, blending morning with afternoon, afternoon with evening. Jenny and the Upper Skagit and Ida stood on one side of the grave, while Bayard stood on the other and he and Jimmy shoveled the gravel and duff into the hole. The Baptist minister stood back to avoid the splashes from the water that oozed up around the coffin until the coffin disappeared and the grave was mounded with sand and humus. It was a neat job. They planted the wooden cross in a hole and wedged stones around its base, Gordon stomping the rocks firmly into the ground with a motion that reminded Tom of a mocking round-dance. Then Jimmy tapped the top of the cross one last time and they stood back.

"She'll stay up there now," Gordon said, patting the top of the cross and winking at his wife.

The hearse, with the same driver who'd brought their uncle, was already gone, and the others began to leave at once. When he was alone in the cemetery, Tom went to the second-youngest grave and looked down at it. Ferns had unfurled already on the sinking mound, and the new granite marker leaned a little in the soft earth. He tried to straighten the stone, but it slipped and fell face-down on the grave. He started to lift the stone again but stopped, dropping it and then smashing it further into the earth with his boot. He teetered on the edge of the granite for a moment and then stepped back.

With both hands he pulled his mother's cross from the grave and sent it spinning out over the river. It struck a boulder, glanced into a wave, and rushed away with the water.

It took several more minutes to pull his uncle's heavy stone upright and drag it to the water and to do the same with Tom Joseph's marker. When he tumbled them in, the glacial river swallowed the granite hungrily and sent the stones pounding downstream with the rest of its boulders, tumbling and smoothing them with its current.

He knelt at the edge of the silty water, listening to the river. There must be a prayer for this, too, he thought, and then he thought of the old ones disappearing. Even Sam Gravey. A hiker had found Sam the same way Sam had found Uncle Jim. Fall was in the air.

When he reached the road the others were gone and his brother was stepping out of the pickup.

"I was coming to see what happened to you," Jimmy said.

He could see that his brother had been crying, and he wanted to explain what he'd done, how he was making things clearer, but he climbed into the truck and said nothing. As they drove toward town he looked hard for glimpses of the river through the trees.

28

They sat in the house, Jimmy on the couch and Tom in the ragged chair. The front door hung open, and a few drops of rain sprinkled the edge of the floor. Decay felt its way through the house, certain but cautious. Rain whispered on the roof and shivered the weeds outside the window.

"Loan me a couple of bucks, Tommy?" Jimmy didn't look at him.

He hesitated, reluctant to let his brother go so quickly. Then he pulled a crumpled bill from his pocket and tossed it to Jimmy.

Catching the bill with one hand Jimmy said, "Thanks. What are you going to do?"

Tom shrugged. "I think I'll be a wilderness ranger, range the wilderness."

Jimmy unfolded the bill and looked at Tom in surprise. "This is a twenty. A couple of bucks is enough."

Tom lifted his hand. "It's okay. I don't need it."

At the door, Jimmy stopped and looked back at him for a moment before going out.

When the pickup was gone, he went to his uncle's room and took the pack from the wall. From the rack he lifted the Krag and opened and closed the bolt. He shoved the box of cartridges into the pack and carried the pack and rifle into the living room and leaned them against the couch. In a kitchen drawer he found his brother's flashlight and a box of wooden matches. He placed the matches inside two plastic bags and then put the flashlight and matches into the pack. There would be too much weight to carry food, but maybe he could find food, scrape the inner bark of trees perhaps. He imagined waves of mountain ranges, black timber rising to snow and ice, wave after wave of mountains and deep valleys stretching far north across Canada and into the unknown territory of Alaska. And there was the Bering

Strait and then still more wilderness on and on forever.

He sat on the couch, feeling the tremendous emptiness of the house, listening to the drifting rain and waiting for his brother to get drunk.

At first the tapping seemed part of the dream, but then he woke to the sound of the door scraping all the way open, and he saw Karen standing in front of him like a spirit. Her bulging raincoat glistened in the light from the single bulb, and her hair hung wet and straight down her back.

"I wanted to come to Sara's funeral, but Buddy wouldn't let me. He went to J. D.'s finally, so I came to tell you I'm sorry."

He sat up, wincing at the sound of his mother's name and brushing his hair back from his face. "It's okay," he said, noticing that her rainboots were caked with mud and a puddle had formed on the wood floor at her feet.

"I heard about Vern firing you," she said. "Will you stay now?"

He nodded. "Haven't you heard? I'm going to be a wilderness ranger. Everything's going to be fine."

When she left, he waited for the sound of her car to die away before he began walking toward the Red Dog.

Only a few bachelors and men who wished they were bachelors had washed up in the tavern on a Thursday night. Jimmy sat alone with a half-empty bottle of scotch at one end of the bar.

Tom looked around the tavern. It would be nice, he thought, to sit beside Jimmy and drink and watch the electric sign above the bar.

Jimmy smiled. "Hi, Tommy. Have a drink?" His face was slack and his words carefully balanced.

"No thanks," he said. "I'd like to borrow the pickup for a while." He studied his brother's dark face. The nose was changed since the fight, and the scar made a white welt across the cheekbone, but it was still the face from long before when they'd hunted cottontails in the creek bottoms.

"You're not going to be no wilderness guard," Jimmy said, squinting at him.

"Yes," he said. "I promise."

"Where you going?"

"Just for a drive. I just want to take a drive."

Jimmy fished the key out of his pocket. "I can walk home," he said. "I sure as hell can't drive anyway."

Tom touched his brother on the shoulder. "Take care, Jimmy," he said before he turned and left the tavern.

He drove to the house and loaded the pack and rifle into the cab of the truck and then turned the pickup toward the Stehemish road. Near midnight the road was deserted. The valley drowsed in the rain, and the old truck breasted the dark clumsily as it rattled down the road.

A few miles out of town, he eased the truck onto a side road that cut a narrow path through the trees. A half-mile later he stopped before a fenced pasture. He got out and stretched the barbedwire strands beside the gate and stepped through. At the back of the pasture two gray buildings hunched under the darkness of a big maple, and he headed toward them, keeping a safe distance from the forest service mules dozing in the shadows of the trees.

A brass lock hung on the door of the larger building, the hasp rusty and the wood behind it soft with age. He pulled his pocketknife out and opened the broken blade. In a minute he had the hasp free of the rotten wood and the lock hung from the door.

The room swarmed with odors of leather and saddlesoap and composting hay. Sacks of oats lay on the littered floor and packsaddles and ropes and harnesses hung from nails and pegs and sawhorses. He found the boxes of forest service powder along one end of the room and pried the top off one of the boxes to expose a layer of yellowish-brown waxed paper. Cutting the paper carefully, he saw the neat rows of dull red dynamite.

He carried the box to the porch and replaced the lock on the door. When the dynamite was in the bed of the pickup, he crawled back through the fence and returned to the far end of the pasture. The trees along the edge of the field made a jagged wall against the lighter sky.

The small building was of concrete blocks, with thick walls. The door was an inch of weathered fir, and he removed the lock as easily as he had the other. The flashlight found the blasting caps in boxes along the back shelf. He knocked spiderwebs out of the way with the flashlight and took one small box from the shelf. The detonators sat in a wooden box near the door, wrapped in plastic bags from the grocery store. Each detonator had its own coil of wire, and he selected one of the boxes and backed out of the room, replacing the lock as exactly as he had the first one.

On his final trip across the pasture, the dark mule shadows loomed at him and the animals stirred and snorted when he passed, one drowsing animal kicking aimlessly with a hind hoof. A breeze picked up and moved across the pasture and carried the mule scent into the trees and sent chills tingling through his shoulder.

As he climbed into the truck, a tall fir beside the road groaned and swayed. The light rain fell steadily, and the truck clambered onto the road and away from Forks.

The headlights cut a dim yellow tunnel up the narrowing valley. By now Jimmy would probably be alone in the old house. The trees rose quickly on both sides. Along the narrow stretch there was no room to turn around. The drainage drew him in like a funnel, and when he glanced into the mirror he saw the night close in behind. The Stehemish River rustled and muttered in the trees downhill from the road.

He stomped on the brake as the shadow leaped out of the timber, hearing the dynamite slam against the back of the cab.

The blasting caps slid out from under the seat as the truck skidded in the gravel. For an instant it was framed in the headlights, frozen in mid-leap—like a coyote but much bigger. It plunged out of the dark into the path of the truck and vanished as suddenly, its head toward him for an instant and eyes an intense yellow.

He shivered again, knowing that it must have been one of the big hunting dogs that roamed the valley at night, from one of the farms lower down the drainage. The headlights must have exaggerated the size.

The truck reached the end of the road and stopped among the machines. He got out and looked at the rusting gate, realizing that he could never break through the two big locks. He'd have to walk all the way. They'd know who did it as soon as they found the pickup, but by then he'd be gone. It wouldn't be much, but they'd notice.

He put the dynamite in the pack and threw the box over the side of the road with the construction debris. The detonator went in with the sticks, but he put the blasting caps in an outside pocket of the pack. He slung the frame onto his back, lifted the rifle out of the truck, and started up the road just as the rain increased its tempo up and down the valley. As he walked, the shadows of the trees along the new road reached out and closed behind him.

He followed the road and then the trail for most of the night, feeling his way through the fallen timber and up the switchbacks. In the dark the small streams pulsated, rising to a crescendo and diminishing in a constant rhythm. By the time the wall of shadows had become individual gray trunks and the edge of daybreak crept down through the timber, he had reached the top of the ridge a half-mile from the lookout. If he was lucky, they would have called the lookout down to the station in Forks because of the low fire danger late in the season, but he couldn't risk meeting Grider near the lake. He crossed the spine of the ridge and descended several hundred yards down the far side to where the mountain hemlock and fir stands thickened.

Racing the light, he slid from the heather slope into the trees, lowering himself in steep spots from one thin trunk to another. The sun came over the wall of Fortress Peak, and clouds started snuffling up around the other peaks until the light grew gray and the morning broke thin and cold.

He ached. The straps cut into his shoulders, and the rifle dragged at whichever arm he carried it in. He crawled into a cluster of hemlocks, their crusty branches drooping to the ground and covered with trailing moss, and sat down against a trunk, moving gingerly because of the sore shoulder and the blasting caps. No one came to this side of the ridge. He wouldn't be seen.

He laid the pack beside him and took out the two blankets. Then, rolling himself tightly in the blankets, he slept. In his dreams, wave after wave of black rain beat its way up the Stehemish drainage, shattering like obsidian against the ridges. Quicksilver specters haunted the edges of the timber, slippery shadows with yellow eyes. And the shadows all around moved closer to the sleeper.

29

Jimmy awoke on the filthy couch at nine with a bad head. The scotch kept up its fermentation process in his stomach, and the rain beat in steady waves against the house. The chill had entered the marrow of his bones, and someone was slapping furiously at the screendoor. Using both hands to steady his head, he lurched off the couch and stumbled to the door to be struck in the face by needles of rain. The screen rapped violently against the wall, and rain pelleted into the room. When he hooked the door closed, the wind worked to rip it free. Failing at the door, the wind shifted and began to cuff the sides of the house. The support post on the porch swung slowly back and forth and came loose, vanishing into the yard. The weeds in the yard bent toward the river, glistening with water.

Jimmy held both hands over his ears to shut out the assault on the house and stumbled to the couch, pulling the ragged spread over himself, blotting out the wind and rain and empty room. The old house seemed to settle closer to the earth, and the roof of the porch fell with a soft thud into the tall weeds.

30

Floyd pulled the curtains aside and scratched the round chin hidden in his white beard and watched the clouds descend into the apple orchard. In wet weather his joints ached. He rubbed the top of his head and shuffled to the kitchen and dumped a handful of coffee into an enamel pot on the stove. Flame appeared through cracks in the stove, and an ancient hound stirred and raised its eyes, the sockets red and sagging. Floyd nudged the dog with the toe of a wool sock and said, "Guess them pipes is somebody else's worry now, huh Maggy?" One hand probed absent-mindedly behind a suspender strap, and he saw the rain feeling its way around the plywood on the broken windowpane and running down the peeling wallpaper. "Better fix that winder this fall, Maggy," he said. He could feel the whole valley waiting patiently for him, the way it had waited for Sam Gravey, the rain tapping at the door and window. Out on the road, Mad John's Plymouth rattled silently by, partially obscured by rain and appletrees.

31

On the roof of the cabin, the rain battered ominously. Jake opened the door of the stove and thrust a piece of pitchy fir into the fire. Heat cut through the small room, and he walked to a window and looked out. A silver curtain hovered over the machinery and broken rock. None of the peaks was visible. His wife was in Forks in the house with the fireplace. He thought of the months he'd spent building the house, falling and aging the logs one year and then notching them and spinning each single-handedly into place with a reverse twist of rope. From the gravel beneath the concrete floor to the split cedar shakes on the roof and the hand-carved knobs on the cabinets, he'd done it all. And now he was in a tin cabin in the mountains in the rain, and she was there with her thin hair in curlers, reading magazines. He was working to pay taxes on a house he'd built and couldn't live in. The others had gone down by helicopter ahead of the worst rain, leaving him to watch. A one-armed man's job. He poured another cup of coffee and picked up a magazine and went to stare out the window.

32

The rain descended over the valley and over the North Cascades. It beat its way into the meadows and stippled the surfaces of the high lakes and shattered against the faces of the granite mountains. In the lower elevations it filled the meadows and forest floor and ran into crevices and depressions and channels cut by earlier rains and flowed down the mountains and canyons to larger streams that tumbled to the big creeks and into the rivers and finally the sea. On the mountains the rain hardened and turned to hail and then snow, first the hard ice pellets shattering on rock and then the soft flakes floating down in layers over the granite and glaciers. The peaks turned gray and then white, and the meadows began to receive a pattering of ice, and the wind began to move the clouds in fast over the valley toward the eastern side of the mountains.

Tom lay on his back in the wool blankets and listened to the hail sweeping down the ridge, and he thought of a story his uncle had told. As the sun climbed over the Cascades, two women were rolling hail. All day they played, rolling the hail from east to west, sunrise to sunset. Their laughter was thunder, and when they loved a man he had power, his wounds cooled and healed by the hail sweeping through the mountains from sunrise to sunset, east to west. He heard the hail soften and watched through the branches as the snow began to obscure the meadows.

He moved his toes inside the stiff boots and flexed his calf muscles to see if the legs were awake. Finally, he worked his way out of the rolled blankets. The shelter of downsweeping hemlock was snug and secure, a dimly lighted lair in the whitening world.

Out of the blankets he sat up and shivered. The short summer had gone from the high country, and fall was coming quickly. Soon the first month, the time the Stehemish called the month of danger, would arrive. The cold and damp, combined with the dried sweat from his hard night walk, made his skin sticky and uncomfortable. He folded the blankets and then removed his boots and stripped off his clothes. The air bit at him and the hemlock needles rasped as he stepped through naked into the outer world. The hail had given way completely to snow coming in fat, determined flakes that flattened and melted against his skin.

He stood on the steep slope, stepping from foot to foot on the cold heather, until the melting snow beaded on his chest and stomach. Then, stripping small branches from the hemlock, he rubbed himself until his skin burned, chanting with the cold. The icy air entered him like a cold knife.

From a clump of mixed fir and hemlock, he gathered an armful of dry branches and moss and then he returned to his shelter. In a few moments he had a small fire going, the light smoke disappearing like feathers in the branches and gray air above his head. He dressed and then sat over the fire warming himself and thinking about the last months, about his uncle, his mother and brother, Karen. "Fast three days. Bathe each day and wipe the water away with hemlock branches," his uncle had explained. "When you are pure, maybe a spirit will find you and you will be a singer, a man with power." His uncle had added, "But it doesn't always work, you know."

He placed small sticks on the fire and listened to the quiet snow and felt the enormity of his solitude, felt himself whirled like a dark spot into the vastness of the mountains. He let his thoughts wander and listened to the wilderness blur with snow and he waited, not hearing the drone of the helicopter that swung in a wide arc toward the far side of the lake.

33

In the cabin, Jake saw the air whiten through the window and heard the sputtering on the roof cease. He cursed and opened the stove to stir the coals and shove kindling and larger sticks into the fire.

By nightfall, the snow had turned to a light rain, erasing the white film on the meadows, and before midnight the rain had stopped and the mountains had turned silent and cold. Tom Joseph curled up in the blankets and felt the air chilling his nostrils with each breath. The three-quarters moon struggled to free itself of the clouds that sped eastward. In a half-sleep, he shivered and tensed his muscles and dreamed of flight through an endless range of mountains where wolves glided down the bare bones of rock ridges. And in his sleep he stirred and bared his teeth.

Jake twitched and jerked in the narrow cot within the cabin. The logs of his house were spinning out of place and tumbling to the ground, the rocks of the fireplace falling with heavy "chunks" to the floor as his wife laughed, her hands on her hips and hair full of pink curlers. Through the open bathrobe he could see pale, shrivelled breasts as he struggled to catch the rocks, to push the logs back into place, but one of his arms refused to work, and he thrashed about awkwardly as the laughter grew more harsh. He mumbled and rolled in the sleeping bag, his feet becoming twisted and trapped in the bag's mummy foot. The laughter turned to sharp barks, and he fought to escape from the dream. Weak light slanted through the window, and Jake became aware of the barking of ravens outside. He sat up and listened to J. D. Hill breathing in the other cot, thinking that Hill was worse than no company at all and wondering why Hill had bothered to come up.

Jake lowered himself carefully and worked the sleeping

bag up around his shoulders with the good arm, and then he fell asleep and dreamed of falling an endless avenue of cedars, each exactly like the last and towering into the clouds. As he slept, the sun broke free of the peaks and pierced the cloud layer, and two dark eyes watched through the window for a moment and were gone.

As the two in the cabin slept, Tom worked quickly, climbing to the base of the water tank with the pack. At the tank, he swung the pack off and crouched on the riprap base, removing the dynamite from the pack and tying it into one bundle with part of the wire. A raven landed on the edge of the tank and cocked its head down at him, the black eye bright with intelligence and skepticism.

He set the bundle on his lap as the raven ratcheted a question at him and then flapped backwards to join its brothers in the nearby trees. He glanced at the disappearing bird, wondering what it had tried to tell him, and then took a shiny pair of pliers from his pocket. Working delicately, he bored a hole in one of the dynamite sticks with the sharp end of one handle of the pliers and pushed a blasting cap into the hole. To the wire on the cap he attached another wire that ran to a coil at his feet. He worked one of the rocks from under the edge of the tank and placed the dynamite in the hole directly under the seam that ran up the side of the tank. The other caps he laid close by, and then he slipped his arms through the straps of the pack and picked up the detonator and coil of wire.

Playing the wire out as he went, he climbed the slope above the rock until he crossed the crest of the ridge. Above the trees now seven ravens circled and swooped, barking excitedly, and he saw the peregrine swing in low over the ridge and then sail out over the cabins, calling in a voice that sliced the cool air.

The falcon's cry cut through the cabin and reverberated on the tin walls and Jake sat upright in the sleepingbag. His eyes stared wildly until, hearing the bird scream again, he relaxed.

Across the little room, J. D. Hill was pulling on his boots. Jake watched J. D. get dressed and grab the expensive Italian shotgun he'd brought up with him when the helicopter dropped him off.

J. D. grinned. "Think I'll try some trap shooting."

Jake shook his head. "The ranger told me that hawk's protected," he said, but Hill had already closed the door behind him. "Fuckhead," Jake muttered as he unzipped the bag and rolled his heavy legs to the floor. The arm dragged after him and he winced with pain. He reached for his pants and pulled them on, tugging the suspenders over each shoulder with one hand. He was sliding his moccasins on over wool socks when he felt and then heard the explosion.

With the T-handle of the detonator in his hand, Tom watched the falcon, mesmerized by the light on the flashing wings. Then, as the clouds swirled over the ridge and streamed up from the river, the hand turned and pressed down, and he felt the impulse rip through the wire and saw J. D. Hill step around the corner of the cabin.

J. D.'s eyes were on the bird when he heard the sound and felt the air hit him like a fist. He stumbled backwards, still holding the shotgun, and then looked up in horror as ten thousand gallons of water exploded toward him.

Tom watched as the water climbed in one enormous wave from the ruptured tank and swept down upon J. D. Hill and the cabin. He saw J. D. dive for safety, but the water caught him and lifted him and threw him against a bulldozer, his back folding strangely as it struck the hard edge of the dozer track. Then the flood hit the closest cabin and lifted the tin box off its foundation and smashed it against the bulldozer. The water broke against the tractor and swept across the clearing, carrying oil drums and boxes and old tires with it. In a few seconds the wave had disappeared, and around the crushed cabin and large machines the ground was shining and clean. J. D. Hill's legs stuck out like twigs from beneath the twisted tin of the cabin.

Tom ran down the hill, stumbling and rolling and running again. Blood soaked J. D.'s pantlegs, and Tom pulled at the tin siding of the cabin, lifting and folding it and carefully pulling the body free. One of J. D.'s eyes stared in amazement at the sky. The other was a round socket of mud. Mud filled the mouth and streaked down the neck that Tom felt in search of a pulse.

Stepping back from the body he heard the shriek of bending metal and looked up to see Jake Tobin crawl out of the crumpled door of the cabin.

Jake rose to his feet and looked around, his face bloody and blank with confusion, and then Tom saw Jake's eyes shift from him to the body and back. Tom turned to run as Jake reached for the pistol in its holster, and he was past the ruin of the watertank before the first shot pounded and echoed over the ridge, kicking heather from the slope ten feet away.

Cresting the ridge, Tom saw the peregrine out over the lake, a dark spot in the distance, and he heard the ravens laughing from the trees below.

Near the crumpled cabin Jake Tobin hugged his arm to his chest and let the gun dangle beside him.

Above the lake, Tom loped along the side of Plummer, angling down toward the trees where he'd slept. When he reached the lake, he trotted across the meadow and dropped over the side of Miners' Ridge.

Inside the hemlocks, he collapsed against the pack, his head pounding and gasping for air. After five minutes he stood and shouldered the nearly empty pack and picked up the rifle. He stepped out of the shelter and began climbing back up the ridge. When he reached the top, he looked at the mountain. On both sides of Dakobed a hundred other, darker peaks stood up in a jagged wall.

He looked at the big mountain carefully. On the north shoulder was White Pass. Once over the pass, he could make it to Canada in two days, maybe twice that if he stayed far away from the crest trail where they'd be looking for him. They would never find him in the deep creases of the mountains.

He skirted the ridge below the lookout tower and started the steep descent toward the river. He'd have to cross the Stehemish, climb over the pass on the flank of the mother mountain, and make his run northward. There was no way of avoiding the mountain; all trails led directly to her, from all directions.

Plunging his heels into the soft duff, he half-slid down the ridge in the near-dark of the timber, leaning in against the slope to balance the weight of the rifle and using the timber to brake himself. In the steepest places he fell to all fours.

34

At the Red Dog, a jam of vehicles blocked the street and a crowd spilled out of the doorway.

"Most of you already know what happened, or at least you think you do," Will Baker was saying. "Somebody blowed up the big water tank up at the mine and killed J. D."

Beside the sheriff Jake Tobin sat on a stool, wearing clean clothes and a bandage on his forehead. He'd managed to radio and get helicoptered out with the body within a couple of hours, and his amazement at his own survival still shone from his face.

"It wasn't somebody, it was Tom Joseph," Jake said. "I seen him clear as day."

Will Baker studied Jake for a moment, avoiding the arm in its sling. "In spite of what Jake says, we don't know nothing for sure. It could of been Joseph or it could of been somebody else. But we need some men that know this country to help us catch whoever did it. We'll have the chopper up and some deputies, but we need men on the ground who know what they're doing out there."

Ab Masingale sat at a table, the casts gone from his legs and a pair of crutches leaning against his chair. "I'll be damned," Ab said. "I'll be double-d damned." Beside Ab, Floyd pulled at his beard and watched the sheriff.

Jake stood up. "Come on Will, that Joseph boy's going to be half way to the border by the time we get out there." As he spoke, he stared at the men gathered around them.

Bayard Taylor pushed through the crowd. "I guess I know this country about as well as anybody," he said. "There's just one thing though. You don't aim to go out there and start shooting, do you?"

The sheriff looked solemnly at Bayard. No one knew the mountains better than Bayard Taylor, unless it was the Indian they were trying to catch. If you couldn't have the Indian, Bayard was the next best thing. Besides, Will Baker reasoned, if they were lucky Tom Joseph would be long gone before they got up there and nobody else would end up dead.

"Course not," the sheriff said. "We ain't going out to shoot anybody. But I want everybody who comes to remember that if it is the Joseph kid he's probably got that thirty-forty Krag of his uncle's, and you all know what that'll do to a man."

"By god, if these legs of mine was working, I'd go," Ab Masingale shouted. "Ain't nobody knows this country like I do, not even Injuns." He started to grin at Floyd and then turned serious. "That's a bad thing he done."

The sheriff looked intently at the old man. "I guess you do know these mountains pretty good, huh Ab?"

"Damned straights."

"How'd you like to go along in the copter as spotter?"

"Damned straights," Ab shouted.

Leroy Brant stood up from the table Ab sat at and said, "I've done a lot of hunting in that area. I'll go along." Behind Leroy, Dinker craned his neck to see the sheriff nod.

"I'm going." Buddy Hill shoved his way to the front of the group. "And I'm taking my two-seventy."

"You can go," Will Baker said, "and you all better bring your deer rifles. But there won't be any shooting if I can help it."

Across the street from the tavern, Mad John stood in the shadow of the Serve-U Market, his hands shoved deep in his pockets and his eyes fixed on the crowd. Muttering to himself, he shook his head and walked toward the junction of the two rivers.

35

Tom left the trail and moved through the timber up the side of the ridge. As he climbed, the cloud cover broke and the evening sun cast slivers of light through the trees. It was two days since he'd eaten, and his stomach knotted.

He climbed steadily, using the brush and small trees. Near the edge of the timber, where the forest began to thin to clumps of fir and hemlock, he found a deer. The skin and crushed bone had been worked by large, sharp teeth, and the animal had already begun to sink into the humus, the line between animal and mineral blurred by a humming mass of insects. For a moment he stared at the carcass with curiosity. Coyotes avoided deer most of the time, sticking to mice and grouse, with an occasional marmot or porcupine. As he turned away, a gray jay rustled onto a nearby branch and cocked its head at him. The hard trickster eye fixed him, and the jay sputtered a warning before fluttering away.

He reached the top of the ridge as darkness moved out of the timber and across the high meadows. Wind caught shreds of cloud and blew them across the sky, but in the meadows only a light breeze stirred the dark lupines and grasses. They couldn't hunt for him at night, but he knew they'd already be camped somewhere below, on both sides of the ridge if Will Baker was running things. He wondered what McBride or Aaron Medicine would say about what he'd done. The night seemed to rock with a bitter laughter, and he felt the enormous dark space around him. The earth was an island in a sea bounded by a great wall. Beyond that wall the spirits lived. Raven dreamed up death and then mourned bitterly for his lost daughter, the trickster tricked by death.

Where the meadow flattened toward the top of the ridge, he paused and watched the clouds push past. The wind blowing from the north meant a coming break in the weather. With a cloud cover, he might have drifted unseen along the ridges, but with each minute the light grew brighter and the moon approaching full thrust its way more surely through the tattered clouds. The growing light threw spears of shadow across the meadow from the clumps of ancient trees, and the moon began to outline the peak above him in silver, the black stitches of crevasses like spiders' webs on the mountain's white sides. The air was warming, and he became aware of the fact that it was a beautiful night. His stomach had ceased to ache, and he felt a growing sense of ease with the night.

He slipped from one cluster of dwarf trees to the next across the meadow, watching for the glint of light that would mean a campfire. But he was alone on the ridge, and his steps on the brittle heather jarred the silence.

He covered two miles in an hour, gliding through the lessening shadows like a predator. Midway along the broad curve of the ridgetop, a coyote yelped and was answered from the distance, the unmusical cries carrying an edge so wild and expectant that he strained to understand.

The trail down the north side of the ridge had been blasted out of a rock face near the top, at the edge of timberline. He had to reach that trail and cross the canyon to White Pass that night, before they could cut him off. The rifle dragged, and he shifted it from hand to hand as the fingers grew numb. He sniffed the air for the smell of fire and hunched his shoulders under the light pack.

Where the ridge fell away to Milk Creek, he crept to the rocky edge and looked down toward the valley bottom. The creek gleamed in a long, twisted thread in the growing moonlight. The valley ran rapidly toward the mountain and ended in a glacial cirque, a sheer wall of rock and ice. There was no way around Milk Creek except over the peak and no way across the valley except by the trail and bridge below. On the far side, the high frozen pass glinted in its narrow saddle. Beside the creek where the bridge spanned the white water, a spot of light flickered yellow and orange.

For several minutes he watched the point of light in the creek bottom, surprised that they could be there already. Then he backed away from the rock and climbed along the ridge as it rose toward the mountain. The late-season snowbanks sent icewater rivulets across the meadowed slopes, and he moved onto the exposed rock of the ridge. As he crossed one of the bare outcroppings, he suddenly stopped and stiffened, knowing he was watched. Ten yards away, a coyote stood outlined against a shoulder of the mountain. Then the coyote slowly turned and walked away, pausing at the crest of the ridge to study him once again before disappearing.

The night turned colder, and he stopped in a clump of whitebark pine—squat, ageless trees battered by wind and snow until they were as bare and indestructable as the rock from which they grew. Inside the shelter of brittle, entertwined branches, he dropped the pack and rifle and pulled one of the blankets out. He sat against a gnarled trunk and drew the blanket to his chin. Around him he felt the hard, eternal quality of a world stripped to essentials: rock with a thin layer of earth and plant, rock and ice rising together to Dakobed and the night sky.

During the night he awoke with tingling cold and pulled the second blanket from the pack. The moon floated full in a nearly cloudless sky and soaked the meadows and stunted trees in a cold light. Above, the mountain loomed intensely white. And as he lay on his side and tried to fit the contours of his body to the rocks and roots, a sound began somewhere on the ridge and moved into his consciousness and welled into a long, wavering howl, a deep-throated and drawn-out cry that filled the night entirely. Different from the wild yodeling of the coyote, the sound fell with great weight across the meadows and down through the timber.

Tom Joseph lay on his side and listened. For an instant it covered the night, and then it was gone and he wondered if he'd dreamed it. For a long time he waited, but he heard only the small streams and the rustling needles of the trees. Then he slept again, and his dreams were of shadows and confused flight. Around him the mountains drummed and the streams sang in rhythmic voices.

The sun burned along the top of the ridge and flamed on the meadows when he awoke. His head ached, and his throat swelled with thirst. He looked out at the bright meadow in shock. Above him, against a blue sky, the mountain erupted in light.

He went to the rocks and stared at the valley. The bridge stood out sharply against the milky water. No one was there. He wondered if he had dreamed the fire, too, but then he saw them. A group of men on horseback threading their way up the narrow switchbacks, a half hour from the top of the ridge.

He stooped and ran to one of the little streams and buried his mouth in a pool, sucking in the icewater until his teeth ached. Then he ran back to the trees, grabbing a handful of hemlock needles as he passed a dark tree and wiping his face with them. Back in the cluster of pines, he shoved the blankets into the pack and swung the pack to his shoulders. He grabbed the gun and stepped from the trees and realized that he didn't know where to go. They had cut off his flight to White Pass, and more of them would be coming up the Stehemish to cut him off there. He looked at the mountain. Once across the peak, he could make it. The mountain filled the horizon, and in the full light the crevasses gaped at him like mouths.

The chop of a helicopter broke into his thoughts, and he saw the machine swing in over the ridge from the Stehemish drainage, one side banked toward the meadow and a figure with a rifle in the open doorway. He leaped into the trees, but still it came toward him, the noise and downdraft beating at the meadow.

He slipped the pack off and crouched with the rifle. The helicopter hovered a hundred yards away, monstrously loud in the thin air. He released the safety and raised the rifle. The figure in the helicopter lifted something to his face, and his name exploded over the wilderness broken by the hammering blades.

He sighted at one of the landing runners but the thirty-forty slug struck higher, ricocheting off the back of the helicopter so that the machine rose like a frightened crow and slipped backwards, banking away from the backbone of the ridge to hover out of rifle shot. He fired again, trying to arc the slug past the helicopter but hearing the plunk of metal again, and then the copter engine began missing, and the pilot swung the machine away in a swift uplift. The helicopter climbed erratically and swung back down toward the lower meadows and out of sight. He heard it settle somewhere below.

He pulled the pack on and scrambled out of the trees and up the ridge, his boots sucking at the heather drowned in snow-melt. In twenty yards he reached the thread of a goat trail along the spine of the ridge, and then he dropped from sight down the opposite side. The ridge bent sharply and hid him in its fold.

He scrabbled up the ridge, leaving the heather behind and climbing on rock and loose talus. His boots stabbed at footholds and slipped on the debris. With his free hand he grasped at holds in the rock, and he moved quickly upward until he was on snow and kicking steps along nearly vertical walls to stay down over the ridge and out of sight. The sun had moved high enough to lance in blinding crystals off the snow. He squinted until his eyes were slits and continued to kick his way along the wall.

Above him the snow ended in a razor-fine line against the blue sky, a line he would have to cross to reach the glacier and his route around the peak. He kept his eyes tightly squinted and hugged the ridge, angling upwards.

A few yards from the blazing line of the ridgetop, he felt the muscles of his back tense. At the top he'd be silhouetted for an unavoidable instant against that skyline.

He tried to leap the last few feet, and his boot kicked out of the snow, sending him sliding back down until he arched his back, dug his toes in and clawed for a hold. His calves began to quiver and he scrambled upward again until the horizon seemed to scorch his face, the egg-shell snow and indigo sky burning into his retinas. He kicked the last few steps more carefully, fighting the urge to turn back and hide, and then his shoulders cleared the knife-blade ridge and he could see the broken glacier below. And at that instant, a pocket of snow exploded at his feet and the report of a rifle echoed across the slopes.

He leaped the final step and was on top and dove face-first onto the steep snow and felt himself lifted for a moment when the second shot struck. Then he collapsed and slid and began to roll until he tumbled onto the broad tongue of the glacier. He lay contorted in one of the big suncups and watched the rifle slide past him to stop in a deeper cup. He waited for the sensation that would tell him where the hunting load had struck.

He felt nothing. He pushed himself to his knees, and there was no pain. Slipping his arms from the straps, he looked at the pack and found the small hole where the hollow-point had entered. On the opposite side of the pack, shreds of canvas and wool protruded from a hole the size of his fist. Clumps of fresh, hard snow clung to the pack and stuck to his pants and mackinaw. Inches away from the cup where the rifle had stopped, the mouth of a crevasse opened.

He crawled to the rifle and looked down into the yard-wide crack in the glacier. White at the top, it grew quickly dark and then black in its narrow depths. A dozen feet up the mountain, the crevasse widened into frightening beauty, white falling to a prism of blues, sky-blue and aquamarine deepening to indigo and violet and finally black. He looked at the glacier sweeping up the side of the mountain, a web of crevasses breaking the smooth ice.

They would probably be working up the ridge now, but they wouldn't be coming very quickly because of the Krag. He looked at the mountain again. The summit hid behind the twin rocky needles of the Teeth. The quickest route over the summit lay between the spires, but between him and the notch were two glaciers and a tangle of crevasses tumbling down into the heart of the world. His stomach twisted, and his hunger came back to him with a jolt. Old Man Coyote, he remembered, had once devoured himself in a fit of greed.

36

"You hit him, Amel." The sheriff looked up toward the ridge-line where Tom Joseph had disappeared.

Amel stared at the mountain. He hadn't meant to shoot at all, not really, but in the excitement he'd just done it, as if Tom Joseph had been nothing more than a mountain goat up there. His blood pounded, and he felt a burning in his chest and hoped the bullet had missed. But he'd seen the body lift in the scope when the hollow-point struck.

"I wish that boy hadn't started shooting like he did," Will Baker said. "You didn't have no choice, Amel."

Dinker slapped Amel on the back, saying, "Finest damn snapshot I ever saw."

Amel tried not to make a connection between what was on the other side of the ridge and Sara Joseph's boy. He wanted to sit on the wet heather, to go no further.

"Spread out and keep down," the sheriff said. "If he's just wounded he might be laying back with that gun." He motioned to the two deputies. "You boys stick close to me."

The sheriff took the point, with the others fanning out on either side. As they began working their way up the heather and crusty snow toward the white ridgeline, Bayard bent close to the ground and swung out away from the rest. He tried to erase the picture of Tom Joseph's body pitching over, and he quickened his pace to move ahead of the sheriff. At the opposite end of the crescent, Martin Grider climbed slowly, his face toward the mountain and Leroy Brant beside him. To the sheriff's left Dinker walked carefully behind Buddy Hill.

37

He backed off from the crevasse and ran and cleared it easily. Quickly he scanned the glacier for the best route through the maze of crevasses. They'd expect him to try to skirt the peak if he weren't already dead or too hurt to run. They'd never expect him to try crossing the glaciers and going over the summit. And they wouldn't follow him once he was across the first glacier.

He ran to the next crevasse, thankful that in spite of the light snow of two nights before, the late summer had laid the glaciers bare. He chose a narrow spot and jumped and then worked back and forth, running and jumping and hunting for the narrow places. Twice he worked his way across the thin blades of icebridges.

In a few minutes he was across the first glacier and onto the shoulder of the second. This one cut its way down the peak in a little hanging valley. On one side it rose up to the glacier he'd crossed, and on the other it ground away at a talus ridge that climbed to the rocks called the Teeth. Large boulders lay at the edge of the glacier on the far talus slope, and he aimed for them, criss-crossing the ice and picking his way around and over the crevasses.

The icebridge spanned six feet of blue air, and in the middle of the bridge he heard a shout and turned to see a man outlined on the ridge where he had been shot at. He jumped for the far side just as a shot kicked up snow near his boot and more shouts faded into the enormous mountain.

He sprinted across the glacier and leaped a crack close to the edge of the icefield. With no crevasses remaining, he ran for the safety of the rocks only to find a yawning gap between ice and rock where the glacier had shrunk away. Several yards across and bottomless where he stood, the bergshrund narrowed to a thin line ninety feet up the mountain.

38

"Next time forget the warning shot," Buddy Hill said. "He's going to fall into one of those cracks anyway."

"Shut up, Buddy." Will Baker looked up the mountain as he spoke.

"Goddamnit, it's my father," Buddy began, but the sheriff cut him off.

"You're not in charge here, so shut the fuck up." Turning his back to the others, Will Baker shaded his eyes with his hand and studied the route the Indian would probably have to take.

Buddy lifted the two-seventy and swung the scope toward the dark figure dancing at the far edge of the second glacier. The crosshairs slid over the blinding whiteness until they caught on the splash of color moving erratically. The fine twin lines made four neat right angles and came together in the middle of the green pack. For an instant they hung there, and then they jerked away as the gun fired.

"What are you doing, boy?" One of the uniformed deputies held the rifle barrel toward the snow and stared at Buddy.

"Goddamn you," Buddy said. "He's going to get away."

Tom was looking down into the bergshrund when the slug hit, and the blue-green ice tumbled over and became painfully brilliant sky, and then the sky merged with a pure pain that soared through his body. He felt the protruding shelf of the icewall when he hit and bounced, and then when he thought he had stopped falling he began to spin down and down into the darkness at the center of the mountain.

"You got him anyway," Dinker shouted. "You knocked him into that hole."

"Let's go make sure," Buddy said.

Will Baker spat at the snow near Buddy's feet. "You want to cross that ice?"

Buddy looked at the glacier and didn't answer.

The sheriff turned to Bayard Taylor. "Bayard, you think you could get over there to make sure he doesn't bleed to death or something?"

Bayard's thin face surveyed the glaciers. "Tom was lucky to get across both of them like that," he said, "but I suppose if he did it I could do it."

"You been up this mountain before, ain't you?" the sheriff asked.

Bayard nodded.

"Think you could reach him by yourself? We don't have no ropes or nothing like that."

"I could do it the same way Tom done it," Bayard replied as he started onto the first glacier.

"I'll go with him." Martin Grider stepped forward. "I've been up this route myself."

The sheriff looked skeptically at the ranger and then back at Bayard. "Might be better not to go alone."

Bayard shrugged.

"Okay, Grider," the sheriff said, "but you'd better take one of these rifles along to cover Bayard with."

"We don't need no guns." Bayard spoke without looking at the sheriff, his eyes scanning the glaciers. He looked at the position of the sun and shook his head.

"I'll take my gun along." Buddy stepped forward. "It was my dad."

"Suit yourself," Will Baker responded. "If we're half lucky you'll lose your ass in one of them cracks."

The three men started across the first glacier, Bayard leading and Buddy following carefully in the footsteps of the other two.

When the three were halfway across the first stretch of ice, the sheriff turned to Amel. "Keep your scope on that spot where he went over to make sure he ain't playing a trick on those boys. Be a shame for something to happen to Bayard."

"He ain't playing no possum after the header he took into that hole," Dinker said from behind the sheriff.

Next to Dinker, Leroy spat a brown stream onto the new snow and shook his head. "Shitfire, Dinker," he said.

39

Far above, a pair of golden eagles swung in slow gliding circles close to the sun. When they banked into the light, their wings flared, and then they turned and became a pair of black points in the immense sky. The eagles called, and the cries disappeared in the great space.

The needles of cold working their way into his body had awakened him. He expected to see darkness and was surprised by the blue vault of sky and the distant floating birds. He lay still and watched the eagles vanish, and then he tried to move. His head was cradled between two sharp-pointed objects, and when he turned it he found that the objects were fragments of ice. He experimented and found that his feet moved, and then the legs. He braced his arms and pushed to raise his body, and one side rose while the other remained on the ice. The left arm wasn't pushing. And then the odd quality he'd been feeling became clear. It was a throbbing in his left arm.

He pushed harder with the right arm and sat up and looked at the other arm. The mackinaw sleeve had a tear in it and was darker than the rest of the jacket. Again he tried to move the arm, and this time was pleased to see it rise to his lap. He examined the small hole in the mackinaw curiously, and then he realized that he was freezing and that someone had tried to kill him, twice.

The pack lay a few feet away, upside down on the floor of the bergshrund. He was in the narrow upper end of the shrund, where it descended only fifteen feet from the surface of the glacier. The sky was close and very bright. Above, the bergshrund ran twenty yards up the mountain and then closed with the rock. Below, the gap between ice and rock widened and dropped away to darkness.

He got to his feet and discovered that the wounded arm hurt

only a little. He retrieved the pack and found the rifle lodged a few feet further down the shrund. The arm began to awaken in measured waves of sharp pain, and he felt himself start to shiver.

He worked his way up the shallow end of the crack until it narrowed to a thin line close to the rock. Squeezing his body between ice and rock, and bracing himself with feet and knees and pack, he inched his way toward the sky, dragging the rifle. His mackinaw caught on a shard of rock and he tore it free. At the surface, he braced himself and peered over the edge. A knot of men stood on the far side of the first glacier. They won't cross, he thought. And then he saw the three working their way over the second glacier.

That the first man was Bayard didn't surprise him. He could think of only one other person who might have the skill and guts to cross the glaciers. And that person was the ranger who followed close at Bayard's heels. Doesn't he know we're in the same business, he thought. Ranging the wilderness. He felt a mushrooming nausea, and he closed his eyes. When he looked again, he recognized Buddy Hill, the one with the rifle who was picking his way precariously behind the others.

He slipped the rifle through the packstraps across his chest and began to climb the easy broken rock, grabbing pressure holds with the good hand and using the wounded arm to steady himself. They wouldn't be looking for him to climb out. They were expecting a good Indian down there in the depths of the bergshrund, and two of them were his friends. He hoped they would be intent on the broken glacier and that his pack would blend with the rock as he climbed.

Amel Barstow kept the rifle scope fixed on the spot where Tom Joseph had pitched into the hole. His mind wandered exhaustedly, and he was glad that he hadn't been the one who killed the boy. He didn't see the dark figure crawling tediously up the rock wall thirty yards further up the bergshrund.

The sun moved past its zenith, and the mountain began to cool. He eased over the edge of the rock face and wormed his way a few feet down the rounded top of the pumice fin until he was sure he couldn't be seen from below. The arm pounded, and he lay in the sunlight on the warm stone, feeling the cold of the bergschrund withdrawing. He shook his head to clear it. On the other side of the pumice ridge, the mountain dropped vertically to another glacier and then to Dusty Creek two thousand feet below. The only way now was directly up the pumice and through the Teeth to the summit. On the other side of the summit, a long ridge swept gradually down between the glaciers to trails northward.

He rested a few minutes. They'd see the blood and think he had fallen on down into the shrund. A lot of climbers dropped into crevasses and bergshrunds and were never found. Down, down, down to where Coyote brought the roof of the ice world tumbling in.

The clatter of falling rock surprised him, and he grabbed the rifle and looked up into a pair of dark eyes and a black nose. A shaggy, white-haired goat stood with its feet splayed where it had skidded to a stop. The mouth formed a dry grin as it watched him, and the eyes seemed the blackest things he'd ever seen. When he rose on one elbow, the goat started and clattered backwards over the edge of the rock face.

He tried to lick his lips and discovered that his tongue was swollen and dry. There was no water on the mountain, and he realized that he had not eaten in three days. Crawling a few feet further down the rock away from the glacier, he rose carefully to his feet and saw the Stehemish River valley. Image Lake made a deep blue point on the green sweep of Miners' Ridge across the drainage, and he imagined the drama on the mountain reflected in the lake. The knotted white river so far below seemed to belong to a different world now, one that had very little to do with the world of ice and rock he inhabited.

He looked up the pumice ridge. A hundred yards away, the base of the outcropping that formed the Teeth rose in front of the false summit. If he could get to the jumble of rock, he could rest again before the harder climb that lay ahead.

40

Amel kept the scope on the bergshrund and let his thoughts wander back to the day he'd picked up Tom Joseph hitchhiking home. The time in between seemed like years, or decades. Now Tom was probably dead because of what must have started as a kind of bad joke, blowing up a water tank. Jake Tobin was a cripple and J. D. Hill was dead because of the Indian kid. The boy's uncle and mother were dead, and the fat one, Jimmy, was all that was left. Amel's arms grew tired, and the crosshairs of the scope wandered slightly over the ice and volcanic rock. What had caused the boy to do it? Why did it seem that for the Indians he'd known in his lifetime something was always going wrong? What, he wondered, was going on down inside that mountain?

Bayard approached the spot where Tom had fallen, and his forehead wrinkled. His eyes searched hard for a movement, and when he peered over the edge of the bergshrund he saw the blood on the ice below.

"See anything?" Buddy pushed up behind the ranger and Bayard, craning to see into the crack.

"Look at that blood." Buddy added. "He must've landed there and bounced on down to kingdom-come."

Bayard looked searchingly down the bergshrund and then turned to look up toward the point where the ice and rock came together. Then he squatted and mantled over the edge of the lip, landing with a grunt on the uneven floor.

He crouched near the blood and then worked his way down to where the bottom dropped away to black space. Bracing himself against the wall, he stared into the dark for a moment, and then he turned and moved back toward the shallow end of the bergshrund, balancing himself between rock and ice as the crack narrowed.

"What the hell's he doing?"

The ranger looked at Buddy and didn't respond. Then he began to follow Bayard Taylor along the edge of the bergshrund, watching as Bayard wedged his thin body and began to stem between the rock and ice walls. Grider saw Bayard pick the piece of red cloth from the rock.

41

Torn moved up the rock ridge on the Stehemish side, out of sight of the pursuers. When he reached the base of the Teeth, he crouched and scurried around the rock rib and into the cleft between the rocks. Here the rock stood in thin, jagged walls overlooking the headwall of the last glacier he'd crossed. He went into a space between the rocks and dropped the pack and rifle, then he stood and looked through a notch in the rock that gave onto a broad view of the glaciers below, the ridge that flowed toward White Pass, and a hundred other ridges and peaks rippling off toward the southeast. The group of men stood a thousand feet down the mountain, waiting patiently at the edge of the first glacier.

He worked his good arm out of the mackinaw and pulled the bloody sleeve off the left arm. Through the tear in the wool he could see a shallow trench in the arm, glazed with blood. He flexed the hand, and a torch of pain flared in the arm as he watched the muscle work. A fleshwound, he thought, and he grinned weakly at the cowboys-and-Indians joke. It was always the cowboys who got the fleshwounds. Heroes got fleshwounds. Indians clutched their chests and fell from spotted horses.

He sat back and waited for his strength to return. Off the snow and away from the shadowy bergshrund, the day turned hot. A horsefly appeared and droned furiously around the hand that lay crusted with blood in his lap. He waved it away with the other hand and listened as a raven made grave pronouncements somewhere in the rocks above. Where his stomach had been there was merely a cool, empty place, but his dry mouth tortured him. He crawled to the snow and scooped a handful into his mouth and returned to the rocks. The raven continued to bark words at him from its hidden place.

He closed his eyes as the sun began to inch down past the icewall of the summit, its rays suddenly red, and he shifted his vision toward the blue arc of sky.

42

Bayard held the threads in his palm. Looking back at the ranger and Buddy, he knew they'd seen his discovery. He climbed up the rock and out onto the top of the pumice rib. There was only one way to go now, and all of them but Buddy knew that way well. He thought about what they could do. He could go back down and they could radio for people to cut off that route on the other side, but Will Baker must have thought of that already. And if he went back down now, and Tom Joseph was wounded badly, Tom probably wouldn't survive the night. There had been too much blood in the bergshrund.

He watched as the ranger and then Buddy made the short jump to the rock wall and began climbing toward him, Buddy carrying the awkward rifle on its sling across his back.

43

The rattle of rocks again awoke him from dreams of flight. He'd been running through thick timber, dodging the face of J. D. Hill that leaped at him from the shadows death-white and muddied.

The air outside his den spun with orange light, and he struggled to focus his thoughts and then realized that the setting sun had thrown an alpenglow across the snow and ice. He grabbed the gun and raised his head to look over the rock. Bayard and the others stood in the open on the ridge three hundred feet away, looking toward him.

He turned in the direction of the summit. Not far away, a twenty-foot wall of ice barred his path. On one side of the wall, the saddle between the Teeth and the icewall dropped a thousand feet to a broken glacier and the froth of a stream and finally the thread of the river. On the other side, the saddle slid away to the sheer headwall of the glacier he had crossed last.

He looked again at the three men. Martin Grider shielded his eyes from the alpenglow, and beside the ranger Bayard stood watching the rocks above with the narrow, intent face of a hawk. Then Buddy Hill pushed past them and began climbing the ridge, carrying the rifle.

Tom pulled the old gun to him and slipped the safety off and rested the rifle in the notch. Snugging the stock against his good shoulder, he sighted down the barrel until the open sight divided Buddy's chest exactly in the middle. His finger tensed, and then he swung the gun down to the talus slope at Buddy's feet. When he fired, the rock exploded. The three men dove for the talus and squirmed over the edge and out of sight.

He saw the rifle barrel appear above the curve of the pumice and he fired again, this time into the darkening sky. The rifle disappeared.

Now they were trapped and would have to wait with him. There wasn't time for the others to get up there before dark, even if they were foolish enough to attempt the glaciers. With the moonlight coming soon, he could try the wall.

In the still-vibrating air he heard Bayard's voice. "Tom, this is Bayard. Come on down so we can all get off this mountain and get you to a doctor."

For a moment he thought it could be that simple, that he could just walk back down. But then he knew it wasn't. You have to make choices, Karen had said. He'd made a choice and J. D. Hill was dead. That was unfortunate and he would undo it if he could. He felt sad for Buddy Hill who lay on the rocks below and who had come to hunt him, Tom Joseph. Around him he felt the mountains and wilderness grow more still, waiting. He shoved the rifle through the notch again and fired a shot into the talus, the roar of the Krag shattering the thin air.

The alpenglow turned from orange to a dim red, and he crouched in the stone lair, watching the color spread across the ice. With the sun gone, the wind began to sweep up the ribs of the mountain, picking up the chill of the ice and probing into the rocky cleft. He flexed his arm to awaken himself with pain, and he studied the point on the ridge where the others had disappeared.

Silver in the blue-black night, the moon climbed over the crest of the Cascades and hung directly above the mountain, sending long fingers of gray and black creeping from the rocks. The shadows crossed the spine of the ridge on which he hid and leaped suddenly upright against the icewall. He looked back to where the others lay. They were trapped more tightly than he.

He heard Bayard shouting again, but the words were lost in the vast mountains. His stomach ached a little to remind him of the long fast. The Cascade peaks had become darker shadows rising one behind another and spreading beyond his vision to east and west, north and south. He slept and in his dream the wolf beckoned, singing as it turned and departed. He tried desperately to understand the words of the song.

He awoke to the shrill yelping of a coyote. Another joined and then others sprang in with a brittle, adolescent cacophony. The chirps and barks and yodelings echoed off the peaks and warbled in the moonlight. He listened to the uneven shrill, and then as he looked again toward the slope below a new sound broke through the cry of the coyotes and silenced them. A deep tunnel of sound welled up in the clear night and enveloped the valleys and rose up around the mountain, a howl that came out of the forests and ascended until it filled the world.

He listened to the rising howl of the wolf and felt the small hairs straighten on the back of his neck. The wolf drew the long howl again and again from the ridges somewhere down the mountain, and suddenly he understood. It was the dream. Below he saw the outline of Bayard's head over the edge of the talus slope. The dizziness left him and he felt strong. Every delicate shadow stood out clear and sharp-edged on the rock and snow.

He left the rifle and pack and walked toward the wall. Taking the knife from his pocket, he opened it and chopped a step two feet up the wall and another a foot higher. Placing the toe of one boot in the first hole, he stepped up and stabbed the knife hard into the ice. When he felt steady, he leaned against the ice and pulled the knife out and chipped a third step. Methodically he chipped a fourth step and a fifth, not hearing the clatter of the knife and falling ice. At his back the wolf howled, and the sound flooded through him and he continued to climb, using the wounded arm as well as the good one.

The moon framed him against the glistening wall and glinted off his black hair, and inside him the song grew louder, and then the explosion of a rifle turned the night suddenly quiet.

He pulled himself over the edge and stood, looking down at the three men wrestling with the rifle below him. And then he turned to run just as the wolf began to call again, and this time it kept growing, louder and louder and spinning in ever-widening circles through the thin air until it was deafening and seemed a part of the air he breathed. He ran with long, smooth strides down the mountain, the moon hurling his shadow northward before him, listening to the rising howl of the wolf that went on and on until the night seemed ready to burst.

END

Photo by Polly Owens

Louis Owens teaches Native American literature and creative writing at the University of New Mexico. Of Choctaw, Cherokee, and Irish descent, he spent eight years as a U.S. Forest Service fire fighter and wilderness ranger before earning a Ph.D. in literature from the University of California. He is the author of numerous stories and essays and several scholarly works: *American Indian Novelists*, with Tom Colonese (1985); *John Steinbeck's Re-Vision of America* (1985); and *The Grapes of Wrath: Trouble in the Promised Land* (1989). In 1989 Owens received a National Endowment for the Arts creative writing fellowship to finish work on *Wolfsong* and to write a second novel, *The Sharpest Sight* (1992). He has published a new work of criticism, *Other Destinies* (1992), as well as another novel, *Bone Game* (1994).